S0-BNQ-944

one little word

Audra McElyea

one

little

word

Andra Watkins

One Little Word

Red Adept Publishing, LLC

104 Bugenfield Court

Garner, NC 27529

https://RedAdeptPublishing.com/

Copyright © 2022 by Audra McElyea. All rights reserved.

Cover Art by Erica Dean

No part of this book may be reproduced, scanned, or distributed in any printed or electronic form without permission. Please do not participate in or encourage piracy of copyrighted materials in violation of the author's rights. Thank you for respecting the hard work of this author.

This is a work of fiction. Names, characters, places, and incidents either are the product of the author's imagination or are used fictitiously, and any resemblance to locales, events, business establishments, or actual persons—living or dead—is entirely coincidental.

For the man who can find me *anywhere*

Chapter 1

If hot meals are deadly to mothers, then my three-year-old son, Graham, saves me from impending death every night at six o'clock. Tonight, I plop down on the couch with Graham and prepare to eat leftover chicken, broccoli, and mashed potatoes—all cold due to the eternal fetching I've been doing for my child since we got home. It never fails. He sees my joyful face anticipating my first warm dinner in weeks, and he instantly needs at least three objects at once. Objects I must retrieve immediately or else.

I know I'm not the only mom who lives in fear of her toddler. My best friend, Violet, also dreads her three-year-old son's colossal tantrums, the big ones where a parent thinks they might need to call an exorcist or construct a padded room so the kid can survive a minor disappointment. Unlike me, though, Vi has the support of her husband, Nick, who salvages her remaining sanity by helping out when he's home from work.

It must be nice to have a partner down in your foxhole every day, dodging stray bullets by your side. Being a twenty-five-year-old widow with a three-year-old wasn't something I planned, but it's the hand I was dealt. And the last thing I want to do is pick a fight with my son. I'm already drowning in a sea of mom guilt over not being able to stay home with him during the day like his friends' moms do, and tonight's looming thunderstorm is likely to freak him out, so I want to keep the peace.

After fetching Graham a different blanket for the third time, I flip on the TV, and WKNX's live news coverage comes on—as if

1

eight straight hours of seeing Tess Miller's face at work wasn't torment enough. She's a decent anchor, but her talent comes with an ego the size of Texas. To her, I'm just a lowly journalist and substitute reporter. Whenever we cross paths, she "accidentally" calls me Madison or Addie, although she knows my name is Madeleine. It's her condescending power play designed to tear down the confidence of a fellow colleague.

"Mommy, can I watch *Paw Patrol*, please?" Graham's eyes gleam with childlike purity or maybe manipulation. Either way, it works. I click the previous-channel button.

"Sure, baby." I catch a teaser for an upcoming news story about a local death, but I've already committed to Graham's favorite show and pressed the button. There's no turning back. "Make sure you eat all your chicken and broccoli so you can have that cookie Meems left you."

With an excited grin, he shoves the meat into his mouth faster than my sprint out the door of WKNX two hours ago.

Tess repeatedly called me "Madison" at our brainstorming meeting today, and the kicker was that Perry, our boss, didn't bother to correct her. He chimed in and called me Madison, too, so as not to call out Tess for her mistake in front of everyone. I sat there and took it, though, and fumed at the workplace politics.

I shove a few bites of dinner into my mouth and roll my eyes as I picture myself sitting silently at the meeting while everyone proceeded to call me Madison, but I pause when I note Graham's full-mouthed, dimple-inducing grin. It's just like his dad's. I drop my fork and squeeze him. Nothing could make me love this kid more, and even though I had a bad day at work, I realize how lucky I am to be his mom.

The ringing of my phone echoes through our apartment as the power flickers. Graham sprints to the kitchen and grabs it for me, oblivious to the shaking lights. "Mom's—I mean—Mad's phone," he answers with a giggle before tossing it to me.

I jump from the couch to catch it, relieved I have decent hand-eye coordination so I don't have to drop another couple hundred I don't have on a new phone. "Thanks, bub." I wince as I answer, hoping it isn't Perry. He's not exactly kid-friendly and would think it unprofessional that Graham picked up my phone.

I stiffen. "This is Madeleine."

"Hey, honey. Did you see Tess Miller on the news just now?"

The familiar voice of my mom sends me sliding back down to the couch as I continue to eat and talk. I'd rather gag myself with my spoon than watch Tess, even though the lead-in to that story did sound intriguing.

"No, we're watching Marshall get himself into another pickle on *Paw Patrol*. Why? What's going on?" I glance to my right, and Graham has shoved his entire cookie, the one meant for his lunch tomorrow, into his mouth. I struggle not to laugh.

Mom gives me a bad-news sigh. "Your favorite author. They found her dead at her house today."

"What? You don't mean Allegra Hudson?"

"Yes. Isn't it awful?"

"Oh my God, what happened?" I can't help picturing those two beautiful boys she shared pictures of on social media. I set down my fork, trying to take it all in.

Allegra's always been one of Knoxville's treasures, like Dolly Parton or Peyton Manning, and it's surreal to think of it existing without her. I don't know how I'll ever drive through Sequoyah Hills without thinking of this dark moment.

"Tess said the cause of death was unclear, but according to Facebook gossip, she fell down her front-porch stairs and broke her neck. You know, I keep thinking of that writing workshop she taught at the library a few summers back and how much it meant to you."

"Yeah, it definitely meant a lot." I hold back tears as I think about the surprise event she held in our quaint little town of Powell, just twenty minutes outside of downtown Knoxville. As an aspiring writer, I felt like I'd hit the jackpot when I learned not only that admission was free and the event was in my hometown but that we would be able to chat with Allegra. Sydney Gray, the librarian, had wished me a happy belated birthday as I approached Allegra for my one-on-one time. As I said thanks, Allegra's head perked up. "Your birthday was yesterday?"

"Yes," I stammered. I wasn't starstruck so much as dumbstruck.

"Mine too!" she answered.

I couldn't believe it. We were bonding, just two Knoxville writers with the same birthday.

"Wish I was as young as you are, though." She winked.

I smiled back at her, unsure of what to say.

"What's your name, dear?" She seemed truly interested in speaking with me.

"Madeleine."

"Love that name! It's always been one of my favorites. In fact, it was one of the names I had picked out to use if either of my boys had ended up being a girl. Alfred Hitchcock used it in one of his movies I watched a lot growing up."

"Right. *Vertigo*. One of my all-time favorites too!" I said.

During our chat, Allegra warned me that the publishing industry was tough. Then she grabbed my hand and urged me not to let that hinder me from working hard and following my dreams. Tears formed in her eyes as, I assumed, she remembered her own early struggles in the industry and the sacrifices made along the way. I could only nod like an absolute idiot, but nonetheless, our conversation had left me feeling... special.

Like many in Knoxville, I felt a connection to Allegra's voice and views on a level I can't explain to my mom, who doesn't read very often. Allegra did everything I'd ever dreamed of doing and did it well. She was a local-turned-national best-selling author, believer in Christ, wife, mother, and philanthropist. And according to a recent article in *Health* magazine, she did it all while suffering from panic disorder, just like me.

I look at Graham and remember how her suspense novels' intricate plots distracted me from worrying about my early contractions when I was pregnant with him, one of the most trying seasons of my life. *Work of Life* hit me the hardest because it was about a single mom who refused to be a victim of the sabotage of a disturbed cousin trying to take over her life. She was struggling with the loss of her husband and was vulnerable, but by the end of the book, she'd overcome a malicious villain and proven herself. That gave me hope and inspiration.

"Apparently, there's going to be a candlelight vigil tonight at eleven at Sequoyah Hills Park," Mom says. "And there's already speculation of foul play."

Of course there is. That's what she built her career on, a good murder mystery. "Leave it to Facebook and nosy Knoxville neighbors to think they know the truth before we can confirm everything and report it accurately."

"I know, honey. It makes your job as a journalist so much harder with people spreading rumors all over Facebook and Tweeter."

"It's okay, Mom. And it's Twitter, not Tweeter." I chuckle. "I'm sure we'll all work hard at the station to get the whole story and allow the glorious Tess Miller to report it and get credit as usual. But in all seriousness, the Facebook groups are sometimes right. Or close enough."

AT NINE O'CLOCK, I collapse onto my bed, still dressed in my work clothes because I'm exhausted after trying to explain to Graham that God did not, in fact, make the Bubble Guppies on the fifth day. I can't stop thinking how tragic it is that the notoriously big-hearted and talented Allegra Hudson was taken from her husband and children at such a young age. My stomach tightens as I think of those she left behind and their anguish, but I can't let myself dwell on their grief, something I know all too well.

I close my eyes and picture Graham and me in a nice house like Allegra's, me with a successful job—one that doesn't consist of writing dull web stories about who won the piglet beauty pageant at the county fair—and feel temporarily elated. When I imagine my perfect world, my boss, Perry, isn't there looking at me like he's mentally undressing me, lingering in my office when it's just the two of us or touching me as we speak.

Perry pushes the boundaries of professionalism, but I'm uncertain whether he'll ever cross the line completely. So far, I've had a stellar ability to squirm out of any touchy-feely moments with a fake sneeze or a sudden itch, and I've created many reasons to call someone else into my office, like my best work-friend, Marcus. But part of me wonders what would happen if I weren't so proactive.

The thought of quitting, however, makes me even more anxious. I don't know how I would pay all my bills and keep food in our mouths, much less keep up my camera-ready appearance for my sometimes-vain job as a journalist-slash-last-minute-fill-in-reporter. Most nice moms in Knoxville are stay-at-home super-moms, nurses, or teachers. Leave it to me to be unconventional, but creativity drives me. At times, for Graham's sake, I wish I'd picked a more normal and kid-friendly career.

My checkbook calls to me from the nightstand as I picture all the things I can't afford even *with* a job. With a lingering, familiar sense of failure, I gather myself off the bed so I can void and rip up a check I wrote last night to my hairstylist for my appointment to-morrow. After finding several overdue medical bills in the mailbox thanks to Graham's recurring bout of strep throat a few months ago, I knew what I had to do, even though my dark roots have grown a good inch and a half out from my bleached-blond hair. With my remaining money, I write checks for the water and electric bills, refusing to touch my savings for something like getting my hair done.

Then I pull out my laptop. Maybe today's the day that someone will have magically posted a job where they pay me to write novels with the promise of a Big Five publisher and a movie deal. *Dream on, Mad.*

I check the listings for the second time today, and my shoulders fall along with my hopes for a better job. No other journalist positions are listed in Knoxville, and I still don't have anywhere else to go. So I must continue to make it work at WKNX, no matter how discouraged the job makes me. I slam my laptop shut, take a deep breath, and face reality. It's time to get ready for bed, and I've got to do this all over again tomorrow.

THE RAIN BUILDS IN the shadowy sky. My empty Riesling glass is in my bathroom sink, and Graham is tucked under his *Paw Patrol* blanket in his bed down the hall, where he's drifted off into a peaceful sleep. I wash my eye makeup off as the power wavers again and the vanity bulbs flicker. Once, twice, three times. Chills cover my body as I envision myself in bed, trying to sleep in the dark alone, something I haven't been able to do since the accident.

The darkness reminds me of a few months ago when the electricity was cut for a few days after I couldn't pay the bill. I'd run over a nail and needed a new tire. Something had to give in my already-tight budget, and paying the power bill late that month was all I could think of without asking my mom for a loan or dipping into emergency funds. When the lights remain on, I exhale a sigh of relief. Then I remember that as I was reading to Graham at bedtime, he told me I must have been invited to a birthday party since he'd found a card for me under the front door.

I walk from my bedroom into the great area of my apartment, where the living room, kitchen, and entryway all sit together in a dated open-concept floor plan that I've tried hard to make up for with my shabby chic decor. I head toward the front door. Before it lies an envelope with my name handwritten on it, but every letter is scribbled in zigzags I don't recognize. I wonder if someone elderly wrote this or if someone deliberately disguised their handwriting. As soon as I touch the envelope, the sky lights up every window in my apartment, and a loud boom vibrates the ground.

The lights go off, and my nervous breaths come in and out, faster and faster, as the carbon dioxide levels in my blood drop. My panic attacks have any number of triggers: fear that I forgot a homework assignment in grade school, overheating in the shower so that I couldn't breathe, the queasiness that comes from giving blood, and the list goes on. But the blinding headaches I've started having recently seem to have no cause at all, and I pray that a headache doesn't come now.

Panic disorder is real, and I've spent my whole life talking myself down from the unreasonable places anxiety takes me, but this situation is a trigger I can't shake. After stuffing the envelope down my tank top, I grow more uneasy as I make my way across the room to the kitchen. I feel my way past the living room furniture, careful not to trip, until I touch the junk drawer by the kitchen sink.

I stumble to my right then lose my balance. My foot grazes something hairy that doesn't belong on the floor, and I trip over my feet and fall to avoid it. The fur-like object doesn't move, and I scoot away from it. Gasping for breath, I wait for the object to make a sound or move, but nothing happens. My fingers inch toward the object, and I wince as I feel for what it might be. I'm probably being ridiculous. Strands of long, humanlike hair wrap around my extended fingers, and I pull my hand back and scream. *What the hell? Is there a dead body on my kitchen floor?* I immediately leap to the worst-case scenario.

I scoot back and take a few deep breaths like my childhood therapist told me to and work up the courage to feel for the object again. It's unlikely to be a dead body and is probably something completely rational. My fingers reach past the head of hair and find something cold, hard, and far too small to be anything human.

When I discover it's only one of my old porcelain dolls, I let out the pent-up air in my lungs, grab my chest, and suck in a new breath. Graham must have dug one out of the storage bin in my closet again, but I know I picked up all the toys before I put him to bed. Surely, I would've noticed this one being out, but I don't know who else could've put it here.

I kick the doll aside, stand up, and reach for the drawer. I dig around blindly, desperate for my flashlight. My hands shake, and I'm terrified that I might not be alone in the room. When I grasp the flashlight, I hold on tight as I press the light on and study my surroundings. No one's here but me. Once more, I look at the envelope tucked into my top. On second glance, the shaky letters look intentional. I tear into the envelope and find an equally zigzagged handwritten note inside. It reads: **Allegra Hudson was murdered—a source.** I jump, and the lights come back on.

Chapter 2

The next morning, Mom knocks on the door at seven thirty on the dot. I'm ready for work, and Graham's dressed for preschool, except his hair looks like a singed wad of rope in the back. I don't know what he does at night to completely maim his mane this way, but it makes him even more endearing.

"Meems!" He runs and gives my mom a bear hug.

"G-man!" She tosses her purse aside. It lands next to several stains on my off-white carpet, and she opens her arms wide for a hug from my boy.

I give her a quick hug. "Mom, can you calm his hair down before you drop him off?"

"Sure, honey. We've got it." She strokes my face and tucks my long hair back with a concerned expression. "Try not to stress. It'll only make those headaches of yours worse."

"Bye, Momma." Graham sulks with glistening eyes as he pulls on my shirt for a hug.

I scoop him into my arms and give him a wet smooch. "Bye, angel." It's been six eternal months since I last drove him to school. That's when my work schedule changed without warning.

I take a deep breath of frigid air as I shut the door to my fifteen-year-old Camry and glance in the rearview mirror. I find no smudges, but there are a few dark circles even my best concealer can't hide. I want to kick myself for being too nervous and afraid to fall asleep until five o'clock this morning. I'd hoped that final glass of wine would do the trick by amplifying my anxiety meds but no.

The letter doesn't seem so bad now. Maybe it's not even true. It's probably some sick joke a bunch of teenagers dared each other to do. Everyone in the neighborhood knows I have my new sixty-second local-round-up segments on Thursdays and that I'm sent out every Halloween to cover the scariest stories and legends around town.

The station. Ugh. My stomach curls as I think about the place. Despite my hard work, I'm getting absolutely nowhere, and Marcus is my only reliable, genuine friend there. Everyone else is only looking out for number one. But if this tip is true, maybe I can get assigned to the Allegra story.

But who am I kidding? Perry will never go for it. Tess will be all over the coverage on Allegra's death, and he'll let her. I can see her smug face now. "Maybe next time, Madison."

There's always that book I started writing a few years ago, the mystery that Allegra herself inspired me to write that day at the library when she told me not to give up. I could finish it and query some literary agents to see if I get any bites, but that would mean at least another year of working for Pervert Perry. The publishing industry works at a snail's pace, and writers' tears don't exactly pay the bills. I'll think of something else. Something outside the box.

WALKING DOWNTOWN IN heels has always been daunting, but the fall breeze and Tennessee-orange foliage I encounter on my way to the office cause my pain to temporarily slip away. After a few blocks, I can't feel my feet anymore anyway. Passing by the Regal Riviera movie theater, the Tennessee Theatre, and the French Market Creperie with its alluring aroma of cinnamon and butter crepes makes me want to skip work altogether and enjoy the lively atmosphere. But as usual, I approach the seven-story Edwardian Miller's Building and step into its gray, marble-floored lobby.

Kevin, our elderly doorman with the kind eyes, always greets me with a gracious smile. "Welcome back, Ms. Barton."

"Thank you, Kevin." His friendly face always makes me feel better.

I step into the office. Waves of conversation fall on my ears as I breeze past huddles of people gossiping around their shoulder-height cubicles, all of them saying the name Allegra Hudson. I'm told that Perry is already down the hall in my office, waiting for me like a circling vulture. I give my burgundy pencil skirt an extra tug and button my charcoal trench coat to my throat as I approach him. I glance at Marcus's office in the left-hand corner—lights off, door shut, computer off, no coat, no cup of steaming coffee from the Beanery. Looks like I'm on my own.

"Good morning, Perry." I force a smile as I walk into my office, which Perry insisted I take even though I'm low on the totem pole at WKNX. I have a hunch why I got that office—it has a door.

Only three women in the building have offices with doors instead of cubicles—Tess Miller, super-anchor, who we all think is sleeping with Perry even though she has a gorgeous younger husband at home; Georgia Wilson, social media manager, who begins every sentence with the phrase "When I was runner-up at the Miss Tennessee pageant" and is still drop-dead beautiful; and me.

I'm not a beauty queen or star news anchor, but Perry obviously saw something he liked when I joined the team a few years ago. Perhaps it was a certain vulnerability he could take advantage of since I'd recently lost my husband, Clayton, and gained a child I didn't even know I was expecting when he passed away.

At first, I thought I'd gotten one of the only offices out of sympathy, or perhaps I'd just won the lottery through excellent timing since some other woman had quit the day I began. Now I wonder if she quit *because* of the office. Maybe it's all in my head. Madeleine Barton: a wounded young woman full of loss and guilt, trying to be wary of even more ugly things life can throw her way when she least expects them. Or maybe I've simply seen enough warning signs from Perry to know I'd better keep my guard up.

"Hello, love." Perry pulls me in for a hug. It's not the side hug many polite men give so they won't feel a woman's breasts pressed against them. It's a full-frontal "so I can feel every inch of your chest" squeeze, which lasts a few seconds too long. For months, Perry has been coming on stronger and stronger.

I gently pull away in disgust. "So, what's going on in this chicken coop today? Something new on poor Allegra Hudson, I assume?"

Perry smooths his salt-and-pepper hair and exposes a dampened armpit. "Word is the police suspect foul play since it's possible she might have been hit in the back of the head before she took her plunge down the steps. Or someone could've snapped her neck after she fell. But for now, they have no real leads, no weapon, no motive, and no arrest-worthy suspects. It's almost like the beginning of one of her suspense novels, so we're going with that for our headline today." He rubs his hands together like a proper villain.

I picture the scribbled note that kept me up all night. "Murder? Are you saying someone wanted Allegra dead?"

He looks me up and down. "It appears that way, love. And I know what you're thinking, but the handsome husband has an alibi. The security cameras inside their house prove he was asleep in their bed at the time of the murder."

I take a few deep breaths to calm my brewing anxiety. "What about security cameras outside?"

"They were in the middle of switching security companies and only had the ones inside up and running."

"Of course they did. That's pretty convenient, right? Ugh. I can't even imagine." I turn to peer through my open door as blood rushes from my face. The thought of the note sent to my home—one that's apparently true—makes my hands shake. I peek at everyone gossiping happily over their desks as if Allegra hadn't been a real person with a real family whose lives were now devastated.

"Yes, yes, it's quite the shock. By the way..." My door shuts, and Perry reaches around my body. "I have a proposition for you, Madeleine," he whispers softly into my ear with a heavy breath.

I scurry to my desk to avoid being pinned between him and the door as I start to sweat. Out of habit, I unbutton my trench and hang it on the back of my chair, instantly regretting my decision. I lift my V-neck sweater as close to my neck as possible without exposing my navel and take a seat. "You want me to work on the Allegra Hudson story?"

"No, no, no. I want you to go to the..." He stops. "Are you interested in the Allegra Hudson story, Mad? I don't know if you're seasoned enough yet. This could be national news, and you report on the fluff. This would require more investigation, possibly more danger. You'll have to talk to the cops, interview neighbors..."

"I'm interested in less fluff, yes, and I'm more than capable. I did work on some big stories before I came here, remember? And this one would mean a lot to me. It feels... personal. I don't have any connections on the police force, but Marcus does. Perhaps he and I can work on this story together."

"Yes, I suppose you have, but..." He moves behind me and places his hands on my shoulders. "I don't know if you really have the time and energy for something like this. Your little boy keeps you completely tied up in the evenings, no?"

I want to haul back and smack him, but I stay professional and wiggle away from his touch. "I can do all I need to do during the day, and if certain things pop up in the evenings, I do have access to a nanny in case of an emergency."

He leans down and whispers in my ear with his hands again on my shoulders. "Is this something you *really* want, Madeleine?"

"Yeah, and I'd be great at it too." I turn my chair to face him, hoping it'll force him to remove his hands. Instead, they find their way straight to my chest. *Wait. That must've been an accident, right?*

Another second or two passes, and I'm paralyzed with shock when one of his hands rubs my chest and the other finds his pants zipper. *They say there's flight, fight, and freeze, and I just froze.* I finally leap to my feet, and my chair rolls backward into my desk. Perry's eyes are wild as I back away. "What do you think you're doing?"

Perry mutters incoherently. "I, uh, I... uh." He shakes his head and turns the tables. "What do *you* think you're doing, Madeleine?" His tone is calm but firm.

"What do you mean, what am I doing? You're the one who just tried to force himself on me. Don't you have a clue how inappropriate this is? That I'd never in a million years engage in this behavior with you?" The unleashed and well-deserved anger drives my anxiety away.

"I thought you wanted to move up, to be somebody here."

That's the thing about narcissists. They never feel remorse or admit they're wrong, not even to themselves, and people are often too intimidated to call them out. I know this from the many stories my mom has told about my father, a classic narcissist who never came back home and never changed his ways.

"I already am somebody here. Somebody who deserves a better position than I've got, somebody who would never sleep with the likes of you, and somebody who's had enough of this toxic atmosphere. I wouldn't stay here another minute even if you quadrupled my salary!"

"Madeleine, wait." Perry rolls his eyes, and I start to gather my belongings.

I walk toward the door, open it, and make my way down the hall, finally allowing my hatred and anger to boil over. "No, I'm not going to wait. I don't work here anymore."

"You can do the story if you just calm down, okay?" He keeps a safe distance, and heads turn our way as he follows me toward the front door, apparently afraid to be the next bigwig to pay for his crimes in the "Me too" era.

"I *am* going to do the story, Perry." I face him before Kevin opens the door for me, and a light bulb of hope clicks on inside my brain. I can do this on my own, especially with anonymous tips like the one I received last night.

Perry smiles, cocks his head, and reaches for my shoulder. "See, now you're starting to use your pretty little head."

"No." I back away even farther to avoid his hands, and Kevin's eyes grow large. "I'm going to take the audience I built covering the news in college, along with the ones who've followed my stories here, and I'm going to let them know that if they want the real news, they can follow me right out of here. I get plenty of likes and retweets anyway. I'll build my own brand and do everything live on my Facebook page before you guys can figure out which end's up."

Perry laughs. "Yeah, you go right ahead. In fact, you have my permission."

"Okay, Perry. Watch and learn. Welcome to the 'I want it now' generation. I'll see you when you catch up to the finish line." I have no idea whether I can actually pull off any of the things flying out of my mouth, and I'm already wondering if I've made a huge mistake, even though Kevin smiles at me with a wink.

I walk out with my head held high. Marcus approaches the building from the Beanery and looks at me with concern. He can always tell when something is off with me. I blink away tears and walk in the other direction, toward the parking lot, because if I go to him now, I'll lose it and start bawling. And maybe something else bad will happen, like Marcus getting fired for punching Perry in the face after I tell him what our boss did. Besides, what's done is done. I take a giant step into my new future and don't look back.

After somehow finding my way to the parking garage, I plop down in my car, slam the door, and am immediately overwhelmed by sheer panic. I wonder what I've done. I don't even have a job now. I'll need to build a bigger online following quickly to support myself and Graham.

My breaths grow closer together, and my head spins as my anxiety spirals, so I roll down my window and inhale the autumn air. I'm experiencing an intense dose of quitter's remorse. The ding of a text interrupts my thoughts.

UNKNOWN: It's true, Allegra *was* left for dead; hit in the back of the head and pushed down the stairs, where her neck was broken—and YOU'RE going to get the story. You're welcome—a source.

Chapter 3

I wonder if this source could be someone I know. **Who is this? Perry?** I text, not expecting a straight answer. But I can't help trying. My sense of urgency is my best quality and my biggest weakness; it makes me a great reporter because I go after the story and often get it first, but sometimes, the first person to a hot dish just ends up getting their fingers burned.

They reply immediately. **Perry? You've got to be kidding me.**

At least we agree that Perry is a jerk. Assuming I interpreted that correctly, of course.

Then tell me who you are.

Someone who wants YOU to get the whole Allegra story. I give you the info I have, and you get the rest of the story. No questions. No police. Find a way to get the *real* Allegra story, or you'll end up just like her—a source.

I suddenly feel as if I'm in a wild suspense novel that just took a dangerous turn for the unsuspecting main character. I can't catch my breath. I've almost hit my point of maximum fear and stress, and chills appear on top of my chills. Only one place can bring me comfort now, so I put my car in gear and drive.

Leaving downtown Knoxville, I approach the interstate intersection, but instead of turning right toward rural Powell like I always do, I go left toward Karns. This community between Powell and busy West Knoxville is the home of new subdivisions, a bridge between city and country.

Violet should be home, and I need to see her. She's seen me through worse; this is barely a blip on our radar compared to the state I was in a few years ago. Violet always knows exactly what I need to hear.

Violet's been my go-to friend since preschool. We've always been as close as sisters, maybe even closer based on many of the sisters I know. Vi's the kind of friend who loves you so much it hurts but in a ball-busting kind of way you didn't know you needed. She's never one to sugarcoat anything, and I trust her opinion.

Vi still has that strange knack for knowing what I need to hear, although she's softened her delivery as we've gotten older. She and I even shared a homecoming date our freshman year when my on-again, off-again male-best-friend-slash-friend-with-benefits flaked on me at the last second. But it was just as well. His loss was my gain because that homecoming dance was where I got to know Clayton Wright—and the rest was history. Maybe Vi can somehow spin this awful day and help me see a silver lining.

I park my car in Violet's leaf-laden, brick-paver driveway. Hers is one of the few old Craftsman-style homes left in Karns. On either side are new homes almost identical to each other: tan-colored brick, black shutters, and two stories tall with basements, small front porches, and lots much smaller than Vi's full acre.

I take a deep breath and put one foot in front of the other. An unfamiliar ringing fills my ears, and a searing pain stabs the back of my head. As soon as I grab my head and moan, the pain ends as abruptly as it came. On top of everything else, I guess I'm starting to have migraines. Frequent harsh headaches have been the norm lately but nothing like this.

After shuffling through the leaves, I arrive at the freshly painted red front door and dust off, trying to reboot before Violet sees me for the hot mess I am. As a toddler mom myself, I know better than to ever ring the doorbell at the home of a fellow mom. Anyone who rings the doorbell at the house of a stay-at-home mom with children under five deserves for said doorbell to jolt them with a couple of hundred volts. Nap time is sacred, and as members of the mom club know, nap times are also subject to change, so no time is considered safe.

I knock three times. Then I wait for Vi to shush Brighton and pull up a chair to the abnormally high peephole on her front door to check and make sure that I'm not a murderer or, worse, a solicitor.

While I wait, I compose myself and take in the fiery maples that distract me from the awful morning. A scuffle from behind the front door and a jiggle from the antique doorknob grab my attention. I take a deep breath and vow that I won't cry right away.

The door swings inward, revealing one of my favorite faces in the world. "Mad! What in the world are you doing here?" She smiles but looks apprehensive.

"I quit my job," I blurt out, "and I don't know what I'm going to do now." My hands cover my face, and I completely lose it. Screw the vow.

"Oh, honey, come inside and have some tea. Let's talk this whole thing out."

I walk into her home and, despite my tears, notice how clean the place is. It only makes me heave harder, knowing I cannot keep my house anywhere near this clean. Her TV is on WKNX, and the headline scrolling on the screen reads "Who Killed Allegra Hudson?" accompanied by a picture of Allegra with her gorgeous smile, long blond hair, and perfect skin and figure. Vi eyes Tess Miller and her gigantic hair with an eye roll then turns the TV off.

"Sit. Tell me everything."

Sitting on her Pottery Barn living room couch, I divulge all the nauseating details of my workday since she says her son, Brighton, is in his playroom, working on a puzzle. "Why do I feel like I did something wrong? Like this is somehow my fault?"

"Mad, you know it's not. Don't you dare think that for a second either. That's exactly why men like Perry get away with this crap. They manipulate women into thinking they've somehow led them on, dressed inappropriately, or didn't take their joke the right way. It's all utter bullshit. He's guilty. You're not!"

"I know, I just feel like maybe I should've stayed. Stood up for myself and gone to HR but stayed—for Graham." I sob, wondering if I'll always question my decisions as a single parent. It would be so nice to have a husband to talk everything over with, even mundane things like what to cook for dinner or what show to watch. Parenting alone has proven exhausting, and I'm sick and tired of always feeling like a failure.

Vi rises to her slipper-clad feet and scurries to the kitchen, where she makes us some much-needed tea. "I think you did the right thing. That was a harmful atmosphere, and what you said to Perry at the end was genius." She smiles with excitement in her voice, and I picture her replaying the scene in her head, only with much more drama. "You really should take a leap of faith and try to brand yourself as the local reporter who works for the people."

I wipe my eyes and sink deeper into the couch as I imagine Graham and me on the side of Gay Street downtown with a homeless sign after my new career tanks. One of my biggest fears has always been not being able to provide for my little boy. "I don't know. I'm afraid it's a little too ahead of its time."

Violet snickers as she carries our mugs to the coffee table. "There's no such thing as *too ahead of its time*, and you know it. You're going to be the creator, the originator, the genius behind this innovative idea. I think it's absolutely incredible, and I hope Perry gets taken down a notch."

"I feel like my life is a constant drama. It's like I'm that girl everyone pictures with a dark cloud over her head." I brush my tears aside and attempt to gather myself, wishing I still had it all together like I did a few years prior when life was simpler. Things were going so well until...

Violet comes in for a hug, the one where her goal must be to suffocate the misery right out of me. Maybe she thinks breaking a rib will make me forget my broken spirit.

"I know, honey. It feels like you've been struggling a lot since Clayton." She pauses midsentence, clearly deciding not to go there. "It's been a tough couple of years. I'll say that. I'm here for you, no matter what. You know that, right?"

I brush fresh tears away as she embraces me. "I do. I really do. It's just... it's so hard sometimes, and I don't always know what I'm doing or who I can trust. I mean, there's someone right now, for example, who I don't know if I should trust or straight-up be afraid of. Maybe I shouldn't even tell you about it." I wince, wondering if telling her will put her in danger as well.

Violet breaks her smothering squeeze and looks me in the eyes. "Do what? You have to tell me now that you've said all that."

I exhale, wondering how much to share. "Someone left a note at my house last night, saying Allegra Hudson was murdered. They also sent me a few texts after the whole Perry thing today."

"Threatening messages?" Vi squints as if trying to decide how perilous she thinks this is.

I take a deep breath and contemplate how I should say this. "Not exactly. They knew some things about Allegra's murder and the Perry episode. They said they wanted to help me go out on my own and get the story on her death. But the thing is, they also said I'd end up just like her if I didn't do it."

Vi's voice rises an octave. "Mad! That sounds like a dangerous person to me. You sure you don't want to go to the police?"

I know she won't understand, but when it comes to getting leads, sometimes it's hard to differentiate a spooked witness leaving tips from the crazy, guilty psychopaths who on some level want to get caught. I try to explain. "I thought so at first, but they don't seem to want anything from me other than to help me catch Allegra's killer, and they said no police. I don't know that they were threatening me. Now that I think about it, they might have been warning me about someone else entirely. Like maybe they know who killed Allegra and that they're still out there." I backpedal.

Violet sighs and rubs her forehead as I continue, clearly concerned about my well-being.

"They seem to know some information, and they're willing to share. They even seemed to be aware of my conversation with Perry as soon as it happened. I guess that part was strange. But if they were trying to decide whether to share information with me about the Allegra story, they might have been keeping tabs on me to make sure I'm trustworthy."

I continue to downplay everything for Violet. She doesn't know how skeptical I am of this source. If I go to the police now, I'll ruin my only lead on my first major story, one I may desperately need if I'm going to make it on my own.

Vi purses her lips. "I don't know. I don't like it. I mean, I want you to make this career work. I just think you need to really watch it with this person. They seem to have too much access to you for my liking."

"I promise I'll be cautious. Hopefully, it's just someone who's afraid to come out of the shadows with their information because going on the record as a source can always backfire. Maybe they *are* privy to the whole truth, for whatever reason, and I can shed light on it on their behalf. God knows Allegra deserves that. After all, her books saw me through some tough times. The women in her books were such survivors."

I gulp the rest of my tea and set the mug down with a sulk, wondering if I've convinced Violet not to call the police. I should've considered that before I started blurting everything out like a fool. This is what happens when I run on emotion.

"Oh, I remember. You related to her like no one else, but you need to be careful, really. Don't engage if they sound like a threat again, and tread lightly."

"Yeah, I admit they don't sound like someone I want to disappoint."

Brighton walks into the living area and starts to fuss, so I take it as my cue to leave Violet's. After our goodbyes and a few hugs, I finally get in my car and drive off into my new life. Not knowing where to go or what to do, I drive downtown, park, and decide to walk. To fully absorb all that's happened and how to move forward, I wander around brainstorming my future business. With every step, a new marketing idea forms until I'm overwhelmed with tasks that will make running my own news program feasible, and for the first time all day, I feel hopeful.

FIRST THINGS FIRST, I need to work on my website and get the word out about my new career path. If I'm going to be a new face and name for news in Knoxville, it's only natural I feature photos of the downtown area. I start in the heart of downtown Knoxville, Market Square, by capturing images of the rooftop dining above Scruffy City Hall with my phone, then I move on to Krutch Park down the road and snap the waterfall, the stream through the walking trail, and the art deco sculptures displayed throughout the walkway.

I capture a few more favorites down Gay Street, the main drive of downtown Knoxville, with its historic Bijou Theatre and the old brick Woodruff building. After I get a few shots of the rocking chairs on the porch of Mast General from across the street, I head home, where my mother is completely perplexed as I enter my front door.

Graham gives me a bear hug and couldn't care less why I'm home in the middle of the day—he's simply glad I am. When Graham becomes enthralled with a TV show, I pull Mom into the kitchen and regurgitate the Perry incident as my eyes fill with tears. She holds me close and assures me it'll all turn out okay and that I'll find my way. I feel safe and warm, proving that I still need my mom, no matter how old I am.

LATER THAT AFTERNOON, a text from Marcus lifts my spirits.

Still can't believe you left me here in this crazy place. Want me to connect you with my buddy Detective Wentworth? Heard he's getting put on the Allegra Hudson case. Just don't tell Perry I'm sharing my contacts with you. I'm working on an exposé of some important figures in Knoxville... potential for some juicy stuff... going to get some real dirt here soon... I can feel it. It's going to be big. I'm on the verge of something with one person especially, someone who has an *interesting* job.

I've never met him, yet I think of all the horror stories I've heard about Wentworth's condescending attitude and vengeful ways. **May take you up on that, even though I find Wentworth intimidating already.**

He's not so bad. Just don't cross him or his family and you'll be fine.

Easy for you to say. He likes you. A good-looking male in his mid-thirties, Marcus has it made when it comes to getting important men like Perry and Wentworth to like him. He has no wife or kids, so he can brownnose and play golf with Knoxville's elite all he wants. He's always available for networking and building relationships with important people. But I can't be bitter, because he's also a good friend.

He was my first friend at the station. I'll never forget my first week on the job when he asked me to lunch. I was terrified that he might think of it as a date, but we both felt an instant sibling dynamic. "You remind me so much of my sister," he'd said and looked down at our table as he took another sip of his Coke.

"Really. Is she younger?" I guessed, based on the way he sounded so protective.

"Older. Five years. You have a lot of the same expressions and mannerisms. It's so weird." He smiled, but his comment was laced with sadness. "She's gone now, though. Three years now." He avoided eye contact as he spread his napkin in his lap.

"Oh my God. I'm so sorry. Can I ask what happened?" I held my hands up. "If you don't want to say, I completely understand."

Marcus had looked as if tears weren't far away. The chatter from the busy Italian restaurant seemed to dissipate as I leaned in. "Abusive husband. One night, he finally took it too far. We never dreamed it was going on, but a friend of hers had proof. It absolutely devastated my parents and me, because if we'd known, we would've stopped it."

Setting aside the memories, I spend the rest of the day revamping my website. Now it's a local-journalism page where community members can offer story tips and tune in for uncensored community coverage. I link my Twitter, Instagram, and Facebook accounts, which I've also updated and revamped, and go on to create an even tighter personal budget in Excel.

Hopefully, I'll get some local companies to advertise on the website and on my Facebook page after I grow my audience. Then I won't have to dip into my nest egg from Clayton and my grandmother, funds I've saved for emergencies only. I share my website on social media and vaguely explain how I'm no longer under the thumb of those who disrespect women. I ask everyone to support me by sharing my page with their friends.

That evening, Mom, Graham, and I go to a brand-new pizza joint down the road, which offered me free pizza for an honest review after I reached out via email to a few local businesses. After we inhale the food, I land a live interview with the owner. During our chat, I realize I'm going to have to get a tripod—my mom's wobbly hands struggle to hold my phone still for my first Facebook Live.

It's a cute interview and almost an advertisement, because everyone in the restaurant becomes involved in the segment and shares their praise. I capture the vintage sports uniforms hanging on the walls, the buffalo plaid tablecloths, and the cow bell that rings every time someone's order is ready.

As we wrap up and gather our things, I get a text that stops me in my tracks. **Where do you think you're going? You don't want to leave yet—a source.** I look around to see who could be watching, and an older gentleman swings open the creaky front door of the vintage building, revealing the dark, rainy sky outside. He's clad in a tan trench coat, and every head in the place turns and recognizes him as Arthur Burns, the Knox County superintendent of schools.

"Linda, Madeleine," he calls to us after scanning the restaurant. "I heard I'd find you two here."

"Arthur, hi," my mom replies with open arms. "What are you doing here looking for us? I haven't seen you at church for a few weeks. How are you?"

"Umm, I've been okay. I've been traveling a bit. I received a text from, um, someone *urging* me to come here because Madeleine's a freelance reporter of some sort now. Is that right?"

"Yes, that's true. I started today, actually. You just missed my first live interview." I wonder who told him he would find me here. "Who did you say sent you here?"

Arthur folds his arms and clears his throat. "I didn't. It's not important."

I smile on the outside, but my stomach drops, and I wonder whether it's the same person who told me not to leave. However, having a bigwig like Arthur on my side can only help my reputation and career no matter how this all came about. He knows everyone in the school system and is a leader at one of the biggest churches in Tennessee, Cedar Bluff Baptist.

Arthur drops his folded arms and grins as he looks around the restaurant. "Mad, I actually do have something for you to share before I go to the other networks tomorrow, if you'd like to have first dibs."

I want to jump up and down but restrain myself. "By all means, yes. That'd be so helpful. What is it exactly?" I lean in, hungry for more.

"As you know, the flu is going around very early this year. We've had over twenty percent of our staff and students out the past week, and we're going to close schools next Monday and Tuesday because of illness. You think you can get the word out on that?"

Is he serious? This story is going to be huge for me. Closing schools for illness at the beginning of November is almost unheard of. "Yes, I certainly can. I can do a post, or better yet, while you're here, we can go live, and I'll share it online." I motion for Mom to grab my phone, and she scurries over and sets up our shot.

Mom beams with excitement and holds the phone as Arthur straightens his tie and checks his reflection in the restaurant's window.

I clear my throat and take a deep breath, readying for my first important story on my own. "This is Madeleine Barton reporting from Farmhouse Pizza in Powell again. This time, I've got none other than Arthur Burns, superintendent of Knox County Schools, here with me for an exclusive announcement. Take it away, Mr. Burns."

Mom pans to Mr. Burns, who explains to viewers what he's just told me. After a quick nod from Arthur, Mom pans back to me.

"There you have it, folks. No school next Monday and Tuesday for all Knox County Schools. Please share this with your friends to help get the word out, and if you or a loved one are sick, I suggest staying home to rest and recover." After Arthur and I chitchat about the un-usual flu season, Mom presses End, and we've made local history. For the first time, a no-name reporter affiliated with no particular news station has announced the closing of Knox County schools.

By the time I tuck Graham into bed that night, my interview has three thousand shares and eighteen thousand views. At the very least, three thousand people now know my name and that of my new busi-ness. I'm feeling incredibly accomplished as I hop into bed to text my mom, Vi, and Marcus with my news—until I receive a text that brings back a haunting reality.

Great inter-flu, I mean interview. He owed me a favor. You're welcome—a source.

Chapter 4

Do I know you? I ask.

The ellipses on the bottom left corner of my phone blink multiple times, but no words follow, and my heart skips a beat. I wonder whether this is a stalker. Maybe I should try to trace the call or go to the police, even though they said not to. *Did they threaten Arthur or blackmail him into giving me the interview, and if so, should I be scared? Or thankful?*

I'm not the one you need to worry about. I'm only trying to help Allegra's truth come out and therefore help you as well. No, the number won't be traceable, if that's what you're thinking. Don't even waste your time.

What do you want me to do? I ask.

No dots appear this time, and they respond immediately. **Get the story. Be willing to wait and truly listen. Trust me. And me alone.**

I can trust you—as long as I don't feel you're dangerous. I'm hoping they'll convince me they're not and tell me who *is* dangerous.

Don't text me back. I text you. More later—a source.

THE NEXT MORNING, I'M in a hurry to begin my investigation into Allegra's death. I can also continue to cover school system–related stories, and I plan to feature residential concerns within smaller communities, business and real estate trends, local talent performances, political events, and charity fundraisers. But before I can get started with work, I need to get Graham and me ready and drive him to school.

When Graham and I arrive at his classroom door, he gives me a ginormous hug and a kiss on the lips in front of his friends and teacher. "Bye, Mom. I love you," he calls as he hangs his backpack on the bright-green wall covered with numbers and letters before joining his friends at the craft table.

I stroll out the door toward my car, my eyes misty with gratitude, and the significantly colder air hits me. I'm so glad I can take Graham to preschool every day now. These moments are so precious. I fold my arms across my chest as the wind picks up. Winter weather has arrived in Knoxville, and the leaves all decided to fall overnight, leaving the trees exposed and naked.

Once in the car, I start it and crank the heat up, thinking about how to begin investigating Allegra's death. *Who would she have truly trusted? Who would know things about her life?* Her family for sure, close friends, her church, neighbors, old friends from school...

There's no better gossip than dirt from a nosy neighbor, so I'll start there. Maybe I'll find a good "mouth of the South" like old Mrs. Warner, the next-door neighbor who was the epitome of a busybody when I was little. We never had a single visitor at our house who wasn't sized up behind her blinds before the caller even hit our front porch. She was the neighborhood watch wrapped up into one ninety-five-pound woman. I'm off to Sequoyah Hills, then.

I pull up on Cherokee Boulevard and drive past Sequoyah Hills Park. Most people in Knoxville dream of owning a house in Sequoyah Hills. It's a hop, skip, and a jump from the University of Tennessee campus, which sits right next to the downtown area. Sequoyah Hills also sits on the Tennessee River, where boats and yachts are often docked.

In front of their ten-thousand-square-foot homes, bundled-up people are throwing Frisbees to their dogs. Others jog down the greenway that runs through the median, and I can't help feeling that they should observe a moment of silence since one of their own has just passed.

I continue on for half a mile and approach a stone-covered English Tudor mansion on what looks like at least two acres of land, and according to Zillow, the home has stood the test of time since 1927. A woman heads out of the Hudsons' front door and toward her worn Highlander parked on the street. Expensive luxury vehicles line the paver driveway. I've got my phone out and my window down, and the woman notices me studying the ivy-covered home. She purses her lips then asks, "Can I help you?" Her disagreeable tone says, "We're all sick of you gawkers."

She probably takes me for another nosy reporter with no boundaries. I wonder whether to drive away or give it a shot, but too late. She's here.

"Oh, hi." I remove the sunglasses that cover half my face. "My name's Madeleine Barton. I actually just started my own—"

She cuts me off with a raised hand. She smiles, and her demeanor changes. "Oh yeah, I recognize you. I heard about you starting your own news operation on Facebook. I think it's inspiring, the way you've branched out on your own."

I grin, thinking I've won her over. "Oh, really? I'm so glad you think so."

"Yes. I hate that they didn't treat you right over at WKNX. I've heard that Perry Brown can be a real jerk. A real *handsy* jerk, actually," she whispers through cupped hands as she looks from side to side as if checking for eavesdroppers.

I cock my head, sizing her up. Freckles and a warm smile give her a girl-next-door look, although she seems about forty or so, and I instantly like her. She seems familiar. "Well, I can't argue with your description. What did you say your name was?"

"Oh, right, I didn't." She shuffles some folders to her left hand and extends her right arm into my open car window. "I'm Ivy Richards. I'm Allegra's—or I *was* Allegra's—best friend. We grew up together. Almost like sisters, actually."

"I'm so sorry for your loss," I offer.

Her friendly face falls, and I have the urge to console her.

"Thank you. It's been awful," she says.

"I'd like to help if I can. Do you know how the family feels about the police not having any real information on the cause of death yet? I know it's only been a few days, but are they happy with the progress so far? Because I've read a few blogs that indicate Detective Wentworth is on the case now and may not be after the truth."

She perks up. "You know what? If I'm going to talk to you, it's not for a story—well, not for a gossip story. I'm only interested in finding justice for Allegra and her family."

I agree wholeheartedly with her ultimatum. "Of course."

She looks back at the Hudson house, perhaps checking to see if anyone's watching our interaction. "I like you, and I'd like to work with you on getting the real story, like you said, if that's what you're asking me."

"Absolutely. I'm not looking to run any stories on Allegra, her family, her friends, or any crazy theories. I'm only interested in finding out what really happened, and when I do, that'll be the story. The only story. No information comes from me except that."

Ivy straightens up and looks around. The wintry breeze blows her chestnut hair back, and she bends down to my level as if she's made a decision. "Let's go sit and chat somewhere else."

"Starbucks on Kingston Pike?"

"See you there in ten." She shuffles toward her Highlander as if we've just made a drug deal.

Before I pull out of the neighborhood, I unlock my phone so I can check on the amount of money in my account, something I'm becoming obsessive about. I'm not sure if I can even afford Star-bucks. My rent check has probably cleared, and I don't know how long it's going to be before I earn another check after this week. I should probably sip from the bottle of water in my purse instead of buying coffee.

MARCUS ROACH'S NAME flashes across the screen of my phone as I cruise past the Ice Chalet, where I had my ice-skating-themed birthday parties in both third and fourth grades, thanks to my amazing mother. I remember he said he was on a big story, so I answer.

"Hey, Mad. How's everything going? I saw your new website, and it looks pretty stellar. Good job."

"Aww, thanks. That means a lot to me, knowing you find it up to par. Things are good. Just got a new source close to Allegra Hudson who's willing to talk to me, so talk fast because I'm on my way to meet her right now. How are things with you and your story?"

Marcus coughs and clears his throat a few times, sounding like a chain-smoker on the brink of death. "Amazing. Juicy. I can't believe how big this is going to be. It could potentially ruin someone. That's all I can say. And yes, they deserve it."

"You still have that cough? You really need to go to the doctor, or you're going to *be* a breaking story. You sounded like you had bronchitis two weeks ago. I'd hate to know what it's become by now. Probably pneumonia. And while you're at it, you probably need to back off the coffee. What are you up to now? Five cups?"

Our brother-and-sister relationship works both ways. Not that I'm the epitome of health or anything, but Marcus has some work to do if he's going to make it to forty without having a heart attack induced by the excessive amounts of coffee and Red Bull he downs on the regular.

"I'll be fine. No time for doctors right now. I'll nail down the rest of this story in a day or two, and I can get checked then. Nothing's going to stop me right now. I can't let them know I'm on the brink of exposing them, or it's all over. After this piece, maybe we can work on the Allegra thing together. If my story goes well, I'll have enough clout to do whatever I want. Maybe I'll join you on your team, or we can team up. I'd love to get away from Perry anyway. Can you imagine what could happen if I break this story wide open for Knoxville and you solve Allegra's murder? We'll both go national, Mad."

I laugh nervously, knowing what he's saying could be true. As much as I want success, I can't see it happening. Maybe I'm afraid to picture what big success would do to me. I might get swept away with it and forget who I really am. "Let's not get ahead of ourselves now."

"Have you phoned Wentworth yet? I think he could help you out."

"No, not yet. I will eventually," I add, knowing it's a stretch. Technically, I might give him a call for something in my lifetime, so it's not exactly a lie.

"I can give him a call for you if that makes it less intimidating. He'd probably be more willing to share information if I talk to him first anyway. I'll give him a ring today or tomorrow."

I sigh. "Okay, that works."

"I'll call you afterward to check up on you and let you know what I hear from Wentworth. Good luck with your new source, Mad."

"And good luck to you on your upcoming takedown. I swear I don't know anyone as ruthless as you. Remind me not to get on your bad side."

Marcus laughs. "Talk soon. And be careful with this one. Something tells me it's a bigger story than you think it is."

THE SMELL OF STARBUCKS coffee reminds me of Clayton and the lake house his aunt used to have in Dandridge. Memories of one particular summer fill me with nostalgia. We'd snuck off to his aunt's log cabin at Douglas Lake when we were each supposedly spending the night at a friend's house. It was the first time I'd told a huge lie to my mom.

The morning after we lost ourselves in each other for the first time, in her master bedroom, I spied his aunt's coffee maker on the kitchen counter and brewed us a fresh cup. Clayton took the first sip while he was clad in black socks and Spider-Man boxers, and he swallowed as if I'd fed him shards of glass. He forced a grin and kissed me on the mouth. "Thanks, baby. It's perfect."

I took a sip from my cup and spit it out in the sink, mortified that I had screwed it up. "Clay, it's disgusting! How'd you even get it down? It tastes like lake water with a sugar cube."

"Yeah, babe, the water from the sink basically *is* lake water. You've got to get it filtered from the fridge." He'd grabbed my waist and pulled me close as he took another giant gulp. "But since *you* fixed it, it really is perfect."

As I remember his face, a single tear stings mine. Then a strange ringing begins in my ears, and the back of my head aches again. It's the same ice pick feeling I had at Violet's doorstep but sharper and more intense. *Not now, please. Not now.* Not when I can practically see Clayton again like it was yesterday. In the blink of an eye, the piercing pain leaves as quickly as it came, along with Clayton.

Ivy plops down next to me as if we're long-lost friends. "Thanks for meeting me here. I didn't want any of Allegra's neighbors or family to get the wrong idea, you know? Did you want to get some coffee?"

I shake my head. "No, but feel free to grab some if you want. I completely understand about the neighbor thing, by the way. Sometimes the media can be overbearing."

"They really can. Some of them know no limitations at all. I'm good on the coffee front for now, too, so feel free to ask me whatever."

"Okay, then. To start with, can you just tell me about yourself and how you knew Allegra?"

Ivy clears her throat, scans the room, and straightens her back. "I'm a stay-at-home mom to a twelve-year-old boy, and my husband, Rick, is an architect. I met Allegra when we were both in the same class in elementary school. We've been best friends ever since, although we've had our ups and downs along the way. She was the sister I never had. We took care of each other."

With her freckles, chestnut-brown hair, and animated gestures, Ivy reminds me of Violet. Perhaps that's why I took to her so quickly. She's so similar, only older. I can't help but picture how devastating it would be for either Vi or me to lose the other one.

"So how is the family doing? How was her relationship with her husband?"

She leans in close. "Allegra's husband, Connor, and the boys are just completely torn apart. I am, too, but I feel like I have to be strong for them. It's what Allegra would want. If you ask me, the police aren't doing a very good job. I mean, how hard can it be? Can they not at least say yes, she was murdered? All the headlines are saying it, but the police haven't confirmed it yet. I think it'd bring everyone a little closure to know whether it was one hundred percent an accident or not. You know?"

"Yes, of course," I say, but I don't mean it. After Clayton's death, I punched my bedroom door and walls until they were stained red. I couldn't deal with my rage or the senselessness of his death. Knowing whether it was or wasn't an accident won't bring them closure. It will only bring them more questions and what-ifs. That, I know.

"Is there a chance it *could've* been an accident?"

Ivy sighs long and hard before she answers. "Remember Allegra's sketchy behavior and appearance when she was selling books on QVC?"

"Who can forget that? I read that she overdid it on her anxiety medication that day because she was nervous about being on air for such a long time."

"Right. Well, that happened more than that one time. And the other times, she wasn't going on live TV. Benzodiazepine can be addicting if abused, and Allegra developed a dependence on it after her mom died. Her death was a lot for Allegra to handle. They were very close. One pill took the edge off, and she quickly discovered that a few at a time mixed with some wine made her forget the pain completely.

"The police don't know any of this, because Connor and I agreed it should be kept a secret, and I hope I'm right and that you can be trusted. She hasn't abused pills for years now, and while they can cause grogginess that leads to falls, we don't want the police using her past problems as a way to blame Allegra's death on her when, according to who you ask, she was arguably hit in the head before she fell. Allegra realized she had a problem after QVC, and she got it together. She threw herself into work and kind of went overboard with being busy, and that's when her marriage problems began, but that's another story. Anyway, my husband and I have heard Wentworth likes to keep things as simple as possible, and we don't want Allegra's reputation tarnished because he's too political and lazy to find out the actual truth."

My heart sinks. I can't believe someone who seemingly had it together could end up abusing antianxiety pills. I guess we're all just one catastrophe away from similar circumstances, especially those of us with anxiety issues. Sometimes, I feel like I need to double up on my meds to do a live report. I know Ivy thinks Allegra's drug abuse is incidental to the investigation, but it's something to keep in mind as I learn more about Allegra. I can't just pretend it's not a possible motive or cause of death just because her friend says so.

Thank God for Graham being in my belly during my time of loss, or I might have ended up with a pill problem like Allegra. And thank God for Allegra's career, because it helped her deal with her pill problem. I realize Ivy didn't touch on Allegra's marriage, so I press her again. "What was her marriage like?"

Ivy appears to choose her words carefully. "They were having some difficulties. Allegra was spreading herself pretty thin over the past few years. I mean, she *was* kind of a big deal. She adored her fans and her career and gave it all she had, but Connor definitely felt neglected at times. And rightfully so in my opinion. Allegra stayed busy with her fans, charities, and career so she wouldn't have to completely accept her mom's passing. But it was hard on Connor, too, because she held her feelings inside. All of that hurt was bottled up, and she was distant at times."

"Did Connor get angry about her absence?" I ask.

Ivy shakes her head. "Connor would never hurt her, if that's what you're getting at. They fought, yes, but nothing like that. Plus, the camera footage from the night she died shows him sleeping as Allegra walked out the front door, and at the time of her murder. He found her, you know. And on the footage, he goes outside after hearing a noise and then, seconds later, rushes inside to call 911." Ivy wipes her eyes.

"How horrible for him to find her like that. I can only imagine how he's torturing himself with guilt over not checking earlier."

She leans in. "Word on the street is that Wentworth is so wrapped up in his police-chief cousin's political career and in tying up cases faster than anyone else that he might be falsely accusing people, which is terrifying. But none of us want to contest it because then we'll likely be the one he pins Allegra's death on. Connor's thought about hiring a private investigator, and maybe he will. I don't know, but I'd love for you to see what you can find out. We need someone out there investigating who's unbiased, because according to the police report, nothing was taken from her. She still had her suitcase, her purse, which had her laptop in it, her wedding rings, and her diamond stud earrings on her when she was found. I find that a little odd."

"Hmm. That's definitely interesting." I'm thrilled she has such faith in me but also surprised. "Of course, I'll do everything I can," I assure her with a nod, knowing I have something no one else has—a source.

Her bottom lip quivers. "I truly appreciate it."

I press on. "So what can you tell me about Allegra? What kind of person was she? Did she have any known enemies?"

Ivy sighs as a tear cascades down her cheek. "Here's the truth. I loved Allegra since we were little, and like I said, we were close until about five years ago, when she really made it big in the publishing world and became a bit... detached. Her free time became limited, especially after her mom and the pills, and everyone wanted to be her friend or fan, and she kind of faded away from me, and I'm not one to desperately chase anyone for friendship. If you want to be my friend, you'll make time for me. If you don't, then you won't."

"Distant and detached? In what way?" I picture Allegra at events for charities like St. Jude's and United Way, a charismatic grin on her face and anything but distant and inaccessible.

"She got busier, obviously. Then she convinced Connor and the boys to move from Powell to Sequoyah Hills. Her youngest and my boy are the same age, and even they lost touch after the move. Everyone knows Sequoyah Hills is one of the ritziest places in Knoxville. You've been there. It's full of historic riverfront mansions with enormous exquisitely landscaped yards for only the elite-est of the elite, and she wanted to be a part of it since they could afford it and all.

"Connor's construction business could probably have allowed them to live there a few years back, to be honest, but Connor's a good ole boy. He doesn't care for the glitz and glamour, and the Allegra I grew up with didn't put much stock in it either. We both came from very humble but happy backgrounds. But they moved, and she slowly began to change. Her new friend and neighbor Mayven Bennett influenced her in the snobby sort of way, if you know what I mean."

"I assume you didn't take well to her new circle of friends?"

"No, not really. It wasn't our Allegra, you know? Not the one I'd known forever. I guess that's what fame can do to you. She and Connor disagreed about a lot of things, too, from then on. She swore the fame and fortune wouldn't change who she was even when they moved, but he found her sudden interest in country clubs, new cars and boats, and rubbing elbows with local politicians a bit pretentious and not at all like the country girl he fell in love with. So many things changed over time, and the boys weren't happy about switching schools either."

I look up from my pen and paper, trying to remember the boys' ages. "She has two preteen boys, right?"

"Gosh, no. Mason's going to be eighteen this year, and Garrett's just turned twelve."

She pauses and touches my hand, and I look up.

"Don't get me wrong, I'm not that jealous friend who couldn't handle the fame and success of her best friend. When she first started writing, I was her go-to beta reader. I was always the person she trusted to read her work, besides her sweet momma, who passed away right after Allegra made it really big. Her mom always struggled with money, having raised Allegra on her own. I was truly happy things were easier for her, just as much as I would've been if it'd happened to me."

Ivy sounds sincere, but she's protesting quite a bit. Maybe she does have some latent animosity toward Allegra, or maybe she's hurt that her best friend moved on and left her.

"So did she stop letting you read her work once she moved?"

"No, she always did that, even with her latest books. We bounced ideas back and forth so well together. Mysteries and suspense have always been my favorite genres since we were little. I got Allegra hooked on Nancy Drew and Scooby-Doo when we were young, and she moved on to scarier stuff by studying Hitchcock in high school. She was hooked on solving every whodunit movie or book from then on, so it wasn't a huge surprise when she decided to create her own. She knew if she could shock me with an ending, it was a worthwhile twist."

"You guys were still pretty close friends, just not best friends, then?" Maybe Ivy was overly needy. Perhaps she required a lot of attention and reassurance once Allegra became a Hollywood hit. Or maybe she isn't telling me everything.

"That's fair to say, yeah." Ivy nods as if she's been carried back to the good old days of their friendship and doesn't remember how things ended for Allegra.

"Did she have any enemies? Anyone who might have wanted to hurt her? Any crazy stalkers or obsessive fans?"

Ivy rubs her temples and frowns. "I have wracked my brain trying to think of anyone, and I've got absolutely nothing. I know it wasn't an accident, but it doesn't make any sense why it wouldn't be. I can't imagine anyone hating her that much. She was a good person."

Her voice trembles, and she's visibly cracking. It's time to wrap this up. "Okay, I can see that you need a break. Tell you what, if you think of any more information that'd be helpful, call, text, email, whatever. At any time, okay?" I jot down my contact information and pass it across the table.

"I will for sure." Ivy wipes her eyes. "Thanks."

Before I leave, I want to get a cup of the smallest decaf they serve and promise to brew my own starting tomorrow. I open my banking app again to see if my latest check has cleared and almost pass out when I see the new amount in my checking account.

I checked it on the way here, and it's grown by three thousand dollars! I go through my history to find the obvious mistake and come across a check that was deposited only ten minutes ago from A.S. Industries. It's made out to me, and while it appears to have been deposited and signed by me as well, I didn't do it, even though the signature is spot-on. When I glance at the bottom left corner of the digital image of the check for the memo, my heart thuds up into my throat, and I take a seat in the booth once more. **Grab that coffee, girl. You're welcome—a source.**

After a few seconds of contemplating whether this person is a psychopath who means to control my bank account in a negative manner later, I gather my things and head to the counter for some much-needed coffee. The source didn't say anything about paying them back, but I'm not sure I want to owe—or depend on—someone I don't even know. I'm already in a panic when I spot the unique profile of a man with a prominent chin eerily similar to my own. My heart rises into my throat until it's about to leap out of my mouth. Surely, it's not...

He turns and speaks to the man behind him, but the face isn't a match. My heart thumps back down, and my whole body unwinds. I've not seen my father since he left my mom and me when I was seven, setting off the first of many panic attacks and insecurity issues. Ever since, I've been dreading the moment God allows our paths to cross again. Luckily for me, today is not that day.

My phone vibrates in my purse, and I reach for it as I move up in line. Another text.

You're gaining their trust. That's a good start, Mad. Keep going. But move quickly, your time is running out...—a source.

I scan the room for someone watching me, wondering whether this person is dangerous. I walk outside and see my breath in the air as I text Vi about my new message. Despite the crisp air, sweat builds around my hairline.

Now my time is running out? I'm freaking out. Should I respond? I ask Violet as my hands tremble.

No, say nothing. If they're as technologically savvy as you think they are, they'll know you read it. You need to let me or someone know about all these texts so we can keep tabs on this situation. Be careful, Mad. They could be watching everything you do.

Her response does nothing for my anxiety. **I suppose I'd say the same thing to you, Vi—so, okay. Better you know than my mom. God knows her heart can't take it. Maybe they want to help me but are sounding vague on purpose so I won't figure out who they are?** I try to rationalize. **Maybe they're intentionally trying to creep me out to keep me at arm's length? Or maybe they truly are what I don't want to admit—a threat.**

SEVERAL HOURS LATER, I tuck Graham in for the night and then myself. I'm in bed and going over the police report that Marcus somehow got ahold of and emailed to me when I was meeting with Ivy, even though Marcus noted that Wentworth had it sealed this afternoon for witness protection reasons. It confirms everything Ivy said, and I'm relieved but still stumped. My phone buzzes on the end table next to my bed. One, two, three, four, five buzzes in a row. *Good grief. Did someone else die?*

I check to see who's texting, and it's WKNX's former beauty queen, Georgia Wilson. I roll my eyes. She obviously didn't realize she left me in one of the station's group texts because I see Perry respond to her as well as others from the station. Everyone seems shocked and surprised as prayers for some family and OMG keep popping up as responses to the original message, which is far from the top of the thread by now. I scroll up, and my stomach tightens when I see the original text.

Guys, I have some terrible news. I just got word that Marcus has been in a terrible accident in his Jeep, and I'm devastated to report that he didn't make it. Please keep his parents in your prayers as they plan to bury their only son, and please love on each other as we endure this difficult time together. We will all miss Marcus terribly. He was such a valued member of our group here at WKNX.

I can't read the rest of the responses. My left hand goes straight over my mouth, tears flow down my face, and my pulse sprints. I just talked to him a few hours ago. He was happy, healthy—mostly—and fine. He was on the brink of a huge story.

And now he's gone.

Chapter 5

The spray of lilies on Marcus's casket, his parents' tears as they console one another on the front row, and the sound of "Amazing Grace" bring back memories of Clayton's funeral, and suddenly, I can't bear the pain of my memories. A panic attack starts building as I stare at Marcus's face in the picture Perry took of him for WKNX's website, now displayed in a dark mahogany frame on a tall metal stand.

Marcus's face morphs into the picture displayed beside Clayton's coffin, the photo of him in a black tuxedo and me in a white lace ballgown. But I close my eyes and try not to remember.

I try to think of something else, anything else, but both their faces haunt me. I excuse myself and head toward the bathroom as sweat pools all over my body and my heart rate soars. I walk faster, afraid I may faint, but once I reach the one-person-only restroom and take a few deep breaths, my panic attack slowly recedes.

After I splash cold water on my neck, I calm down. Once I'm gathered enough to return to the service, I open the bathroom door, and next in line is Perry. I walk right past him as if he doesn't exist, and when I pass by, I sense him eyeing me from behind.

A nagging feeling comes over me. Ever since Marcus's death a few days ago, a part of me has been wondering if he could have been murdered, and my gut says I'll never forgive myself if I don't do some digging.

"Wait, Perry. Can I ask you something?" I turn and hold up my index finger as I notice his lowered eyes, which must have been studying my rear end.

He lifts his eyes to my face. "I suppose."

I take a deep breath. "Believe me, you're the last person in the world I want to have a conversation with right now, but this is about Marcus. Do you know whose secret he was about to expose in his story? Because he kept telling me it was big, and I can't help thinking, 'What if someone caused the accident intentionally because they were onto him?'" Maybe he was secretly doing something with the Allegra Hudson case. He already had access to her police report.

Perry steps toward me and whispers even though there's no one around who can hear us. "Marcus was tight-lipped about the details of his story, and he didn't want to tell me who it was about until it was complete. What I do know is no one could've caused the accident, because the autopsy showed that his death was caused from anaphylaxis. Apparently, a barista accidentally put almond milk in his coffee that morning when he went to the Beanery. The wreck was caused by his severe allergic reaction behind the wheel, not someone running him off the road or whatever you were thinking."

I can't believe it. "There's no way he would forget to mention his nut allergy at the Beanery, and I thought almond milk was a special order kind of thing?" None of what Perry is saying sounds right.

"Seems like an honest mistake, according to the police. A very unfortunate one. I don't think it has anything to do with his exposé, Madeleine. I really don't."

"What about his laptop? Can we take a look? Maybe there's something—"

Perry shakes his head. "Destroyed in the wreckage."

I sigh in frustration. Marcus never made a hard copy of anything he was secretly working on, because it might get leaked. "Of course it was."

"Listen, nothing's going to bring him back. And if you go rooting around after his death, it's only going to make it that much harder on his family. And I don't think Marcus would want that. Do you?"

Perry makes a valid point, especially since his parents have already lost their other child tragically as well, but I don't think Marcus would want me to ignore the fact that this all seems a little too convenient for whoever he was about to out. I play along, though, because Perry might be trying to get me off the case so he can exploit Marcus's death and suspected murder for his own reasons.

"Of course. Well, I'm going back in. Thanks for answering my questions." I no longer want to engage with him and whatever motives he may have.

"Yeah," Perry answers as he walks toward the bathroom. He turns again. "Impressive, what you've done for yourself."

I'm shocked to hear him admit it. "Thanks."

He hangs his head and gives me a slight smile as he walks into the bathroom and shuts the door. Perhaps that was his way of hinting at an apology. I don't know. I've never seen him apologize to anyone.

"HELLO?" A FEW DAYS after Marcus's funeral, I answer my phone, not knowing who is on the other end as it reads Private.

"Ms. Barton?" The older, scruffy voice sounds like Sam Elliott.

"Yes. This is she."

"This is Detective Jeff Wentworth. I got the message you left me at the office this morning. You said you have concerns about the unfortunate death of our mutual friend Marcus Roach. Is that correct?"

I'm nervous about speaking to Wentworth. "Yes, it is. I know he was working on a big story. An exposé, actually. It was going to out someone important, and I know ruining someone's life like that is a valid motive for murder. I was wondering if I could convince you to look into it, since you were friendly and all. Maybe his death is even connected to Allegra Hudson's."

Wentworth sighs as if I'm exasperating and clueless. "Now, Ms. Barton, I really don't think this is something you need to worry—"

I jump in. "What if the Beanery didn't mess up his order? What if someone else tampered with his drink after he left? We don't know where he went that morning, after all."

Wentworth clears his throat. "The case seems pretty cut-and-dried, unfortunately. Someone brand-new was being trained at the Beanery last week, and they say it's possible they mixed up his order with someone else's or reached for the wrong milk. I'll do some additional digging if it makes you feel better, but this was clearly a mistake. We do have more pressing matters that require our immediate attention right now."

"Right. You mean the Hudson case, because it has national potential."

He laughs as if to belittle me. "Ma'am, I don't know how you think we do business around here, but we don't work that way. We work on our cases based on the evidence, not based on what's popular."

I want to say that I know all about how he conducts his investigations, that he tries to close murder cases as quickly as he can and make them seem less serious than they are. That's the reason they haven't referred to Allegra's death as a murder yet. They don't want the public to panic and think his police-chief cousin is doing a bad job of keeping crime down in Knoxville, and they don't want the media to get the idea that it's a dangerous place to live. But I hold my tongue for Marcus's sake. "I'd appreciate it if you looked into it. It could be something..."

"Is that all, Ms. Barton?"

We both know he's not going to give Marcus's death another thought. I know a blow-off when I hear it.

I roll my eyes and bite my tongue. "That's all. Thanks for your time."

Once again, it's up to me to do Wentworth's job. If anyone reveals the truth about Marcus and Allegra, it'll be me. As tears roll down my cheeks, I pull up the cell phone picture of Marcus and me eating pizza at Barley's last year. He was such a good friend, like the brother I never had. It feels like losing Clayton all over again, and the grief tries to smother me.

I quickly pray not to go back to the awful state of mind I was in after I lost Clayton. I became consumed with anger and sadness, and I can't afford to go there again. I have a strong hunch that if I can find Allegra's killer, Marcus's death will make sense somehow. Perhaps the big exposé Marcus was working on was about Allegra's killer. The two deaths could easily be related, but I haven't one shred of evidence to prove it. I guess I have a story to get back to.

A WEEK HAS PASSED SINCE Allegra's death, and despite my research, I haven't found any evidence pointing toward her killer. The police said they had all the evidence needed to continue investigating and allowed Allegra's family to cremate her and have a funeral. No press were allowed anywhere near the church.

I flip through the church directory of Second Baptist of Knoxville, where the funeral was held, hoping to find information on Allegra. Maybe she was part of some close-knit groups within her church, or perhaps she was a leader or teacher. Nothing sticks out except a list of the names of those in her and Connor's Sunday school class. The roster means nothing to me, but there might be some loose-lipped ladies I can check out. I circle the names of those whose addresses are closest to Allegra's and decide to scope out the neighborhood again.

Only four women from the list live in Sequoyah Hills, and three have already slammed their door in my face after claiming they have nothing to say—except that Allegra was a good Christian woman and no one had it out for her. The fourth lady claims, "It had to be an accident, and anyone who says otherwise is simply trying to torture her sweet family in order to sell dramatic stories to the press."

That stung.

I prepare to exit the neighborhood but get another text before pulling out onto Kingston Pike, so I pause. **Leaving the neighborhood so soon? If at first, you don't succeed...—a source.**

My window is still down since I've been peering at the gigantic homes, and another vehicle pulls into the neighborhood and a familiar voice calls out.

"Madeleine, hey! Wait a second."

I throw my car in Park and look in the rearview mirror. Ivy sticks her head out of her window and waves. No one else is on the road, so I throw my car into Reverse until we meet face-to-face.

Ivy lowers her Ray-Bans and pulls her scarf close to her neck. "I was going to call you today. I spoke to Connor about you and the 'investigation,' and he's all in. If Wentworth doesn't provide any answers for him in the next few days, he says he'll tell you everything he knows."

I wrinkle my forehead, surprised people have such faith in me. "Really?"

"Yeah, he says he knows of you from your Facebook page and thinks you're the real deal. Honestly, he wants answers, and if he thinks you can help, he's going to do whatever he has to do to help dig up the truth."

Perhaps my luck is changing. "Tell him to call me when he's ready."

"I sure will." Ivy smiles. "You should go feel Mayven Bennett out. We're not exactly each other's biggest fans, but she did know and love

Allegra too. Maybe she'll have some information from their hoity-toity social circle. It's worth a shot. She lives right there."

She points at what must be a ten-thousand-square-foot river-front mansion that somehow looks cottagey. Tranquil landscaping and old charm make it the perfect combination of livability and luxury. If I were Ivy, I'd have a chip on my shoulder, too, if the resident of this home stole my best friend.

I APPROACH THE TWELVE-foot-tall mahogany front door with a gulp of intimidation. To my surprise, the lady of the house answers her front door all by her itty-bitty self—and itty-bitty is an understatement. Clad in what appears to be a snug size-two Victoria Beckham sheath dress, Mayven Bennett is no more than a hundred and ten pounds soaking wet, and she's at least five foot six.

"How can I help you?" she asks robotically.

I can't stop staring at her raven-colored hair slicked back into a perfect ponytail draped over her right shoulder. She looks ready for a cover shoot. I imagine she could "help me" in several ways I don't care to mention, like how to sip my tea correctly, how to lose a few pounds, or how to enunciate like a lady.

"Oh, well, I heard you were friends with the late Allegra Hudson. Is that correct?" I shuffle papers around so she can't read her scribbled and underlined name on the top of my stack.

"Can I assume Ivy Richards has informed you of my relationship with Allegra, then?" When she says Ivy's name, it's as if she's trying not to snarl and I'm guilty by association.

"Why would you assume that?"

"Dear, my cameras picked up you two in front of the house, having some kind of 'street conversation' before she pointed you to my front door." Her voice doesn't elevate as she accuses me of lurking around her house with someone she clearly doesn't like, not even when she makes air quotes around "street conversation."

"To be perfectly honest, yes. She did inform me of your friendship. She also said you may be willing to help her and Connor figure out what really happened to Allegra. Is that something you'd be willing to be a part of? As you probably know, they aren't very pleased with the progress the police have made thus far."

Mayven seems to consider my words. "I'm very well aware of that. I'm not too impressed myself. I feel terrible for the boys, to have their mother taken away like that. Who could do such a horrific thing?"

I pat my stack of papers and raise my eyebrows. "That's what we want to get to the bottom of."

Mayven opens the door wider. "All right. Come on inside. I'll assist you however I can."

I follow her into the living room—one of them anyway. I lower myself onto a stiff but no doubt expensive armchair across from Mayven, who sits on the matching French provincial sofa. I glance around the space and inhale the swanky décor.

I'm surrounded by ornate moldings, twenty-foot ceilings adorned with ancient wooden beams, and pristine curtains over enormous windows that reveal a beautiful view of the Tennessee River. I take a deep breath to gather myself. What I really want to do is drop my jaw, gawk, and ooh and aah over this incredible house. Instead, I grab my BIC ballpoint pen from the purse I bought at Target and attempt to remain professional. "To start, just tell me about how you met Allegra and what your relationship was like. I need to know as much about her as I possibly can." *And as much as I can about you too. Because as far as I'm concerned, everyone is a suspect.*

Mayven crosses her ankles and clasps one palm over the other, her perfect posture making me aware of my slumped back.

"When Allegra and Connor moved here from Powell, as I'm sure Ivy has informed you, Allegra and I instantly hit it off. She and I were unalike personality-wise, but we really connected on interior design and décor since our tastes are similar. She wanted to integrate herself into this neighborhood, and I took her under my wing as far as introductions went.

"My husband and I head up several charities. He's a stockbroker and an investment adviser to everyone who's anyone in Knoxville, and I'm a former adviser myself, but I now serve on the HOA board for our neighborhood. Many people knew of Allegra, especially after her first book was turned into a movie, but not everyone is a mystery reader, you know. I helped her redecorate their home when they moved in, and she shared her writing with me before she sent it off to her editor since I've always been an avid reader."

I finish my notes on how they met and wiggle my pen back and forth between my first two fingers. Nothing points toward any conflict.

"Do you know of anyone she didn't jive so well with? Any enemies, frenemies, or people with a chip on their shoulder over her success, perhaps?" I picture Ivy's face and wait for Mayven to confirm my thoughts. I like Ivy, but I can't help thinking something's a little off about how her friendship with Allegra disintegrated.

Mayven glances at the ceiling then me. "No, not that I recall. Unless you include Ivy Richards in the 'frenemy' category. I'm not so sure she was always genuinely supportive of Allegra's success. She always seemed to be making her feel guilty for the time she spent furthering her career. When Allegra was on her last book tour, Ivy let her know how selfish she thought it was that the boys had to be without their mother for a whole month. But if Allegra had been a man, no one would've said a word, would they? Allegra wanted to bring the boys along, but they would've missed baseball and football camp, and she didn't want to take away from that."

My eyebrows rise, and I'm interested in the drama surrounding Ivy and Allegra's friendship.

Mayven continues, "I'm not saying I think Ivy did anything. In fact, I'm quite positive she didn't, and never would, but there *was* bitterness and strife between them, and you did ask about any frenemies." Mayven switches ankles without missing a beat.

"Was the problem Allegra's success or simply how much she changed?" I stop taking notes so I can study Mayven's body language.

Mayven uncrosses her legs and tugs on her dress with her perfectly manicured blush nails. "Ivy always said it was Allegra who did all the changing, but maybe it was just growth. Ivy wanted Allegra to remain stagnant so they could be on the same page, if you want my thoughts on the matter. Ivy was particularly irritated that Allegra made so many new friends with her rise in fame. She didn't think anyone who hadn't known Allegra her entire life could possibly want to be her friend for the right reasons, and she made that known, especially to me."

She doesn't seem to be lying, but she does seem a little agitated and perhaps biased when discussing Ivy.

"If you don't consider her worth looking into, let's move on. Was there anyone else you can think of who might—"

Mayven bounces up in her seat. "I can't believe I forgot! There was that one teacher at Garrett's school. You know, Allegra's younger son. This man was assigned as Garrett's teacher last September, but then Allegra and Connor moved Garrett out of his class because he and Allegra had dated before she met Connor. It caused quite the stir among the school staff. I believe his name was Lane something. He never could get over Allegra. He would randomly but conveniently bump into her at the grocery store and gym. It always bothered Allegra. Connor didn't like it either."

I start scribbling, my heart racing at all the possibilities this information brings. I lift my head to drop a question in. "Was he actually bothering Allegra, or was Connor the jealous type?"

Mayven interlaces her fingers on her lap as if reining herself in from showing excitement. "I wouldn't say Connor is the jealous type, no. I think Lane made quite the idiot of himself years ago after she moved on with Connor, and Connor never forgot about it. Connor's a gentleman, always was, but Lane pushed him to the edge a few times. Connor even encouraged Allegra to pursue a restraining order against Lane, but Allegra insisted Lane was harmless and ignoring him would be best. Ultimately, Allegra didn't feel comfortable having Garrett in Lane's classroom. She thought he might be tempted to pump Garrett for information about her or her marriage. It just wasn't a good fit."

My wheels are spinning an intricate web of facts, suspects, and insights that propel me into another unbearable headache. Ivy had jealousy issues with Mayven and Allegra, Mayven doesn't care for Ivy, and Connor seemingly stole Allegra from her ex-boyfriend, Lane, who apparently couldn't let go of their relationship. With so many possible motives, I grab the back of my head and hear that awful high-pitched noise in my ears again. Only this time, it's completely deafening.

Mayven's lips are spilling more details that I desperately want to jot down, but I hear none of them. I cover my ears and wince in pain. Mayven's hand touches my knee, and I open my eyes to see her face mere inches from mine.

"Are you okay?" she mouths, almost in slow motion and with a look of concern.

I have an urge to run out like I did at Marcus's funeral, and nothing else matters at the moment. It's like I'm trapped in a darkening haze. I grab my belongings. "I'm sorry. I've got to go to the doctor. I promise, I'll look into the Lane thing."

Mayven's hand is on the small of my back, guiding me toward the front door as I hold my head with one hand and my things with the other. I scurry across the crunchy frozen lawn to my car, the noise in my ears still shrill but subsiding once I'm outdoors. When I'm in the car and moving, the sound gradually fades away, and I dial my family doctor.

When I explain my situation, the nurse says to come in right away. I arrive in the waiting area and bounce my knee up and down until the nurse calls me back into an exam room. There, I explain the problems I've been having to Dr. Davenport's nurse as I smell and taste the fresh Lysol spray in the air. She purses her lips, tilts her head, and leaves, and I text my mom to fill her in as well. Before she can text me back, Dr. Davenport walks in.

He arrives with a frown. "Hi, Miss Madeleine. My nurse says you've been having headaches and a loud ringing in the ears, and you thought you should run this 'new thing' by me?"

Dr. Davenport looks uncharacteristically concerned. Migraines are my obvious assumption, so despite the pained expression on his face, I remain calm. "Yeah, that's pretty much it. I mean, it kind of sounds like textbook migraine issues to me. Don't you think?" My eyes grow large, begging for reassurance.

Dr. Davenport takes a seat on his rolling chair and wheels right up to my face. I lean backward as he looks into my eyes, studying me. "Madeleine, I have to ask. You aren't trying to play some kind of joke on me, are you?"

I look around the room like I'm on *Candid Camera*, getting punk'd, or something. "A joke? Me?" I laugh nervously even though Dr. Davenport knows me almost as well as his own children. I was in school with them from kindergarten on.

He moves closer and sighs. "You came in here two days ago with this exact same theory. I gave you some migraine medication to try and said we would do more testing if it didn't work. We also talked about the possibility of it being your PTSD again that was triggered. Are you telling me you have no memory of that visit?"

I'm dumbfounded. It's like my brain can't produce a thought well enough to form words, so I say nothing and scramble through my purse until I stumble upon a prescription bottle dated November 10, which confirms what he's saying. I hear my phone vibrate and pluck it out to read a new text from my mom.

You've gone to the doctor again? Is everything okay?

My face grows warm, and my head tingles as if on fire. I dwell on the word "again." The air is thin, the room is spinning, and I have the urge to run, so I rush to pick up my belongings before I have a full-blown panic attack.

Dr. Davenport reaches for me. "Are you okay? Don't leave. It could be as simple as your PTSD symptoms returning from the accident. If you're embarrassed about it or in shock, we can sit down and talk this out, just the two of us. You did just go through another significant loss in your life, so setbacks can be expected."

I pull my phone out and check every day of the last two weeks on my calendar. A dot appears on November 10. I click the date, and it says, "Dr. Davenport 11am." My head aches as I read the entry I have no recollection of making. None of this makes sense. *How could I have forgotten this?*

I muster a few excuses on my way out the door. "Nothing to talk about. I remember being here, I just... I didn't really want to take the medicine yet. That's all. I've got to go. I forgot I have an appointment in fifteen minutes across town, and it's important."

"Please, call me when you calm down. I'm here if you need to talk, Madeleine," Dr. Davenport says just before I hit the hallway and speed-walk past the lobby. It's like I've held my breath for the last two minutes, and when I reach the parking lot, I finally gasp for air.

How do I not remember coming here? Are there other things I've forgotten too? Am I that stressed out? Is this something serious like a brain tumor?

I close my eyes and focus on how I got the prescription now in my purse, and everything is blank and dark. An image flashes through my mind, and I glimpse my hand reaching for the prescription bottle at the pharmacy drive-through. But I can't be certain whether it's an actual memory or an assumption my mind has somehow made up to fill in the blanks. I start to spiral out of control as I consider what memories I *can* actually trust, if any, but get distracted when I hear a familiar ding from within my purse.

So, you forgot something...Big deal! Don't freak out so much, and don't forget the *real* story here... keep digging. Your time's ticking. You're not Mad, but you *are* getting warmer—a source.

This time, I read and don't respond. "A source" doesn't think I'm crazy, but I'm starting to wonder. Mad is capitalized, but maybe that's just a typo. They're right. Time *is* ticking, but in which direction, I wonder. Everything suddenly seems backward.

Chapter 6

The next afternoon, luxury vehicles of all makes and models fill the parking lot of Westview Academy as the pickup hour approaches. On the private school's twenty-five acres of perfectly manicured landscaping, no piles of leaves are available for jumping in. They have someone on top of it, it seems. I can't help wondering how many of these kids are picked up daily by their nannies and, of the ones who are, how much time they actually spend with their parents.

As the students file out of the newer building, which is designed to look very Gothic Revival, I work my way in. I've done my research. If I walk in like I'm supposed to be here, I can blend in all the way to room 203 on the west wing of the second floor.

I approach the door labeled "Mr. Stone—6th grade Reading" and peek through the glass to see him speaking with a young female student, and I get cold feet. As a single mom working alone, I may not want to be involved with someone who has a reputation as a stalker. At the same time, I recognize the financial independence that breaking the Allegra story would bring me and Graham, especially after the surge in likes and followers I saw after my interview with Mr. Burns.

A source appears to be reading my mind or watching my every move as I think things through in the hallway, because my phone buzzes with a brand-new text. **Leave no Stone unturned, Mad.**

I take a deep breath as I turn the knob, enter the room, and patiently wait by the door for them to finish up. I lightly clear my throat to announce myself. Lane Stone's instant double-take tells me he notices my arrival.

"We'll talk about this more tomorrow, Anne. You can go now." He quickly shoos his student away with a kind grin and lowers his glasses. "I'm sorry. Do I know you?" His wrinkled eyebrows almost meet in the middle.

"No, you don't. I'm Madeleine Barton. Nice to meet you." I smile and step toward him with my hand extended.

"Lane Stone. Great to meet you, Madeleine. Whatever brings you my way?" He has a happy twinkle in his eye as our hands meet. He seems about the same age as Allegra, forty-five-ish, but dresses like a hipster in his twenties—skinny jeans, Vans sneakers, and a newsboy cap.

"I'm doing a story on Allegra Hudson, and I heard you two used to be quite close. Is that right?" I narrow my eyes.

His face drops, and he steps backward. "I don't have anything to say to the press, thanks."

I'm losing him fast, so I backpedal. "Look, Lane. I promise, it's not like that. I've actually been asked by Allegra's close friends and family to conduct my own assessment of the situation. I'm trying to help them out by getting all the facts. Until we get to the bottom of what happened to her, there will be no other Allegra story on my part. No embellished reports or manufactured drama."

Lane's skeptical eyes meet mine, and his head cocks as if he's still trying to place my face. "Wait. Are you the girl who used to work at WKNX and started her own online gig?"

"The one and only." I laugh and take a bow, trying to lighten the mood and gain his trust.

He smiles, and his tense shoulders finally drop. "Okay, have a seat. I've got a few minutes before I meet my buddy at the gym, so shoot."

I take a seat at the desk closest to his, set my papers down, and shuffle through them.

"Are you sure we've never met before?" He leans in closer and tugs on his sweater vest.

With my pen in my mouth, I look up. "No, I think I'd remember you. You don't look familiar." I grin afterward to dull the harsh truth. It sucks when someone remembers you and you don't recall them, though I suspect he may be saying he knows me as a way to flirt.

"You must just have one of those pretty faces I think I've seen before, then."

I can see every tooth in his head and realize I was spot-on. I'd better get us back on track before this charmer asks me for a date.

"My first questions for you are..." I flip through my list, and I imagine he's still making moon eyes at me as I get organized. "How long did you know Allegra, how did you meet, and what was your relationship with her? Let's start with those and see where we end up."

Lane's playful eye contact breaks, and he shifts in his seat, looking uneasy. I suspect he's wondering how much I already know about him and who told me.

"We, uh, we met in 2001, I believe. She and I went to the same gym. We were friendly in passing for a while, nothing romantic or anything. Then after a few months of running into each other, I finally asked her out, and she said no. She said it was because of Mason. He was about two and a half then, and she said she couldn't see herself dating anyone while having a toddler to tend to. I told her I had no problem with her having a kid, I loved it, actually, but she didn't want him to meet any men at that time. I think a lot of it was truly about Mason's dad. I never got the full story on why or how he left them, because she didn't like to discuss it, but I don't think she wanted any other men in Mason's life. Almost like she didn't trust anyone to stick around, you know?"

"Oh, wow. I guess I can really relate to that. I didn't realize Mason isn't Connor's son and that Allegra was married before. What else can you tell me about her first husband?" *He might have had a motive for killing her as well.*

Lane purses his lips and shrugs. "All I know is he left and never came back. She could never talk about him without crying, so I didn't push it. Nothing else to look into there as far as an investigation goes. He never came back around."

I eagerly click my pen. "Okay, so you asked her out, and she said no. Keep going."

"After a few more weeks of nos, she said yes. She insisted we keep it casual and light. She was quite reserved, always playing hard to get. She said she wasn't looking to get married again anytime soon, but I could see sparks flying all over the place whenever our eyes met or I made her laugh. She was falling hard for me, even if she wouldn't admit it. We dated for three and a half months, until she met Connor." Lane pauses, and I feel tension.

"How did they meet?" I prompt as I jot down more notes.

"He was the contractor for her mom's home renovation. That jerk snatched her away from me right under my nose. The guy had no respect for our relationship from the get-go."

Lane's fists grow white as he tightens them. "He's been front and center on *Knox Mag*'s Best in Business edition for years. Everyone thinks he's such a great, stand-up guy. But I can tell you that he isn't!"

I nod, fearful of disagreeing, and lean backward as his spit spews my way. He seems nerdy but passionate, and he's probably harmless underneath, but he is definitely overaggressive and dramatic when it comes to Connor. I need more time with him, but he's clearly overheated right now.

Lane seems to catch himself losing his cool and glances at his watch while he adjusts his glasses. "I'm sorry. We'll have to continue this later."

Maybe if I goad him, he won't be able to help divulging more information. "So you two weren't serious, but you felt like maybe you could have been, eventually. If given enough time?" I try to sound supportive, although he now has stage-five clinger written all over his pink face.

Lane picks up his bags and smooths his vest down as his mood reverts to breezy and charming. "I'm sorry. Like I said, I really do have to run now."

I dig in my bag and pull out a business card. "My work information is obviously different now, but my cell is still the same. Call me, and we'll pick up where we left off," I say as if I don't secretly consider him suspect number one.

He shoots me another dreamy grin and takes my card. "Sounds good. I'd be happy to chat with you again. Maybe we could do it over dinner?"

The thought of leading him on creates a sinking feeling in my stomach, but I do need to get to the bottom of their relationship. And it's called a business card for a reason. "That would be fine. A business dinner, that is," I clarify.

"Of course." Lane nods as we part in the hallway, likely ignoring the part about it being a business dinner.

I step toward the school's entrance, and he heads toward the back parking lot. I have the distinct feeling I'm being watched, so I turn to check, and there he is—walking backward, beaming at me. *Oh dear God, this poor guy thinks we've just hit it off.* I wave goodbye, and he throws up a finger gun and winks. I turn around and cover my mouth to conceal my laughter, then I frown, knowing exactly what Marcus would say if he were here. "This dude is cheesier than Mr. Rogers eating Velveeta."

Allegra and Lane appear to have been polar opposites. I guess she needed a little pick-me-up in her life, and Lane is nothing if not entertaining. He was obviously under the impression they would end up in a serious relationship one day. I'm not certain, but it seems like he was a quirky way for Allegra to pass the time on her journey toward Mr. Right, whether she intended it to be that way or not.

I arrive home that evening with a plain cheese pizza for Graham and grilled-chicken salads for Mom and me. I got salads for us so that when we graze off Graham's uneaten pizza slices later, we'll consume only a few hundred calories for dinner as opposed to a few thousand.

Graham tugs on his pizza with his teeth, and the cheese stretches at least eight inches. "Hey, Mom. Tanner is having his birthday party at his dad's house. Can I please go?"

I stare at the elongating cheese, and my willpower goes right out the window. I grab a slice and eat it over my untouched salad. "I don't know where Tanner's dad lives, baby. Is it close to where his momma lives?"

"Um, no. His dad has a place on the water," Graham mumbles as he chews with his mouth open.

I quickly swallow a chunk of pizza. Vivid images of Douglas Lake and its splashing water fill my mind. "On the water? Are you sure, baby?"

Graham swallows. "Yeah, at the lake. They have a boat and everything, Momma."

I drop my pizza slice on the table as Mom's wide eyes try to warn Graham to stop talking. "Absolutely not!" My voice rises, and I feel powerless to stop it. It's not Graham's fault his friend invited him to a party on the lake, but I'm certainly not going to let him go. The thought of my baby so close to the water, with so many people there and no one watching him, sends me overboard.

"But why?" Graham whines with his arms crossed.

"Because I said so. That's why!" I take a swig of water and wipe my brow as I stand up from the table. I hate getting upset at my sweet boy, but my heart races with pure fear.

"That's not fair. Everyone else gets to go. You're being mean!" Graham picks up his cup of milk, takes a gulp, and slams it on the kitchen table.

Mom pats Graham's leg to quiet him. I slam my hand down on the table next to his milk and can't stop the words from coming out of my mouth, even while I hate myself for crushing his heart. "For the last time, I said no. Stepping foot in that water is the dumbest, most dangerous, selfish, and irresponsible thing a person can do, and I'm not having it."

Graham's face scrunches into a ball of confusion as I make my way to the kitchen sink. "Huh?"

"Never mind!" I yell, knowing I've made no sense to him. "You're not going."

Tears of anger build behind my eyes, and I smear them away with a splash of water, recognizing that Dr. Davenport could be right about my PTSD returning. I take a deep breath. "I need a minute," I tell Mom as tears start to fall from Graham's eyes as well. She of all people knows why this is so important to me. I head toward my bedroom, where I gaze into my dresser mirror. I throw my dampened hair into a ponytail and take another deep but shaky breath at the sight of my splotchy neck.

The top drawer of my jewelry box catches my eye; I haven't allowed myself to open it for months. I give the drawer a tug and reach toward the back, where I grasp the two metal circles, still soldered together. I clutch them in my palm, close my eyes, and remember the day I buried Clay in his matching ring. The lake—the same damn water Graham wants to go to—took Clay from me far too soon. But instead of focusing on the dark day my life was forever changed, I force myself to remember the time Clayton gave me my ring.

I had sported a perfect replica of the "Rachel" haircut at my second cousin's wedding, which was held at the convention center downtown. Snowflakes floated from the white sky, the bride and groom had just departed for their honeymoon in New York City, and the DJ was still spinning music for the rest of the guests. All the songs were upbeat, and everyone was dancing their velvet-wearing butts off when the DJ suddenly switched to a soft ballad, "I'll Be" by Edwin McCain. Clayton gave me a sly grin, revealing his dimples, pulled away from me, dropped to one knee, and pulled out the ring.

The DJ had given him a second microphone before the song began. Clayton had hidden it in his back pocket, and in front of God and everyone, he pulled out his mic and clicked it on. "Madeleine Barton and random people who I don't know, I realize the success rate for high school sweethearts who get married at twenty years old is probably staggeringly low. But what most of those marriages don't have, and I luckily do, is God at the center of them and you by my side. I know we're young, and many will say we don't even know who we are yet. That may be true, but what I do know is that I want to find out who we both are together. Mad, my li'l Mad Hatter, will you marry me and grow up and grow old with me?"

My hands fluttered to cover my mouth, and happy tears filled my eyes. He'd won over the crowd, most of whom we didn't know from Adam, and they all stopped and held their breath. He'd already stolen my heart, but that night, he captured my soul as well. My love for him always scared me, because I knew if I ever lost it, it would cost me everything. And it would have if it weren't for the surprise he left me—a piece of himself growing inside me.

And that was Graham. I had to take special care of him because his survival depended solely on me taking care of myself. I didn't have the liberty or luxury of giving up simply because Clay was gone—I couldn't let him down like that.

That same little boy now owns the pieces of my heart and soul that were left after Clayton died, and I have the same worries and fears about him that I had about his father. The last thing I'm going to do is permit Graham to set foot in that lake.

I KISS GRAHAM GOOD night. I know he's forgiven my outburst by the way he hugs my neck. "I love you, Mommy, even if you hate the lake."

I chuckle at the simplicity of his conclusion. "Baby, it's not that I hate the lake, it's just..." I sigh. I can't expect him to understand the fear, guilt, or pain I feel when I picture him near the water, especially without me. "It's complicated, baby."

Later, after Mom's left and Graham's asleep, I throw on an old, oversized tee of Clayton's that always calms me down and hop into bed. I throw my phone on the charger, and it lights up with a new text message notification. After I read it, I gasp and leap out of bed.

He loved you too—a source.

Loved. As in past tense? I wonder how this person could know that I was thinking about Clayton or that he loved me too. I spin around, suddenly sick at the thought of someone watching me in my bedroom as I held my rings earlier and when I just now put Clayton's shirt on. My mind races through the possibilities, like someone spying through my window or taking photos with a secret camera. I wonder what else this person has seen me do. Or, I think to myself with a slight laugh, maybe I'm being haunted. *Right, a ghost who can text message.*

For protection, I grab the flashlight in my nightstand and the letter opener in my desk drawer. I tiptoe to my closet door as the letter opener wobbles in my sweaty right palm. In one fell swoop, I thrust the door open. My heart skips a beat as I rifle through my wardrobe, finding nothing that shouldn't be there.

I take a few deep breaths and continue to look behind every picture frame, lamp, and drawer for any recording device or camera. Still nothing. I make my way to the living room and kitchen area, where I step on a rogue Lego that Graham neglected to put away during bedtime cleanup. I jump, and my whimper scares me half to death.

The floor of hell is sure to be lined with these microscopic toys. I flip all the lights on in my apartment, and tears fill my exhausted eyes. Three more times, I search every spot—minus Graham's room since he's sound asleep—with the letter opener before me.

The thought of my bed brings zero comfort, so I leave every light on and cuddle up on the couch with a few blankets. At two o'clock, my eyes are still wide open. The silence makes me anticipate something alarming even more, so I turn on the TV for background noise and allow my eyes to finally close.

The TV helps, but it can't drown out the endless questions filling my mind. *Who is "a source"? Are they just trying to drive me crazy?* If so, it's working. I don't feel safe in my own home anymore, but I feel stupid calling the police and don't know what I would say. "Hi. A mysterious text says my dead husband loves me." The police would definitely think I'm crazy then. As I stare into the darkness, I wonder how this "source" knows so much, how they have so much access to me, and whether they could've killed Allegra or Marcus.

Chapter 7

"Restless sleep is putting it lightly. I had nightmares all night." I'm on the phone with Violet, finally revealing all I'd kept from her since our last chat—even my fiasco at the doctor's office. "I dreamt that I woke up in the hospital in this foggy room 101 with no one around, and I didn't even know why I was there. I was hooked up to several machines, and I had a panic attack so intense that I woke up sweaty and gasping for air."

"My dream after that was even worse. I was being chased by killer clowns at a medieval festival I was covering live on Facebook. I kept screaming my script on air as I was running for my life. Okay, maybe that one's a little funny, now that I say it out loud." I laugh, but on the inside, I'm still disturbed by the text about Clayton loving me.

Violet snickers. "I think you're just under a lot of pressure right now. You just lost a good friend, this Allegra Hudson deal is a huge story, and you've completely changed your entire career plan. If I were you, I'd probably be having weird dreams, migraines, and tinnitus too. You need to calm down, hon. Are you still running at the gym?"

Tears well up at the reality of Marcus being gone forever, and I sigh. "Yeah, I am, but not as much as I used to. Only once or twice a week. I should probably step it up. It does tend to help me relax, but so does wine." I laugh half-heartedly.

My phone beeps, and I hold it away from my face to read the notification. On some level, I still expect a phone call or text from Marcus, but it's a number I don't recognize. "Vi, a weird number is calling me right now. I'd better answer it. It could be a tip."

"You think it's 'a source'?" Violet asks with a loud gulp I can hear through the phone.

I wince, because the truth might actually be scarier than what I've been imagining. "God, I hope not. I'd probably shit a brick if I found out who it was."

"Maybe it's a ghost who stalks you and watches you when you get naked at home, and they just now learned how to communicate via text," Violet jokes, but I want to smack her.

"Seriously, I do worry about crap like that. Anything's possible!" I laugh to cover up the sensation in my stomach that something really is wrong—with me, with this situation. I can't put my finger on it, and I don't want to worry Violet, but I'm scared.

Another beep. "Okay, Vi. I've really got to go."

"Bye, Mad." Violet makes a kissing sound and hangs up.

I click over to the other call, and my stomach fills with dread. I answer with a slight break in my voice. "Hello, this is Madeleine."

"Hi, Madeleine. This is Connor. Connor Hudson. Ivy Richards gave me your number and said you two had been discussing my late wife, Allegra. She said you'd be expecting my call."

Knock me down with a feather. Although I'd hoped, I never thought Connor Hudson would actually call and want to meet with me. So Allegra's husband is on the phone. *The* Allegra Hudson's husband wants my help. "Oh, Connor. Wow! Yes, she sure did. And we have talked a few times. How, uh, can I help you today?"

"I thought we could meet and discuss all the information I know at this point."

"Sure. I have one appointment later today, around three thirty. I can meet you anytime before that," I offer, hoping we can work something out before he changes his mind.

"I have to drop by my son Garrett's school at eleven. Could we meet for lunch at noon? Somewhere busy downtown perhaps, where people won't recognize me?"

I try to think of somewhere with a loud atmosphere, somewhere that he won't be overheard by bloggers, reporters, and busybodies. "How about Downtown Grille and Brewery, then? It's nice and loud."

"That sounds great. I'll see you there. I'll be wearing a red flannel shirt if that helps. I just realized you probably have no idea what I look like." He laughs.

"That's right, I don't. I'm not dressed yet, but I'm sure I'll be wearing my signature color, black." I giggle and make a mental note to google his picture before our meeting.

He kids me with a warm tone. "I remember you from your broadcasts, so I'll recognize you. Come to think of it, you do wear a lot of black."

"Yeah, it's a real problem." I grin and laugh nervously, surprised at how nice he seems. Then I realize I told him I wasn't dressed yet, and I hope he doesn't think I meant I was naked while on the phone with him. I should've just said I was still in my pajamas or kept my big mouth shut altogether.

"I'll see you there, then," he replies.

"You do too," I say as he hangs up. *You do too?* My cheeks grow warm as I replay our conversation. He probably thinks I'm a complete moron, and honestly, I would judge him a little if he didn't.

A SCRUFFY-FACED MAN in a cobalt-blue sweater walks into the Downtown Grille just before I do. He doesn't see me but apparently senses someone behind him and holds the door open for me like a true gentleman. I catch his profile and note how ruggedly handsome he is, so I give him my most pleasant smile accompanied by a very Southern "Well, thank ya, sir."

"You're so welcome, Madeleine. Should we try to sit upstairs or down?" He points at a table upstairs and waits for my reply.

I step back with rosy cheeks and study his shirt again, suddenly remembering I forgot to google a picture of him. "Connor? That's not a red flannel shirt by any stretch of the imagination."

"Oh, right. Coffee." He tilts his head to one side as his lush, dark hair falls in front of his face.

I squint, confused. "Your shirt's not really brown either..."

"No, coffee. As in, I spilled coffee all over myself on my way out the door and grabbed this at the last second." He laughs, revealing perfect white teeth.

"You really should've texted me. This has thrown my entire day off," I say with a playful smirk. It's distracting, but I can't help noticing how good-looking he is. He doesn't seem forty-something at all.

Connor laughs as we seat ourselves by the downstairs window. "Thanks for that, by the way. I was long overdue for a good laugh."

"Glad I could help you out." I giggle, embarrassed at how I tried to flirt with him when we walked in. We have a seat and begin looking over our menus. I drop mine almost as soon as I pick it up to say my piece about Allegra and clear the air.

"Can I just say, it's so nice to meet you. I hate that it's under such terrible circumstances, of course, and I know you're probably tired of hearing this, but your wife was such an inspiration to me. I met her at a workshop once. I used to write a bit of fiction myself and was inspired by old Hitchcock films, just like Allegra. So I really connected to her words on every level, and her books helped me get through a rough time in my life. It's an honor to do whatever I can to help her and her family."

Connor has tears in his eyes. "No, don't apologize. I never grow tired of hearing how Allegra's words made an impact on others. That was always her dream, you know?"

I pat his forearm three times before retracting my hand, and he wipes away a tear. "I know this is hard for you. Just tell me as much as you can. If you feel comfortable, that is."

Connor sniffs back a sob and rubs his eyes. The love he clearly has for Allegra touches me. After all, I sat in his seat not too long ago.

"All right. I'm sorry. I promised myself I wouldn't get emotional till we spoke for at least ten minutes. Yet here I am, crying before you've even asked your first question."

I pat the table and perk up to lighten the mood. "All right, my first question is pretty easy."

"Okay, let me have it." Connor takes a deep breath.

I place both hands on the table and lower my voice, leaning in. "What would you like to order for lunch? The white pizza is my personal favorite." I point at my menu and smile, hoping he'll feel more comfortable.

Connor nods. "I love it too. Let's both get it, then." He motions the waitress over and orders for us.

Once we've ordered and the waitress is out of sight, I go ahead with another, more serious prompt. "Why don't you just take a deep breath and start at the beginning. Tell me about Allegra. How did you two meet, and when?"

I take a sip of the water the waitress dropped off and hope Connor can gather himself together enough for me to gain some valuable information. He's clearly a man torn apart, deeply in love with his late wife, and boy, can I relate to how he's feeling. I've been there, and the longing is agonizing.

He clears his throat as if trying to keep it together. "We met in 2002. Her mom was one of my clients. She was renovating parts of her house, and I was her contractor. Allegra came by almost every day with Mason to visit her mom and make sure we weren't swindling her out of thousands of dollars or anything. Mason was almost three then, and he was really craving some male attention, so sometimes on my breaks, I tossed a ball with him in the yard for a few minutes. Mason never knew his father, unfortunately, and we ate up our time with each other. Allegra and I spoke here and there, and I fell hard for her and her sassiness rather quickly." He smiles, and I do as well as I continue to write.

"Allegra was dating that goofy Lane Stone, who teaches at Westview Academy. They weren't very serious. You could tell. She thought he was endearing at first, but then his neediness and mood swings rode on her nerves."

I narrow my eyes, and as the waitress drops off our pizza, I wonder if there's more to the story about Allegra and Lane's relationship. Connor's face is open and earnest; I think he's being honest with me. He seems to have no animosity toward Lane Stone but maybe a little irritation. "So, you asked her out, even though they were seeing each other exclusively?"

Connor gives me a half smile and a plate full of pizza. "Not exactly. One day, when the three of us were playing ball in the yard at her mom's, Mason asked her if we could all get pizza together. Allegra said yes. I drove home, changed, came back, and we were all four on our way to her car together when Allegra's mom whispered in Mason's ear, after which he announced he had a tummy ache. He said he wanted us to go ahead without him. Allegra said absolutely not, like any mom would, and made a fuss over him big-time, only to realize he was faking. I think he tipped her off when he giggled and said he wanted us to bring him back his favorite extra-cheese pizza when we 'got done on our date.'"

Connor laughs. "So we continued our 'date' as ordered, and Mason stayed with Allegra's mom, who was beaming as we left. We had a fantastic time. Just clicked, like magic. She broke up with Lane the next day, and we got married one year later with Mace as our little ring bearer. I adopted him before we left for our honeymoon because I couldn't wait to be his dad, and Allegra got pregnant with Garrett two years after that."

"Did she start writing her books right after you two got married, then?" I jot down more notes. Only a truly good man would be so generous to his new bride and her baby. Taking the baby as his own before heading off on his honeymoon showed he had the right priorities.

"After we got married, Allegra finally had the stability and flexibility to do what she'd always wanted but never had time for—writing books. She started writing her first book, got her agent, and landed a great publisher within two years. The rest is really history. Five years later, she had four books out, one movie under her belt, and two more films in the works—she'd made it big, and fast."

Her story almost sounds like a book she would have written. The way the stars aligned for her and her career are inspiring but also a cautionary tale about getting too much success too fast. I bite my pen and cock my head, wondering how such success would affect an average family of four.

"At first, it was great. Mason was in elementary school all day, and she wrote mostly during Garrett's naps. She'd also write after we all went to bed. So even though she'd sold her debut, nothing really felt different as far as her being busy. Then after her first five years of selling books and cowriting screenplays, we really noticed a change. She wanted the boys to be safer, so we hired security to accompany her on her book tours and moved into a fancier part of town. Allegra's mom died from a heart attack around that time as well, and it really caused her to prioritize, as busy as she was. She and her mom were extremely close, and it was beyond hard on her. She thought if she stayed busy enough, she wouldn't completely cave to those intense emotions. So after some tough times with her anxiety issues, she began flying to New York and LA every other week for something or another and going on tour for longer. It really started to take a toll on our marriage and on her friendship with Ivy. One thing she always did no matter what, though, was make time for the boys."

I gaze up from my notepad to dig a little deeper. Connor doesn't know that Ivy told me about Allegra's pill problem, and I admire the way he keeps it a secret to protect her. He stayed vague by saying she had anxiety issues, but I already know the problem was much bigger than that.

"How did her busyness affect your marriage specifically?"

His jaw tightens, and there's a hint of pain in his expression. I wish I could take the question back; I don't like to see someone look so hurt. But then he answers, his voice slow and careful.

"She was gone a lot. And when she was here, she spent time with the boys and wasn't very present with me. So we slowly became friends who happened to coexist in the same house. Before that, we'd always prided ourselves on our closeness. We were *that couple* everyone envied. We finished each other's sentences and were annoyingly cute together, and I hate the word 'cute.' But alas, we were."

"What about the boys, then? How did it affect them?" I sneak in another bite of pizza. The husband is usually the number-one suspect, although I'm not getting any inconsistent answers from him. He seems like a man who truly loved his wife, and their marriage was going through some difficulties they could've gotten through—if they'd only had more time.

"Don't get me wrong. Allegra had major mom guilt. She loved those boys more than anything in the world, but she slowly let work take over. And to put it simply, they missed their mom. She was gone a bit too much toward the end, and for so long, they were used to her always being home." He seems to regret saying that, like he hates himself for saying anything negative about his wife.

I purse my lips, wondering about the drama with her friends. "How about Ivy? How did she cope?"

Connor shuffles in his seat. "Ivy's a dear, but she also calls it like she sees it. And she didn't hold back when it came to Allegra. Ivy told her she was doing too much and she needed to get her priorities in order, which didn't sit too well with Allegra. Especially since deep down, she knew Ivy was right. She was escaping to avoid dealing with her loss and her anxiety head-on. Mayven pushed her to be involved with her many charities, to make public appearances, and to get involved with the community, which was great, except Allegra was only one woman. And as hard as she tried, she couldn't do everything without falling short on a lot of things."

He stops and rubs his face. "I'm so sorry. I never thought I would spill so much to you today. I guess I just needed to talk to someone."

After taking another bite, I look around the room and sigh, processing everything he said. I feel terrible for Connor and Allegra because they seemed to have so much unfinished business despite their love for each other. Now they'll never have the chance to tell each other how they really felt. This whole situation is such a shame—for him, for her, for their children. For everyone.

"Okay, I think I've got the gist of it now. Let me ask you this, though. Is there anyone in Allegra's life, past or present, who might have had reason to harm her? Anyone ever send her, say, a threatening note?"

Connor looks me dead in the eyes. "No," he answers convincingly.

I feel a rush of disappointment hearing that Allegra might not have been receiving threatening notes like me. I was hoping for a connection there. I wonder if he realizes he should probably be pointing me toward anyone but himself. Despite my belief in his innocence, the public will still think it's the husband, alibi or no alibi, especially if there were marital issues.

"Not even Lane Stone?" I narrow my eyes, knowing he's an easy target.

"Honestly, I know he doesn't care for me, but he's harmless." Connor shrugs as if unconcerned.

I dab my napkin around my mouth to check for pizza crumbs. "Are you sure? I heard he had a hard time letting go after the breakup."

Connor's mouth tightens. "He did. I mean, he would show up places he knew Allegra would be to try to win her back. It was pathetic if you ask me, and Allegra wasn't into it at all. Thinking of how long he had to wait around to run into her at the gym, the grocery store, and the gas station really gave her the creeps. But I think he was desperate for closure and a little out of his right frame of mind."

I scrunch my brow. "That doesn't seem like a red flag? He sounds like he googled 'stalking 101' and put it to use. People like him can be dangerous, you know."

"I know. I really don't think there's anything there, but if you think it's worth looking into, by all means, do it."

"I've already spoken to him once, but I have another meeting with him scheduled for today, actually. He's the three thirty I told you about."

"Oh, really? Well, there's obviously something I don't know. I just keep thinking it had to have been a random crime or an accident somehow. She didn't have any enemies. Everyone liked her. The police are really leaning toward calling it a random act of gang violence. I just... I don't know. But I feel like there's a story there, which is fitting, because Allegra was all about those dramatic stories."

"Yes. Yes, she was." I frown as I look at the table and think of her debut suspense novel, the one I read while pregnant with Graham.

"Listen, I'd better go. I've got a job site to check on before I pick Garrett up from school. If there's anything else you need from me, don't hesitate to call or text. At any time." He passes me his business card and throws a fifty on the table. "My treat."

"You didn't have to do that," I argue with a smile as we both stand to say goodbye.

"No, but I wanted to." He shakes my hand then holds it for a second. His eyes meet mine, and something in them feels familiar and safe. "Thanks. For everything you're doing. I appreciate someone having Allegra's back, and I know she would too. I'll speak with you soon."

As he exits the restaurant and makes his way across the street, my hand lingers in the position where he last held it, and my eyes have stars in them. I shake it off and gather my things. *No, Madeleine. You can't develop a crush on Allegra Hudson's husband.* This is beyond ridiculous, not to mention inappropriate. The poor man's wife just died, and he's probably fifteen years older than I am.

The more I try to talk myself into being repulsed by his age, or by the situation itself, the more romantic it seems. I keep picturing myself with him. *What the hell is wrong with me?* I mean, he is hot and seems to be sweet, loving, and a great husband and father. Of course I would feel attracted to him. Maybe I should give myself a break. I've never even thought about another man in this way since—

The clearing of a throat makes me jump.

"Ms. Barton?" a man's raspy voice asks from behind me.

"Yes. Can I help you?" I turn and immediately notice his white hair, round frame, and tall stature. If he had a full beard instead of just a mustache, he would make a perfect Santa Claus.

He reaches into his coat pocket and pulls out a badge. "Detective Jeff Wentworth." He states it as if I should be impressed or surprised. I can't help eyeing his clichéd black trench coat. He hasn't disguised himself very well if that was his goal.

"I can see that." I stretch out my hand. "Madeleine Barton, Marcus's friend and colleague, but it seems you already put my face with my name." I cautiously wonder if Wentworth's even thought of his "friend" Marcus since his passing, especially since I don't recall seeing him at the funeral.

He ignores my friendly handshake, pulling out a pen and a piece of paper from the other side of his coat pocket instead. With my rejected hand, I scratch my head and wonder how long he was watching Connor and me.

"Can I ask what your business was with Connor Hudson here today and how long you've known him?" He scribbles on his pad.

I gulp as I recall what Ivy said about him wanting to quickly wrap up a case so long as there's someone around that it's relatively believable to pin the murder on. It seems irrational, but I can't help wondering if he's going to zero in and watch me closely.

"We only met today, actually. And if you must know, he's asked me to look into Allegra's death."

He stops scribbling and eyes me like I have three heads. "You a PI?" he asks as if considering such a ridiculous notion is about to blow his mind.

"I'm a freelance reporter and journalist," I answer confidently.

The corners of his mouth turn up slightly. He looks like he's trying not to laugh. "I knew that. I was just yanking your chain. And you and Connor only just met today, huh?" he asks again, presumably to see if I change my story.

"Yes. Why?" I hope he'll clue me in to what he's getting at.

"You seemed to get along rather well for two people who just met. Don't you think?"

His accusatory tone instantly makes me defensive.

"Not particularly. We didn't *not* get along. We just had a lot to say because we're both taking this case very seriously, and there's a lot to discuss." I'm not letting him put any words in my mouth, intimidate me, or insinuate anything.

He closes his pad of paper and buttons his coat. "Honey, don't you think you're in a little over your head here? Someone like you could get really hurt out there, and you have very limited resources." He pats my shoulder with what he probably considers fatherly concern, but it comes across as condescension.

"I think I'll be fine, thanks." I play along as if I'm naive.

"Let me walk you out." He guides me toward the frosty front door. "I'm going to let this one slide for now, but if my calculations are correct, your parking meter ran out of time about three minutes ago." He makes his way across the street, where his black SUV is parked.

"With all due respect, I would've left five minutes ago if you hadn't approached me, Detective Wentworth." I let him know I came to play.

He reaches his car and smirks as he opens the door. "Touché, Ms. Barton. Touché."

I PULL MY COAT TIGHT. As Lane approaches, I rise from the concrete picnic table on the grounds of Westview Academy. I grin as our eyes meet; his smile could light up the world if he could harness its energy. Admittedly, I can totally see how hanging out with him enough would build Allegra's self-esteem and optimism. He seems fiercely loyal to her, but his supposed clinginess after the end of his relationship with Allegra makes me keep my guard up. He might be dangerous. I shake his hand. "Nice to meet with you again, Mr. Stone."

He turns my offer of a handshake into a hand hold that lasts too long for my comfort.

"No, no, no. Call me Lane, please."

"All right, Lane. I think I can handle that." I force a smile as I gently pull my hand back and have a seat. My phone dings. "Let me just turn this on silent really quick." I reach into my bag and glance at it as a new text flashes across the screen. My shoulders tense up as I read it.

So, Mad. Which one are you going to believe? —a source.

Chapter 8

"It's deceiving, huh?" Lane buttons his coat and looks me straight in the eyes as if he knows something.

"What's deceiving?" I look at him in confusion as my heart beats heavily in my throat. *How long has he been looking my way? Did he see my text?*

Lane points toward the blue sky. "The temperature. From the inside looking out, it legit seemed much warmer than this."

I sigh in relief; he doesn't have a clue about what I just read, and I'm being paranoid. "A hundred percent. It's so sunny and bright, right? I thought I might be able to get away with a lighter coat today, but nope."

"Yeah, we're basically into strict winter weather now. Won't be seeing any light coats for a while. If you'd rather move our meeting inside, that's perfectly fine."

I look around at the surrounding bare trees and inhale the crisp air, which temporarily soothes my worries. "No way. This fresh air is just what I had in mind today. I can take it if you can."

"I'm perfectly fine. I love the cold weather, actually. Or I don't mind it. 'Love' may be an overstatement." He snickers. "I'm sorry I had to move the time on you today. I have to go out of town tonight, unfortunately. So we'll have to raincheck the dinner we discussed."

"No problem," I say, although I hope I won't need to see him again after today. This time, I'm not going to let him leave without getting answers about the school incident and without addressing the fact that others paint him a stalker. I don't want to get stuck at dinner with someone who might become obsessed with me.

"So, I'm going to jump right in. Hopefully, we can get through all my questions today. Can you talk to me about your relationship with Allegra after your breakup?"

Lane takes a deep breath and laughs as he exhales. "Oh, okay. We'll get straight to the tough part, then, won't we?" He fidgets in his seat, seeming uneasy. "Um, Allegra claimed Mason 'tricked' her into having dinner with Connor one evening, and that's how things got started with them. She said Mason really took to Connor when they met at her mom's house, and the whole explanation really irked me for a couple of reasons."

I cringe with secondhand embarrassment, mortified for Lane as he names the reasons one by one, holding fingers up for each item on the list. "One, she never let *me* meet Mason, which was a huge point of contention for me. Yet she allowed Connor to play with him several times over at her mom's house while he was working. I didn't get that. I was her exclusive boyfriend, and he was just some contractor. I mean, I know she couldn't control that he was there, but in my mind, it was a big slap in the face. Two, she wouldn't have appreciated it if I hadn't been exclusive with her, so why should she have a different set of rules for herself? And three, Connor knew we were together, yet he went along with it. Not only that, he really went for it! Apparently, he went for it so hard, Allegra dumped me the very next day. She said she wanted to pursue things with Connor and didn't think it was fair to date me any longer. After just one date!"

Lane's eyes roll so far back in his head that all I see is white, and he has a point. If I omit his alleged compulsive tendencies from the equation, it sounds like he was pushed aside because of Connor. Like he might have had a shot at a relationship with Allegra, otherwise.

I purse my lips, contemplating the possibility of his skewed perception as I take it all in. "So you'd rather she go out with him and feel something but not let you know?"

He grimaces. "Obviously not. I was glad she was honest. I was just surprised and hurt she'd throw our whole relationship away after one measly date and that she felt compelled to go on the date at all. She could've at least tested the waters a bit. I would rather she'd dated us both for a while, to compare, to give me a fair chance."

I nod. "I get why you'd feel that way. I do. Did you and Allegra communicate after she broke up with you?" But what I really want to ask is: *Did you or didn't you stalk her around town like a total creep after she severed ties?*

Lane scratches the back of his head as if he's trying to recall something I suspect he knows. "No, not really. She pretty much cut me off cold turkey. I needed closure, though. I wanted to make sure she was happy and that Connor wasn't just keeping her from talking to me, which I suspected at the time and still do. I tried my best to contact her, but she always refused my calls. I ran into her several times on purpose, just to check on her, but she always brushed me off. It was pretty awkward. I finally gave up, and we lost touch completely."

Lane takes in a breath of cold air as tears form behind his eyes. "When I found out she'd passed, after all these years, I was torn up about it, as if we'd remained friends all this time. I truly loved and cared for Allegra. She was such a great woman. I wish things had gone differently for us."

The corners of my mouth turn down, and I can almost feel his pain. Whether it's the truth or not, I sense he believes what he says. He truly thinks he had Allegra's best interests at heart when he was trying to run into her. He thinks he had a reason to check on her.

"Listen, Lane, I can tell you truly cherished her and the time you two had together."

He sniffs and wipes his eyes. "I did. I really did."

I lean in and whisper softly while he's in a state of mind to open up. "Was there ever a time, when you were close with Allegra, that she told you she was afraid of anyone? Or was there anyone that you can think of who wouldn't wish her well?"

Lane leans in farther, as if he's going to divulge something important. "The only person around Allegra who gave me a weird vibe was Connor. I don't think he's all he's cracked up to be."

I narrow my eyes, suspecting that all Lane has to base that on is his general dislike for Connor. "And why is that?"

Lane sits upright and crosses his arms. "Just a vibe, a gut feeling. She seemed jumpy around me after we broke up, like he made her scared of me or something. Maybe she felt like she'd get in trouble with him if she talked to me or any other man. I don't know."

"So you're saying Connor was the jealous type?" I wonder if Lane is simply still miffed or if any shred of this could possibly be true. I certainly didn't get a jealous vibe when I spoke with Connor. He could've easily pointed me toward Lane as a suspect if he'd been bitter, but he said he didn't think Lane was a threat.

Lane shrugs. "I'm saying it's definitely possible he was jealous and controlling. Maybe he had some woman on the side, even. I wouldn't put anything past him. When the school placed their youngest son, Garrett, in my classroom last year, they went berserk and had him removed immediately, like I was carrying the bubonic plague or something. That really humiliated me, and I have no doubt it was all Connor's doing."

The school incident clearly struck a nerve with Lane, but was it enough for him to do something drastic? I scribble down my notes as I ask one final, important question. "So was the incident with Garrett last year the last encounter you had with Allegra?"

Lane shifts in his seat, looks down, and answers softly, "Unfortunately, yes, it was."

He's hiding something. I'm sure of it. His demeanor completely changes when he answers that question versus the others. He might not have killed Allegra, but they definitely had another run-in before she died.

"YOU WANT TO DO WHAT?" I ask Violet the next day as I slam down my cup of hot green tea. Liquid splashes on her white coffee table, but I don't care.

Vi waves her arms up and down to caution me. "Shh, you'll wake Brighton up."

"Please tell me you're kidding." I roll my eyes at her over-the-top idea.

"Listen, you said he's cute and you don't know whether to believe him or Lane's wild accusations. So let's put him to the test. Then you'll know who's trustworthy." Violet sips her tea as if trying to prove that flirting with a man whose wife has just died is a perfectly ordinary thing to do.

"That won't prove anything, Vi. His wife's dead." I gulp my tea, wishing it were something stronger.

Violet leans in close to me on the couch. "Yes, but she hasn't been dead for long, so it'll still feel wrong to him on some level—or it should. And as far as he knows, I have no idea who he is or that his famous wife just died. I'm just some lonely, horny housewife." She winks. "If he was ever a wanderer before, he'll take the bait. Guys like that don't change overnight, babe."

My eyes widen at the balls this woman has. "Aren't you forgetting two things?"

"What?" Violet asks before she sips her tea.

"Um, remember Nick, your husband? And your child, Brighton? What would they say?"

A coy grin grows on Violet's face as she pushes her boobs up in the mirror. If anyone can get a man going, it's Violet. Back in the day, she was one of the best—a legend—when it came to flirting. She even managed to charm Bryce Miller, the hunky quarterback at the University of Tennessee, with the classic line "I seem to have lost my number. Can I have yours?" Plus, she's still as gorgeous as ever, even when she's wearing sweats and a messy mom bun. "Nick won't ever have to know. It's only investigative flirting, and Brighton will be at preschool."

I rub my forehead to press away the tension as I imagine this insane scenario playing out. So many things could go wrong. "And what if he wants to get down and dirty with you?"

She whips her head around. "Then I'll go all mental and scare him away at the last minute. I've been watching a lot of *Real Housewives of Beverly Hills* on Hulu. I think I can go from sexy to crazy on a dime."

"Ugh, let's just get it over with, then." I slump into the couch and cover my face with one of her throw pillows.

"For your sake, I hope he passes." Violet grins as she grabs my phone then copies and stores his number.

"What do you mean, for my sake?" I peek out from the side of the pillow.

"You're crushing on him, hard. Hey, maybe something could happen for you guys, eventually. I mean, way down the road, of course, assuming he's not a complete skeeze or a wife murderer."

"Gee, thanks, Vi. I'm so glad to have your sweet, demented blessing." I bury my embarrassed face under the pillow again and groan. It must be obvious that I have a crush on Connor, and that's causing me to have a biased opinion of him. "A source" did ask me who I was going to believe, so I guess I need to decide. This wild scheme of Vi's seems to be the only way to get a clear answer about Connor's loyalty to Allegra. But if I'm being honest, I'm going to be disappointed if Connor fails the test.

"I can't be here for this. I have to go home and see my son. Text me later when he gives you an appointment date, okay?"

"Okay, babe. I'll text you." Vi gives me a friendly wave. She's enjoying this project a tad too much.

MOM, GRAHAM, AND I have plans for dinner at her house, and I'm hoping a home-cooked meal in my childhood home will distract me from the Connor-and-Violet thing. I pull up to Mom's all-brick basement rancher, built in the seventies. She's been saving for years and can almost afford to give it the makeover she's always wanted: a new sunroom in the back, new tile and hardwood floors, and several coats of paint inside and out.

I rap on the pineapple door knocker that's been there since I was born. Since the doorbell is out of order and no one comes to the door, I reach under the third landscaping rock to the left of the small front porch and grab the hideaway key. I unlock the door, return the key to its place, and walk into Mom's foyer.

They've got the radio blaring in the back toward the kitchen, and the smell of marinara sauce fills my nostrils, making me feel at home and more relaxed. "Mommy, Mommy, I made the skeetos, and Meems helped a little!" Graham yells when he sees me.

At first puzzled, I realize Graham associates Mom's spaghetti with my own specialty from a can, SpaghettiOs, which he calls skeetos.

"Great job, bub!" I exclaim as he leaps into my arms for a monster hug and fifteen kisses. "I missed you, baby. Did you miss me too?"

"I did, Mommy. I really missed our hugs the most." He smiles and tilts his head with apparent adoration. It's as if he's tugging my heart out from my chest by a tiny rope. The happiness I feel with him, especially when he's this sweet, is almost too much to handle. Many times, I can't help but think it's unfair. His dad never knew him, and he never knew his dad. *Why am I the one who gets to raise him and love him? How did I end up being the one who receives his special hugs and kisses? Will I always be enough for him, and will I always fear I'm going to lose him too?*

"Our hugs are the best, aren't they, baby?" I beam with love and kiss his head, knowing how important it is to cherish moments like this because nothing lasts forever. Sometimes, I can't help picturing what life might look like if Clayton were still here. I imagine an alternate world in which my dad never left and my parents are still in love all these years later, stealing knowing glances at each other from across the dinner table. Clayton's cutting up Graham's spaghetti for him and promising to play catch in the yard later if he cleans his plate. The truth is that while there are gaps in our family, Mom and I have managed to fill them with extra love of our own.

LATER THAT EVENING, after I tuck Graham into bed and we say his prayers, I hear the faint ding of my phone in the living room. When I check, I'm glad to see it's Vi because I've been dying to know what happened with Connor.

Hey, babe. So, Connor answered, and he's coming by tomorrow morning for a quote on my en suite. I'll give you the play-by-play when he leaves. You sure you're okay with this?

My finger hovers over the reply box. *Am I okay with this?*

Another text comes in and startles me as I'm deep in thought. **Focus on the investigation, Mad. Not your schoolgirl crush on Connor. I don't want to have to get ugly here—a source.**

After a twinge of hesitation and fear, I type my reply to Violet before "a source" changes my mind. **Yes, I have to know who to be-**

lieve. This is the only way. You're the only person I can trust to do it.

Vi replies. **I mean, he'll eventually learn we're friends. I can't let him think I truly hit on him. You know?**

She's right, but I seriously doubt we'd ever date in a million years. He's way out of my league, and this is purely business. I promised to get to the bottom of this story. My life may even depend on it. **We'll cross that bridge when we *don't* get there.**

WHAT A MORNING. I GET Graham to school, grab a coffee, then do a live interview with one of my new advertisers, Taylor Bowery, owner of Taylor'd Fit, a new clothing boutique in an all-red building across town. I drive back home, and once I'm inside, Violet calls. My phone barely has time to ring once before I answer it and jump up off the couch. My pulse races. "Tell me everything."

Violet's giggles sound like a machine gun. "Are you ready for it, Mad? Are you really ready for it?"

"Yes, I am. So for the love of God, just spill!" I raise my voice, because I'm in no mood for games. She loves to drive me insane by holding information over my head.

"Gosh, you're no fun at all." Violet huffs. "Okay, so I answered the door in my robe, which had a short, sexy nightgown underneath it. And I had on full makeup, and my hair was done, of course. He acted like the perfect gentleman when I apologized for not being fully dressed yet, and he even asked if he needed to give me a minute."

She pauses, but I stay silent.

"Can you believe that?"

I pace from the front door to the kitchen as I bite my nails to the quick. "Keep going," I beg, feeling like I'm going to jump out of my skin. "Did Connor pass or fail?"

"All right, all right. Well, I said no, of course, and showed him around the house as I explained how I wanted to add some square footage and create a larger master bedroom suite. Which I actually wouldn't mind doing, by the way. I let my robe fall open a few times and drape down my shoulder, especially when we were in my bedroom. I mentioned I was a single mom and asked if he was single too. And you know what he said?"

"No, what?" My stomach knots up.

"He said he was married!" Violet shouts, and I smile into the phone.

"Good. He *should* say that," I say as my stomach relaxes. I'm proud Connor was the stand-up guy I believed he was and didn't hook up with some woman he doesn't know.

Violet sighs. "Guess Lane was wrong, then. Doesn't seem the type to have a woman on the side or anything."

I wipe the grin off my face. "Why do you sound so disappointed?"

"Well, for two reasons. One, I didn't get to go all *Real Housewives* on the guy. And two, the quote he gave me for the addition is actually so doable that I seriously want to talk Nick into it. Only I can't now, because I totally came on to the guy." Violet cackles.

I snort. "You know how I always say don't ever lie about being sick because you'll get sick? It's like the boy who cried wolf, only you're 'the vixen who cried construction.'"

Violet huffs as if irritated. "Well, you're welcome. Now my dream en suite is gone with the wind."

"Get over it, Scarlett. After all, tomorrow *is* another day." We laugh, then I get a beep on my phone. "You're the best. Thanks so much for what you did. You get, like, a million best friend points today."

Another beep.

"Only for you, babe," she says as I look at the caller's name.

"Oh my gosh! The beep on my phone, it's Connor! Do you think he knows about what we did or that we're friends? Did you say anything that might've tipped him off?" Beads of sweat form around my armpits.

"No, you nut! He's just calling you. You need to relax. This is why your brain is trying to explode on you, you know. Take a deep breath and answer. It's fine!"

I take a deep breath, count to three in my head, and let it back out. "Okay, I'll text you after."

I answer the other line quietly, as if I could hide on the phone. "Hello?"

"Hey, Madeleine. It's Connor Hudson. I just got some really bad news. Do you think we could meet?"

"Oh, I'm sorry to hear that. I'm free right now, actually. Where would you like to meet?" I scramble to come up with a reason he might have bad news. Maybe he's been bumped up to suspect number one despite his solid alibi. But surely not.

"My house, if that's okay? The boys are at school still, so we can talk there. I'm headed that way now. It'll take about five minutes for me to get there."

I glance at my clock then down at the outfit I changed into when I got home. Nothing too fancy. I'm casually cute in leggings and a cozy peach sweater. "Yeah, okay. It'll take me about fifteen. I'll see you in a few."

"Sounds good, thanks." He hangs up.

I don't get the impression he's upset with me, but he's definitely upset about something. Maybe he has cold feet about sharing information with me, or maybe he wants to quit the story entirely and let the police do their thing. He did tell Violet he was still married, so maybe he wants to let Allegra rest in peace and not do this anymore—for the boys' sake. There's only one way to find out, and it's not by sitting on my butt.

Chapter 9

M y fingers grip the steering wheel at ten and two, like my destination may bring about my ultimate downfall. It's been frigid outside for months, it seems, but today, it's so frosty that I wear my coat in my car as the heat blasts on high. I'm normally cold-natured anyway, but when I'm scared or nervous, I can never stop shivering.

After Clayton passed away, I shook for days and couldn't wrap myself in enough blankets to feel warm. My body was in shock. And when my dad left us when I was seven, I shivered for days and cried myself to sleep, wondering what I'd done wrong that caused him to leave. Right now, the million-dollar question on my mind is: Did I do something to upset Connor Hudson, and does he know I'm behind Violet's ruse?

DESPITE MY NERVY, ANXIOUS outlook, Sequoyah Hills is as picturesque as always with immaculate lawns and perfectly maintained grand homes. I see the park, the greenway, and bundled-up neighbors exchanging tidbits outside, but other details escape me. I'm focused on getting to Connor and Allegra's home. Until I know what's on his mind, mine will not rest.

I walk up the stairs that lead to the enormous front porch where Allegra's body fell. I don't want to linger in the place where she was killed, though. It freaks me out. Before I can knock or ring the doorbell, Connor opens the door and peeks out as if he doesn't want anyone to see me waiting there. "Come on in, and thanks for coming so quickly."

"Of course, of course." I enter the house.

"Can I take your coat?" His hands move toward my frozen shoulders.

I don't want to show my insanity cards yet, so I comply. "Yes, that'd be great. Thank you."

As he pulls my arms from my coat, his hand grazes mine. "Oh my God, you're freezing! Do you want to keep this on?"

"No, no, no. I'll warm up eventually. I'm kind of weird, I know. Maybe I have circulation issues." I laugh, embarrassed, as I fold my arms across my peach sweater to keep warm.

He motions me toward a den in the back of the house, but my mouth gapes open as we pass the enormous library on the way there. "Let's go sit in this den. It's the coziest place in the house. I'll turn the fireplace on, and we can talk on the floor right next to it. If you don't mind roughing it a little, that is."

The simple but classic French country décor, along with the cottage-like charm of the house, make it grand and homey at the same time. The original built-in nooks and shelving around the stone fireplace are over twenty feet tall and full of antique books and down-to-earth decor. There's a TV so large it just about covers one wall entirely, and it's adjacent to a wall full of family photos.

I'm grateful I already changed into leggings today instead of a dress, or I would be wildly uncomfortable sitting on the floor. "I don't mind at all. I'd love more than anything to sit by a warm fire and take these blasted heels off." I pull my shoes off one at a time then sit on the rug as Connor hands me an ivory faux-fur blanket.

"Here you go. This one was Allegra's favorite. It should keep you nice and warm. Oh, and here's an extra scarf too."

"Thanks," I mutter.

"Like I said, I have some bad news. It's about the police investigation." Connor sighs as he takes a seat on the floor across from me and hunches over.

"Oh no." I cover myself with the faux-fur blanket, which *is* fabulous, just like Allegra's house, her career, and her husband. She had great taste all around.

"They're not closing the case entirely, just until new evidence comes up, but tomorrow, Wentworth says, he's declaring it a random act of violence to the press. He says he got a confession that her killer was a gang member named Claude Van Morrison, who they arrested a few weeks ago before he died in prison. I don't remember hearing on the news about his arrest for another murder, but maybe you do? Anyway, this guy's ex-girlfriend confessed to police that he killed Allegra when he was running around Sequoyah Hills drunk one night with other recruits as some initiation thing. Then he got caught for another murder. They think it was simply a case of Allegra being in the wrong place at the wrong time." He shrugs and speaks clearly even though tears well up in his eyes.

"And what do you think of that?" I lean toward him, trying to decipher whether his emotions are an act. Or whether I'm being blinded by my attraction to him.

Connor glances at the burning fire. "I think it's bullshit. That's what I think!"

"Good. I do too! I mean, I'm sure they're doing their best, but there's clearly something fishy going on here. She was hit in the back of the head and pushed down her front doorsteps in the wee hours of the morning, right before a six a.m. flight to New York. If someone was doing a gang initiation or trying to rob the house and she ended up dead, wouldn't they have tried to enter the house afterward? Or at least taken her cash and belongings?"

Connor nods. "Before this 'confession,' they thought it was possible she just surprised someone before they had a chance to fully break in, and they freaked and hit her. Or it could've been someone out-of-their-mind drunk or on drugs or something. But this confession they're trying to sell us wraps the case up with a pretty red bow, especially since the murderer happens to be dead already."

"Right, and Wentworth knows the public will feel safer if they think the killer is already dead. That looks good for the police and the police chief, who happens to be Wentworth's cousin."

"*And* who happens to be up for reelection next year." Connor frowns.

"Do they know what she was hit with? Did they figure that part out, at least?" I hope to be spared the gory details.

"A bat." Connor stares blankly at the fire. "Something most robbers or gang members would be carrying around for breaking and entering."

I touch his hand. "I'm so sorry. I shouldn't have—"

He touches my hand in return, cutting me off. "No, you need to know. And listen, I'd really like to compensate you somehow. I know you're out on your own now, and you're really sticking your neck out for us on this story. So I hope you'll consider accepting this." He hands me an envelope with my name on it, and it contains a wad of Benjamin Franklins.

I shake my head and hand it back to him. "I really didn't mean for you to—"

"I know you didn't. That's why I did it." He places the envelope in my palm with one hand then covers it with the other. "Take it, please. This investigation is taking up a lot of your time right now. I know that. But I feel like I can trust you to get the truth out there. That's worth more to me than getting the best PI in Knoxville, who's likely going to be in Wentworth's pocket anyway."

I give him a reluctant half smile. "Thank you." I place the envelope on the black coffee table and don't dare count the money in front of him, even though I'm dying to know how much is inside.

While I feel awful taking his money, this is truly a godsend. I'd rather receive money from Connor than have "a source" give me a handout they can hold over my head.

"I hope the wrapping up of their investigation doesn't encourage you to quit," Connor adds.

"If anything, it makes me want to try harder. Like I'm the only one who can figure this whole thing out."

Connor nods. "You know, what if they're right and it was random? What if there's no premeditated murder to uncover?"

My eyes fall to the shaggy rug we sit on. I remember going through my own version of this agony and having similar questions. "Then you move forward, without thinking it through or making a plan. It just happens. Minute by minute at first. Then hour by hour. Then day by day and year by year. You'll never forget, and she'll always be with you, but you have to go on for those kids of yours. It's what she would've wanted."

Connor looks at my ringless finger then again at me with a knowing glance. "You've been through this, too, haven't you?"

I rub my face and sigh; the jig is up. "Yes, I have. So I can tell you from experience, as much as you're doubting yourself right now, you're stronger than you realize." I touch his arm. "I can promise you that."

Connor scoots in closer. "I'm so sorry. Can I ask who?"

I shift my legs around on the rug and end up sitting cross-legged to get comfortable. "Um, yeah."

Connor waves his hands. "I'm sorry. If you don't want to talk about this, I completely understand. I shouldn't have pried."

I shake my head. "No, I'm fine. I just—I didn't want to make this all about me when I'm supposed to be helping you. That's all."

"Hearing you talk about your experience would actually help me tremendously. If you don't mind," he adds with raised eyebrows as he turns up the gas on the fire.

I blow out some more air through my mouth. Normally, I wouldn't open up and share this with someone I just met, but there's a familiarity between Connor and me. "It was my husband. His name was Clayton. He was my high school sweetheart and best friend. We married when we were just twenty years old, and after the best year of my life as his wife, I lost him." My lip quivers, and I fan my eyes, embarrassed to be crying in front of Connor when I'm supposed to be consoling him. But having him trust me as a friend could be beneficial to the case.

Connor's eyes widen, and he scratches his head. "Wow, I'm so sorry. How long ago was this?"

"Almost four years ago. We have a son together, Graham, but they never met. Clayton died very suddenly. It wasn't until after his funeral that I discovered I was pregnant."

Connor's hand covers his mouth, and his face pales. "Oh my God!" He stands and walks to a window, where he leans over and catches his breath.

His extreme reaction strikes me as awkward. Maybe it's too much sadness for him to take in along with his own. Or maybe he's having a panic attack. I wipe my eyes and ask, "Are you okay?"

He rubs his temple and stares at me as if I'm now someone else entirely. He looks out the window again then comes and sits beside me. He leans in close, studies me, and touches my hair. "I know that story. I remember that story. It was—" He starts to say something but stops himself. "You mean, you don't know who...?"

He's not making much sense, and I wonder if his grief has caused him to take one antidepressant too many, like Allegra. "I don't know what?" I ask.

Connor begins again. "I remember hearing about that story from... a friend of mine who was friends with Clayton Wright. I didn't put it all together until now. Oh, Madeleine. That's just awful.

I mean, awful that he passed and never knew his son and you had to go through that difficult time all alone."

"The whole thing was so tragic and so terrible. I never thought I'd get through it. And maybe I wouldn't have if it weren't for Graham. He gave me a reason to go on. This is how I know you'll be okay, because you have to be, for your boys."

Connor sniffs and studies the fire again. "Yeah, I know. It's been hard keeping it together for them. Sometimes I just want to break down, but I can't. Not in front of them."

I feel for him. At least my child was still in the womb, where he wouldn't be traumatized by my constant meltdowns. "If you ever need someone you can fall apart with, I'll listen. Gosh, I don't know how many times I went to my best friend's house, V—" I almost slip and say Violet's name. "Uh, Vivian." I start again. "She was 'my person.' The one who'd listen to me at my absolute worst moments after the accident. Everyone needs someone like that, or else you'll go mad."

Connor gives me a hopeful smile. "I'd hate to unleash all of that on you, especially with all you're already doing for me, but I could use a friend who gets it. And by the way, I hope you'll keep that scarf. It's the least I can do."

I finger the red cashmere scarf and run it through my hands. "Thanks, and the offer to talk is always on the table."

Connor grins and opens his arms for a hug. It seems like I'm crossing a boundary that I shouldn't with a client, but having mutual trust is also important, so I lean in for the embrace.

"Thanks. I feel so much better already." He sniffs as we hug, almost like it's the first real hug he's received since Allegra passed. After another second or two, a shadow crosses the window behind him. I jump back and gasp.

"Is everything okay? Should I not have done that?" Connor scoots away from me.

"No, no. It's not that. I thought I saw someone in your window." My voice trembles.

Connor makes his way out the French doors into the yard and looks for himself. "Probably a reporter or blogger. Some of those guys have no boundaries. Not you, of course."

"Yeah, something like that," I agree, although I know good and well it was likely "a source" out there keeping tabs on me. Or even worse, it's Allegra's killer, biding their time before murdering me next so I won't figure out who they are. I pray that's not the case, or I'm a goner for sure.

Connor leaves my sight as he searches the back and side yards, so I inch toward the French doors he left ajar. I peek outside, facing the freezing wind toward the right, and squint when I can't see Connor anymore. I start to worry because it's eerily silent, and I hope nothing terrible has happened to him. My neck strains while looking for him, and a *creak* on the hardwood floor behind me makes me scream.

"I'm sorry! I didn't mean to scare you."

Connor winces, and I grab my chest and breathe a sigh of relief that it's him and not someone else sneaking up behind me. After this, he'll probably assume I overreact to everything.

"No, it's okay. I just didn't expect you to come back inside another way. I guess I'm a little jumpy today."

"It's all clear. Whoever it was is long gone now," he assures me. "Glass of water?"

Connor asks me to stay awhile to make sure I'm okay. To lift our spirits, we snack on popcorn and watch a few episodes of *Friends* together. We do a lot more talking than watching, and I tell myself it's not unprofessional—it's research. Although I can't remember a time when I enjoyed research half this much.

After I announce I must go, Connor smiles as he walks me to the front door. "Thanks for keeping me company. I'm really enjoying getting to know you."

I grin as my cheeks grow warm. "No problem. I had a great time. I'm here if you need to talk," I remind him before I open the door to leave, feeling guilty about our budding friendship since I have a crush on him I can't seem to squash. I walk to my car with a dopey grin plastered on my face. Somehow, the wintry breeze feels snug and inviting.

When Ivy Richards pulls up in Connor's driveway, a flabbergasted expression on her face, I feel sick to my stomach.

"Hey there!" Ivy calls as she exits her car and walks over with what seems to be a pie. "Didn't expect to see you here today. What's with the big smile? Another interview with Connor? Or something new about the case?" She cocks her head as if suspicious and eyes the red cashmere scarf wrapped around my neck.

I tuck my hair behind my ears and look away. Maybe she won't see the glow on my face if I don't look right at her. "Yeah, something like that." I don't know whether Connor wants anyone else to know about the new status of the case, so I stay mum. And I didn't come here for another interview, but we did both ask each other some very personal questions, so it's not technically a lie.

"Well, how'd it go? Obviously, it went pretty well if you're leaving with my best friend's scarf." Ivy inserts her face right in my direct line of sight and touches the scarf, her expression skeptical. As Allegra's friend, she's the shark, and I'm the fish. The only way to fend off a shark is to bop it right on the nose. Standing my ground, I look her in the eyes.

"Very well, actually. It's cold and I... I just borrowed it. I didn't steal it or anything. Then Connor gave it to me. So what are you doing here?" I add to stop myself from overexplaining.

She scrunches her eyebrows. "I'm here to check on Connor, of course, to see if he needs anything." She answers like it's none of my business. Somehow, this conversation is taking a defensive turn for both of us.

"Okay, I'm just going to ask, because there's a big elephant in the room. Is something wrong? Did something new happen?" Ivy steps closer, making me uncomfortable.

"Just... go talk to Connor. I don't know if he wants me to say or not." I narrow my eyes and wince. As a reporter, I need to maintain confidentiality, and that means not sharing every single detail with Ivy, even if she did give my name to Connor. She *is* a potential suspect, after all, although I doubt she sees it that way.

"Wait. So now he's telling *you* things before anyone else and giving you Allegra's things?" Ivy places a hand on her hip, and her forehead suddenly has several wrinkles.

"I don't know why you're getting upset. You're the one who asked me to be involved with this case. So here I am, doing my job. Why are you acting like I've done something wrong?"

Ivy snaps back. "That's right. *I* got you involved. So you're supposed to be in this with *me*, not Connor. I thought we were going to run things by each other." She stops and studies me. "Oh my God! Do you have some kind of crush on him or think you're going to replace Allegra?"

She's jumping to irrational conclusions based on little to no information, and she's drawing an aggressive line in the sand I don't intend to cross, but I will stand directly on it to prove a point.

My face grows warm, and my temper gets the best of me. "Are you seriously hurt that he told me something first and didn't want me to leave cold? If so, that may be something you should discuss with him, not me. And no, I don't have a crush on Connor. I'm just trying to do my job, and I can't tell you everything I learn because it's an ongoing investigation."

"But I'm the one who—"

Ivy starts to argue, but I jump back in with a calm tone. "I get it. You feel like I've somehow betrayed you by befriending Connor in the same way I've befriended you. And you lost your best friend, too, so there's no one here to call you out when your wild thoughts get the best of you."

"This has nothing to do with—" Ivy points at me, but I interrupt again.

"Just know that I'm in your corner as well as Connor and Allegra's. Call me later when you calm down."

Ivy's mouth gapes open so wide her uvula probably catches the winter breeze. I hop in my car and drive away, for once feeling like I'm not a pushover. The shark's nose has officially been bopped.

IN THE MIDDLE OF THE night, I wake with another headache and mild beeping in my ears. Ever since I got home and counted the money Connor gave me, I haven't been able to think about anything else. It's on my mind again now that I'm up. It was great when I realized the sum was going to be over two thousand dollars, but as I flipped through the remaining hundreds and it seemed like they were going to add up to a grand total of three thousand dollars—just like the deposit I received from "a source"—my gut felt queasy. *What are the chances of this being a coincidence? And if it isn't, what exactly does it mean? Can I trust Connor?*

Maybe I should start taking those migraine pills. I tiptoe to the kitchen for a glass of water and an aspirin when Graham's mumbles from his room stop me dead in my tracks. I hurry down the hall, scared he might actually be talking to someone in there. Perhaps "a source."

When I reach his door, I swing it open, and he's tossing, sweating, and talking in his sleep. "Baby, wake up. Wake up, Graham cracker. You're having a bad dream," I softly say as I rub his back to soothe him. He wakes with a stir and instantly hugs me like I've been gone for days.

"Mommy, I missed you! You were gone, then I found you, but you couldn't see me. I couldn't get to you, and I was so sad." He squeezes me tightly with his sweaty head tucked under my chin.

"I'm right here, baby, and I'm not going anywhere." I pet and kiss his head as he gives me a tighter squeeze. I hate seeing him so distressed, but it's nice to know that I'd be missed by someone if I were gone.

"Can you please sleep in here with me, Mommy?" he begs with misty eyes, and I can't resist.

"Of course, baby. Let me go grab my phone and bring it in here so I'll wake up on time. Okay?"

"Okay." He tucks himself under the covers. "Can you get my treasure map off my table too?"

With a furrowed brow, I turn to see a detailed map of his school on his bedside table, and the *X* for the treasure is marked at the playground fence, along with a smiley face.

"Where'd you get this, bub?" I study the map and smile.

"A pretty lady gave it to me at the fence outside the playground today. She said to share the treasure with you, Mommy. But... I couldn't find any." He sulks.

I turn the paper over. My body trembles, because there it is, just as I feared. **Mixing business with pleasure, are we? I thought I told you to back off with Connor—a source.**

I put the shaking paper down with a fake smile and race to the kitchen to grab some aspirin. "A source" has access not only to me but to Graham as well. I notice my front door is standing wide open. After I sprint to the door to lock it, I turn and scan the room with quick breaths. *Am I losing my mind? Did I leave that door open?* I stand against the door and rub my forehead as I think. No, I did not open this door. I'm absolutely sure of it. Then I see a doll sitting on my sofa, a doll I've never seen before in my life.

I tiptoe over to it as I look from side to side, making sure no one's inside the room with us. The doll's hair is a dirty blond, like mine, and she's dressed all in black. Against my better judgment, I pick her up to study her further. As soon as I lift her, her head tumbles to the floor, revealing a note stuffed down her neck. I scream and throw the doll's headless body onto the couch.

After a few deep breaths, I pluck the note from the gaping hole in the doll's neck and open it. No zigzags like before. This one is printed in twelve-point Times New Roman font with no signature and simply reads **Stop Looking.** My heart rate soars, and the deep breaths I took moments ago seem light-years away.

Someone wants me off the Allegra Hudson case, and they mean business. This can't be from "a source" unless "a source" is just playing elaborate mind games with me for kicks. But I wonder what the alternative is. And whether I possibly have two enemies with very different goals.

Chapter 10

I'm walking down a hospital corridor and searching for room 101. I must see the person in this room; my life depends on it. I'm in a maze of hallways that keep changing and twisting as sporadic fog blocks my view. Room 100 appears a few times, and room 102 does as well, but I never see room 101. After an eternity, the fog clears, and a new corridor is within view. I rush down the new path. It's a long, dark hallway that leads to a door with a blurry number on it. I run toward it. The harder I run, the larger it becomes, until I'm finally upon it—room 101. I grab the knob and twist it. A rush of cold air comes over me as machines beep from inside the room, and I view the outline of feet at the end of the hospital bed. I stick my head in the door farther and—

Graham's arm swings across his bed and hits me in the face. "Mommy, your alarm's going off."

"Damn. I wanted to know who it was," I grumble to Graham, who has no idea what I'm talking about.

"Who what was, Mommy?" Graham asks, and I'm suddenly aware I said the d-word in front of him.

"Oh, never mind." I turn off my buzzing alarm and swing out of his bed.

On the drive to Graham's school, I'm haunted by my vivid dream, the treasure map, and the doll incident. Graham chatters as usual, but my responses are like those of a distracted robot. I don't know if I should call the police, and I'm questioning whether I even trust my own mind. The police might not do anything about my concerns even if they think it all sounds legit. And the report could trickle down to Wentworth, providing him with more ammunition to throw at me about how I'm in over my head.

Once I drop Graham off and hop back into my car, I notice a missed call from Ivy. I brace for another clash. She might hate me now, or this phone call could be an olive branch. Perhaps our friendship can be salvaged since we got along so well at first. I felt drawn to her as a friend and thought the feeling was mutual.

"Hello, Madeleine." She answers on the first ring as if eager to talk.

"Hey. Listen, I wanted to say that I'm sorry."

"No, no, no, I was a total jerk. I'm the one who called to say I'm sorry," Ivy says.

"But I get it. I was in your friend's territory, wearing her scarf, and you were only trying to protect what's hers."

After a long pause, Ivy speaks. "I mean, yeah, you pretty much nailed that. Except she's not here for me to protect anymore."

"Listen, protecting Allegra's husband and her children is the most honorable thing a friend can do. I respect you so much for that. I just hope you feel like you can trust me." I'm telling her the God's honest truth. As much as her behavior frustrates me, it also makes me admire her loyalty.

Ivy exhales, and I take it she's ready to make peace as well. "I do. Let's just forget the whole conversation even happened. Can we do that?"

"It's already forgotten." I smile, thankful to be on good terms with her again. Maybe we can stay on the right track, where we started.

AN HOUR LATER, MY PHONE gets a new text: **Chelsea Knight, the unreliable girlfriend—a source.**

What the heck does that even mean? Whose girlfriend? I consider asking but decide it's a waste of time. They've made it perfectly clear they're running this show, and I'm just the lucky participant. I google the name and search for an address on White Pages online, where I find half a dozen matches. One is a woman in her seventies with a husband named Dave. I doubt she has anything to do with this, so I move on to the next name.

Chelsea Knight of Farragut—married to Steve, who has two young children, according to further Facebook searches—is also unlikely. Then I get to thirty-something Chelsea Knight, who lives on the notoriously rough street of Marigold. She has no Facebook account I can find, but further googling turns up a mug shot associated with her drug arrest last week. With her record, she sure sounds unreliable, but I hop in the car and drive over to her address to check it out.

As I approach Marigold Street, I press the door's lock button. At the interstate underpass covered with explicit graffiti, several homeless men huddle together, looking back and forth like they're up to no good. The area is known for drugs and prostitution, and the first thing I see when I park across the street from Chelsea's house is a nice black SUV parked along the street in front of her crack-filled sidewalk. In her driveway is a beat-up Chevy Cavalier I assume is hers, meaning the SUV likely belongs to a visitor. I park close enough to see who comes and goes but far enough away so I won't look like I'm lurking.

After ten minutes of waiting, I notice her front door swing open, revealing a painfully thin, gaunt-faced woman who looks much older than thirty-something, likely due to a rough lifestyle of recreational drug use. Behind her walks a man with his head down. He's wearing a hat and a dark trench coat. When she waves a white envelope, he pushes her arm down and to her side. She tucks the envelope under her arm as if to hide it, and the man seems appeased.

I lean closer to my windshield and narrow my eyes. When the man finally turns toward me and walks toward his black SUV, I gasp. The white mustache and large belly are hard to miss, and I instantly recognize him as Detective Jeff Wentworth. I scrunch down lower in my seat until I've slithered underneath the steering wheel completely, scared he'll recognize my vehicle.

After counting to one hundred, I creep up toward the driver's-side window to make sure Wentworth isn't staring me down on the other side. Once he's gone, I decide that now is my only chance to learn the truth about his visit with Chelsea. I wonder what she could possibly have to do with Allegra's murder.

Three knocks on the front door and I feel like I'm about to burst with fear and anticipation. I need answers before I end up dead like Allegra. I can't leave Graham without a mother. I just can't.

"Yes?" The woman I assume is Chelsea cracks the door open just wide enough for me to see her left eye.

"Chelsea?"

She raises her eyebrows. "In the flesh. Who's askin'?"

"Hi. I'm actually a reporter working on a story about—"

She rolls her eyes, and her voice is raspy as she puffs on a cigarette. "I'm not commenting on Claude Van Morrison."

I take a step forward and wear my most sympathetic smile. "Claude Van Morrison?" I find it odd that she would jump straight to the guy Wentworth pinned Allegra's murder on, but I play along. "You did know him, though, right?"

"Isn't that why you're here, lady?" She purses her lips.

"No, it isn't. I'm working on a story about the new neighborhood watch. My cousin, John, lives down the road, and I'm going to be staying with him for a bit starting soon. He said he knows you. Anyway, we wanted to start one and raise awareness about it. Would you be interested in joining?" I give her my friendliest smile, impressed that I came up with such a plausible story. Everyone knows a John, after all.

She opens the door wider and looks down the street each way. "Since you know John, I guess I could see what all it involves. It'd be nice to feel safer around here. It'd probably help if we all looked out for each other, I guess."

"Exactly." I grin again.

"Come in, but just for a few minutes. Okay?"

"Sounds great." I step inside and immediately want to gag at the smell of old laundry, smoke-stained walls, carpet that practically oozes yellow, and God knows what else. I fish for information as I look around the place and avoid taking a seat on the tattered, soiled couch. "I couldn't help but notice someone just left your house a few minutes ago, by the way. Was that your father?"

"God no." She laughs in an even raspier voice. "That was just... someone I used to work for." She laughs again until she chokes with a smoker's cough.

I get the impression she doesn't want me to know he's a cop, but I note the revealing words she used. *Does this mean she actually works for Wentworth? And what does any of this have to do with Claude Van Morrison?*

"Oh, okay. Just wanted to make sure that was a vehicle we could trust when looking out for your house on the watch," I assure her as I pretend to take notes.

She answers confidently, "Nah, he's fine."

"Good to know. I'm sorry about Claude, by the way." I hope she'll spill some information on how she knows him.

"Yeah, well, he had it coming. Telling me about killing that famous lady and all," she quips without a drop of sorrow, like only a woman scorned would do. Then it hits me that she's the ex-girlfriend who said Claude confessed to killing Allegra. I now remember hearing her name on the radio the other day.

I glance over at the table by the door, which Chelsea was blocking when I first walked in, and see an envelope marked CK on the front with a few twenty-dollar bills spilling out the top. An instant fever rushes over my entire body as I realize what's happened and how dangerous a situation I've put myself in. Wentworth likely dropped her drug charges last week in exchange for the false confession about Claude. And I bet he paid her off today in return for her continued silence.

With a shaky hand, I grab my phone from my back pocket and create a way out. "Oh, shoot. I've got to go. I've got to take this call. But I'll make sure John knows you're in for the watch. He'll come by sometime next week to get you all signed up." I hurry toward the front door, afraid Wentworth will return and recognize me.

"When are you moving in with John again?" she yells from the front door as I scurry to my car, but I never turn to answer her.

The rumors must be true. Wentworth's either too lazy, politically motivated, or both to find Allegra's real killer, and I'm Connor's only hope for finding out the truth.

Chapter 11

A new wedding venue is opening in Maryville today, Cottage Grove, and I'm grateful to cover the opening after last night at Chelsea's. I'm going to do a live broadcast from the grand opening and interview the owner to capture the vibe of the upscale indoor-outdoor venue. For the interview, I change into a black sequined gown with a slit up the middle of my right leg, just past my knee. I don't recall being this dolled up since my wedding, and I enjoy feeling fancy, even if it is just for work.

At the conclusion of my coverage, which draws two thousand live viewers, I reach my car, still feeling like a million bucks—except that I can no longer feel my toes, which are crammed into four-inch-high heels.

A familiar voice calls out from across the parking lot. "Hey, friend. Is it too soon to need to talk?"

I turn to see Connor, who's wearing a tuxedo. "Wow!" I accidentally say aloud for God and everyone else to hear. My face grows warm. "I mean, you look..."

"A tad overdressed? Ridiculously handsome? Like a penguin?" Connor laughs as he makes his way across the parking lot.

I giggle like a schoolgirl with a crush on her teacher. He reaches me and bows like a gentleman. "Can I show you something, since we both happen to be so dressed up? I caught your story on my phone while I was getting fitted for my new tux and thought I'd ask if I can take you somewhere cool and see what you think of it. So here I am." He laughs at his silliness.

I place my hand in his and grin as he pulls me to his car. "Now I know that at least one of my friends watches my live news broadcasts."

As he drives to an unknown location, I wonder what Connor has in store, but all he'll say is that it's a surprise. Perhaps an important clue awaits at this secret destination. But judging by his happy demeanor, this doesn't feel like research at all. My stomach knots up as my conscience tells me I'd better get back to work and focus on Allegra's story before something bad happens.

After a car ride full of nonstop conversation about our mutual love of everything from HGTV and old homes to pickles and the Dave Matthews Band, we reach a large, rustic barn in the countryside of Powell. We pull into the spacious gravel driveway in front of it, and Connor takes a deep breath. A majestic willow tree stands in the back yard, next to a small stream among rolling hills of gated farmland and an old farmhouse in the distance. The views are amazing.

"I know what you're thinking. An old barn is the last place you'd want to go in a formal dress, but just bear with me. Stay here." He runs inside the barn for a few minutes then rushes to my door and opens it for me. "Okay. Come on in."

We make our way to the enormous chipped red barn door, which he also opens for me. As it creaks open, lively music comes from inside. I peek in, expecting to see a party, but find only empty black rustic tables, elegant white chairs, and a lonely black-and-white-checkered dance floor. Like icicles, lights trickle down from the rafters, and the scene takes my breath away. "Wow! What is this place?"

Connor beams as I take in the view. "This is a *real* wedding venue. Maybe you can cover it when it finally opens to the public."

"Is this yours?" I spin in a circle, absorbing it all. From the outside, I would never have expected the interior to be so modern.

"Yeah. Allegra and I fell in love with it. I renovated it and never got around to finishing the exterior. There's a hundred-plus-year-old farmhouse a few thousand feet away that we wanted to restore as well. At one point, we thought maybe we'd live here and have a mini farm with the boys. But Sequoyah Hills happened instead, and this got placed on the back burner. What do you think? Is this perfect for weddings or what?" Connor regards the barn as if it's a long-lost child.

"I absolutely adore it. Truly." My eyes widen.

Ever since our fireside chat yesterday, Connor seems to have more interest in me. Maybe it's because he knew someone who knew Clayton or because he found out I have a child, too, or because the whole thing with Clayton humanized me. Nevertheless, I think of Ivy and Allegra and how hurt they would be over Connor and me growing closer. I'm a girl's girl, through and through, so the thought of being untrustworthy really hits me in the gut. What if I'm the shark?

When an upbeat eighties tune plays, Connor walks out onto the dance floor and motions for me to join him. I reluctantly walk out and allow him to spin me once then twice, but when I lose my balance on the third spin, he grabs me midfall and holds me upright.

When he starts to lift me back up, Connor and I lock eyes like two teenagers. I fear we're in dangerous territory as our bodies touch in all the wrong places. After we stare at each other for the longest two seconds in history, I stand, say thanks, and pull away before we make a huge mistake.

Connor clears his throat awkwardly as I wander around the barn.

"Thank you so much for bringing me here. It's such a magical place." I mosey around the tables and finger the white table runners.

"I guess that's my cue to wrap it up, huh?" Connor replies with a look of disappointment I can't quite figure out.

"I really do need to get back. I'd hate to have to pick Graham up from preschool while I'm wearing a black sequined gown." I laugh, stroking my dress.

ON OUR WAY INTO TOWN, we get stuck at the notorious train tracks in Karns. No cars are around, and we've stopped anyway, so Connor suggests we do a quick Chinese car drill in our formal attire, just because it seems ridiculous.

"Are you serious?" I ask with a furrowed brow. *Aren't you, like, forty years old?*

Connor looks at me like I'm the old one. "Oh, come on. I haven't done it in years, and I'm feeling like living a little in this ridiculous getup. You may need someone to force you to have some fun even more than I do. Come on."

A smile grows on my face, and with a nod, we're off. We laugh and run toward the front of the car, smacking into each other like a couple of dim-witted kids. We continue to cackle as a car approaches from behind, likely thinking we're both insane or on something, and we run into each other again as we attempt to pass on the same side. Finally, he plants his hands on my waist and steers me to the driver's seat of his car to avoid another collision as we continue to laugh.

I drive to the lot of Cottage Grove, where we left my car, and my shoulders fall as soon as I realize we must part ways. Our conversations flowed like rushing water all afternoon, without those awkward, cringe-inducing lulls when getting to know someone new. When I put his car in Park and pull on the emergency brake, Connor turns to me and continues a conversation about Clayton and Allegra. "I think they'd want us to have fun and be happy. You know? And maybe we were put in each other's path to help us do that."

My eyes grow large. I wonder whether he's insinuating we become a couple or just friends.

He holds up a hand. "As friends, I mean. I know you're working on the case as well, and we have to communicate with each other to an extent anyway, but beyond that, I enjoy your company and understanding," he clarifies, and I smile at his compliment. "It'd just be nice to hang out with a friend who gets the fact that I feel like dying with grief one minute and living my life without dwelling on Allegra's death the next, because that's what she'd want me to do."

I cock my head and give him a frown full of sympathy. "That, I do understand. And I kind of already consider us friends."

"Good." He smiles.

I open my door and turn to Connor. "I had fun today, by the way. And I'd love to cover the barn for you when it's ready. Whatever I can do to help out." I hop out of his car and leave it running, hoping it'll set a breezy tone for our departure. He meets me at the driver's door and shuts it behind me.

"This is one of the best days I've had in... in a long time," Connor confesses with his arm propped on the car. "It was nice to act like an idiot again." He opens his arms for a hug. I feel heat and tension between us as his warm breath reaches my neck. It may be all in my head, but it feels as if the universe is trying to pull us together.

LATER, I ACTUALLY DO have to pick up Graham in my sequined gown; my impromptu friend day with Connor didn't allow me enough time to go home and change. Beaming, I drive toward the school and walk into Graham's classroom, where the other moms give me loads of compliments on my gown.

When he spots me, Graham leaps into my arms at his classroom door, and his dirty shoes leave two perfect footprints on my dark sparkles. I wince but don't push him away. What's done is done, so we might as well enjoy the moment. Then I realize the same applies to my new friendship with Connor. We might as well enjoy what we have while we have it, despite the obvious mess it's sure to cause.

AS MOM, GRAHAM, AND I enjoy homemade tacos at home that evening, I receive a scathing text from Ivy.

Remember our conversation this morning? It was so easy for you to lie about you and Connor. You know, easy, like *you* obviously are.

My head spins in bewilderment, and I can't swallow my mouthful of taco. Acid finds its way up to my mouth from the pit of my stomach. *Did she really just call me easy?* For a second, I wonder if maybe she sent the text to the wrong person, but we did meet this morning, and we did discuss Connor.

Ivy, what are you talking about? I brace myself.

Really? You're going to play it that way? Don't worry. I won't beat around the bush—you and Connor were clearly playing on the wrong side of the tracks today.

Oh, shit! Ivy must've been in that car behind us. Neither of us paid any attention to the vehicle or the driver inside. I cringe at the image of Ivy fuming in her Highlander as Connor led me around his car by the waist, both of us giggling in formal attire. This looks really bad. So bad.

That was not what it looked like. Can we talk? I cross my fingers and wait, assuming the worst but hoping for the best. This is such a horrible misunderstanding, and I don't have a clue how to fix it.

No, I know all I need to, and now you do too. You can consider our friendship "off the rails." You almost had me fooled, Madeleine.

I repeatedly try turning the three ellipses in my text box into actual words but hit Delete every time. There's nothing I can say right now to cool her down, and nothing can come close to explaining what happened with Connor and me this week. Our connection is something I don't know how to explain to myself, let alone anyone else.

ANOTHER STABBING HEADACHE awakens me that night, so I reach for some medicine in my nightstand only to remember I'm out. I roll out of bed and scuffle to the kitchen for some more, and the beeps in my head begin, growing louder with every step. I see flashes of the dream I was having before I woke. It's the same dream I've had before: the hospital corridor engulfed with a blinding fog, finally finding room 101, the rush of frigid air as I open the door, the machines beeping inside, and the foot of the bed with a blanket covering the patient I can't see.

Despite my pain and nausea, I tuck myself back into bed and close my eyes, and I drift to sleep, only to have my recurring dream once again. This time, I'm in the hospital, hooked up to all kinds of machines, not knowing why I'm there or why I'm all alone. The disturbing dream keeps me awake most of the night, and I can't shake the sense of familiarity. It makes me feel... haunted.

The next morning, Graham and I are about to head out the front door when someone knocks on it from the other side. I approach the peep hole with my finger over my lips so Graham will shush, then I see if it's anyone I recognize. In the circle, I see Wentworth and another police officer and instantly panic. I duck and motion for Graham to shush, but he doesn't see me in time.

"Mommy, are you going to answer the door? Is it Meems?" he yells loudly enough for them to hear on the other side of my cheap, thin front door. My palm hits my face hard, then I turn the dead bolt and twist the knob. *Here we go.*

The door cracks open, and I stick my head out.

"Hi, Madeleine." Wentworth gives me a smug grin as the other cop scrolls on his iPad. Maybe he really is going after me.

"Um, yes. Can I help you?" I narrow my eyes. *Is "a source" setting me up for something I didn't do?*

"Yes, ma'am. We just have a few questions to ask, if you don't mind," Wentworth says.

"We're on our way out the door right now. Can we do it later?" I anxiously tug on Allegra's scarf that Connor gave me.

The other officer chimes in, "Sorry, ma'am. We'll only be a few minutes, we hope. I'm Officer Hunt, by the way. If you need to have a friend take your son to school, you can certainly arrange that. We'll wait." He doesn't look up from the iPad he's typing on.

Wentworth checks his watch.

"Um, it's okay. It's just preschool, so I guess we can be a little late. Come on in. Let's go ahead and do whatever this is. Graham, you can go play in your room for a few minutes. Okay?"

Graham drops his backpack onto the carpet and runs to his room, probably thinking the police are going to haul him off to jail if he doesn't do what I ask. It's a threat I now regret using in rare moments of desperation. I take a seat on the recliner across from the officers, who are now parked on my sofa. "What's this all about?" I ask with crossed arms.

"It's come to our attention that you're working on your own story on Allegra Hudson, per request of the family. Is that correct?" Officer Hunt asks.

I exhale slowly, desperately trying to assure myself I haven't done anything wrong. "Yes, the family and a close friend of the family asked me to, like I told Wentworth before. Is that a problem?"

"No, ma'am. We're just trying to get all the facts straight," Officer Hunt says as Wentworth now takes notes on the iPad.

"We were also informed you and Mr. Hudson may have some romantic relationship. Is that correct?" Wentworth cocks his head and appears ecstatic to see what my response will be.

I rub my chin, flabbergasted, feeling like I *have* committed a crime now. *What the hell kind of question is this? Ivy must've called the police on me!*

"We're friends only," I say with a clenched jaw.

Officer Hunt reluctantly reads the next question on the iPad while Wentworth types. "So you were never romantic with Mr. Hudson during your outing yesterday? And you only met him after the death of Mrs. Hudson, is that right?"

"No, I wasn't. And yes, of course. You were there in the restaurant the day we met, sir."

Steam builds inside my head. If I could get to Ivy Richards right this second... I don't know what I would do, but it wouldn't be good. Suddenly, after being grilled, I can relate to Lane and his hot temper. "And I know who's feeding you all this crap too. She's the one who asked me to investigate all of this, and she introduced me to Mr. Hudson, so she knows good and well we just met."

Officer Hunt responds, "We have to check out every lead like this, ma'am. It's nothing personal against you. As of right now, we have to take all allegations seriously."

"Are you going to question everyone all over town about this?" I huff at how this speculation will tarnish my reputation. *How could Ivy do this to Connor and me? Can't she see how this will affect Connor's children if they hear about it?*

Hunt chimes in, clearly trying to calm me. "There will only be a tight-knit circle of people needed for questioning. Nothing to worry about there, Ms. Barton."

The men look at one another and nod.

"All right, ma'am. Thanks for answering our questions. We'll be in touch if we have anything further to ask," Hunt says as they head out the front door. Wentworth continues to type with a smirk on his face.

Wentworth passes the iPad to Hunt, reaches in his pocket, and turns to me with a confused expression. "Oh, this postcard was lying outside your door, by the way," he says in the tone of an experienced smart-ass before they walk off.

I look at the picture, which is a painted scene of railroad tracks with a red dot on one side of it, a dot labeled Madeleine. I flip it over, and it reads, **"There you are, Madeleine, on the wrong side of the tracks. Better get back on the other side and leave Connor to his family—remember what I said—a source."**

Now that they've left, I'm forced to go through the mom motions required for taking Graham to school, although the postcard and Ivy's betrayal consume my thoughts the entire way there. I wonder whether Ivy could be "a source." Both she and the source did mention the train tracks and don't want me getting sidetracked by romance.

Their motives seem to line up, and I can't ignore that. But I can hardly think straight, and I don't know if I'm more angry or embarrassed about my visit from the police. Ivy's lit a fire under me, and she's about to understand what it means to get in my wrath path. It takes a lot to make me angry, but when I finally get there, I see red.

Wentworth couldn't have been happier to see me squirm. Maybe he's the one who left the doll with the note down its neck, the one warning me to stop looking.

I text Connor. **Hey, it's Mad. Just wanted to warn you Ivy has started a huge ruckus with the police because she saw us together at the train tracks yesterday. They may question you, so be warned.**

Two minutes later, he replies. **Two officers just left my place. When I called my lawyer, he didn't want me to answer any of their questions, but I did. I guess they went after us at the same time so we wouldn't be able to coordinate our stories. It's probably good for us that we both went ahead and told the truth. Did you answer all of their questions?**

I reply. **I did, well, most of them were just about yesterday and how I got involved with the story. That's really it. P.S. I'm so sorry this happened.**

I think that's perfect. No reason to be sorry. I'm not. And they're just doing their job. I don't think anyone is really taking Ivy's claims to heart. Now, the real question is... what are we going to do about Ivy and her vivid imagination? She's not going to believe us.

That's one question I definitely have a good answer for. **I'll handle her.**

And I'll let you... I'm home today, by the way. Come by if you're in the neighborhood and say hey.

Will do. But all I want right now is to find Ivy and tell her off. If Wentworth uses Ivy's wild imaginings as a way to suggest there was an affair between Connor and me before Allegra died, then I have my Chelsea Knight card to play against him. If only I'd thought to have a camera on me while I was at her house.

Chapter 12

I text Ivy and ask her to meet me somewhere. If I don't nip this, there's no telling what she'll do next. I thought she seemed trustworthy and reasonable, like Violet in many ways, but maybe I was wrong.

Ivy, we need to meet in person and clear this whole thing up. What do you say? I hope she'll take the bait. In reality, though, I want to ream her up one side and down the other for the mess she's made. I don't understand how she could possibly think Connor and I had an affair while Allegra was alive. It makes zero sense. First of all, Connor wouldn't do that. And second of all, we couldn't have gotten away with something like that without Allegra knowing. I would never be the other woman, and I would think Ivy would realize that from the little she's gotten to know me.

She responds faster than I'd imagined she would. **Fine. Same Starbucks—in one hour.**

Okay, I reply but wonder why she always gets to be the hurt one. As far as she knows, I've done nothing except engage in a silly game of Chinese fire drill with Connor. She has no real meat to her side of the story. No secret conspiracy, just paranoia and speculation. And her accusations are eating away at me because there's nothing worse than being falsely accused.

My anger stems from my need to be liked. When someone doesn't like me, it drives me insane, and I get defensive. I know that in her eyes, it appears that I've done her and her best friend wrong,

125

and I truly want to help her see the truth from my perspective. I just hope Connor's kids don't get wind of all this drama.

STARBUCKS IS BUSY, which is good. Maybe our raised voices and name calling won't alarm anyone since it's loud in here already. I take a seat inside a booth toward the back, just in case. Fewer rubberneckers this way. Ivy walks in five minutes later, gives me a nod, and waits in line to order her coffee without coming over to say hello first. I can't say I'm surprised by her slight; I would expect nothing less at this point. Instead of checking my phone to occupy myself, I make sure I look good and impatient by clicking my nails on the wooden table.

The line takes a while, and Ivy looks my way and shrugs, accidentally bumping the man in front of her on the back of the head. I can't hear her, but she clearly apologizes to the man, who turns around and yells at her.

Her hands motion for him to stop, but he points at her face, and all heads in the coffee shop twist their way. Blood pumps through my body in preparation for something. Fight-or-flight is kicking in, and I don't know which one it's going to be, but it's definitely not "freeze." Once the man touches Ivy's shoulder, forcing her backward, "fight" has won. I see fear on Ivy's face, and despite our issues, I jump up from my seat.

I step between the two of them with my hands stretched out, trying to create as much distance as I can without touching anyone. "Whoa, whoa, whoa, sir. C'mon now. There's no need for anyone to touch anyone else. She said she was sorry. She was trying to signal something to me from across the room and obviously didn't mean to hit you on the head. Her hand's so dainty it couldn't have hurt that bad anyway." I laugh to lighten the mood, but he isn't buying it.

The man is a jerk and an outnumbered one at that. Two angry men glare at him from behind Ivy and me, making it clear whose side they're on should things escalate.

"Fine!" The man yells at me as he turns around to finally place his order with the terrified barista. Everyone else in the shop gradually turns away. The show's over.

"Oh my God. Can you believe that man?" Ivy whispers as if exhausted from the episode. She takes a deep breath and places her hand on my shoulder. "Hey, thanks for that. It was really nice of you to defend me."

I take her hand in mine since the momma bear in me has emerged. "Why don't you go sit down, and I'll get your coffee. Black, right?"

"Yes, that's fine. And thanks again." Ivy walks over and unfolds into the booth, like an overcooked spaghetti noodle.

When I approach her with two cups of steaming coffee, she asks, "Why did you do that?"

I roll my eyes and smile. I would think it's obvious that despite everything, I sympathize with Ivy and don't want anything bad to happen to her. "You're not exactly my favorite person right now. I came here to tell you off, but obviously, God had other plans for us today. Did you honestly think I'd stand by and let some strange man get physical with you?"

Ivy looks down as if she realizes she's pegged me incorrectly. "You know I went to the police yesterday, don't you?"

I tilt my head to the side and lift an eyebrow. "Sure do. They paid me a nice visit this morning when I was trying to take my son to school. He was late, by the way."

"If I'm wrong about you, I'm sorry. I just have to know for sure, for Allegra, that this isn't some twisted game. I'm so worried I missed something somewhere, and all these what-ifs keep popping into my head. Like, what if you and Connor are playing me like a fiddle and he was having an affair this whole time?" Ivy throws her head back onto the booth's headrest. She must realize how silly she sounds.

I place my hand on top of hers and lean in from across the table. "I get it. But you *know* I just met Connor, so even if some crazy scenario *was* true, it wasn't with me. And while I'm on the subject of cheating, he's clearly not the type. Trust me."

"Not the type? Really? He's running around with you not even two months after Allegra's been dead." Her accusatory eyes are bloodshot and hardly blink.

"That's different. We're just friends, honest. We've really connected over experiencing the same kind of loss. I opened up about losing my husband while having a child to take care of soon after. That's why we've been hanging out." I hope she'll understand. "And I did my homework on the cheating thing, by the way. For the case's sake, I had a very attractive friend of mine run a test on him. He passed with flying colors. Cheaters don't normally pass up a good opportunity like that, and he even lied and said he was married, for Pete's sake. So no, he's not the cheating type."

Ivy jerks her head back again, and I'm not sure whether she's surprised that we tested him or shocked that he passed. "He really said that?"

I nod with a grin, knowing she won't have much to say against him now. "Yes, he did."

She sighs, and I wonder if she's beginning to see the light. "Maybe I'm wrong, then. And if I am, I'm sorry. Truly, I am."

"You're still not convinced we're just friends, are you?" I sense her uncertainty.

"I don't think you two had anything going on before she died, but you might right now."

I sit and say nothing. I can't bring myself to tell her I sense genuine feelings between us at times, because it could all just be in my head. I can't even say that out loud because it will undoubtedly sound absurd.

I sit in silence and get lost thinking for a few more seconds, and Ivy suddenly gets mad at me all over again.

"Guess your silence answers it for me, then." Ivy rises from her seat as if to leave. "I assume your 'relationship' means the whole story is compromised now, doesn't it? That's quite the conflict of interest." She grabs her bag, jerks her coffee from the table so fast that some of it spills, and walks out the front door without another word. I don't bother trying to convince her the story will go on as planned. And just like that, "a source" has something quick-witted to say.

Finding out who our friends really are is always a good thing—a source.

"DRAMA DOESN'T EVEN begin to describe your life right now," Violet says over the phone. I can hear her munching on popcorn as we talk. In her wild mind, my life is playing out just like an episode of *Desperate Housewives* or *Pretty Little Liars*.

"I think you're enjoying this a bit too much," I whine. "You know this isn't a soap opera, right? This is *my* real life." I turn onto Connor's street to stop and say hey.

Vi retorts with what I imagine is a straight face. "Yeah, I know that. Of course I *know* that. It's just so entertaining. How in the world did you get into this giant pickle, Mad?"

"Personally, I blame Perry. He started this crazy train," I snap as I pull into the Hudson driveway and turn off the engine.

"But you wouldn't take it back, though. I know you." Vi throws the harsh truth in my face. She's right; with all that's happened, I've already learned a lot about myself. I feel like I'm on the verge of some huge epiphany with the case, despite my fears about being in danger.

"Probably not. I didn't do anything wrong, even if Ivy Richards thinks otherwise. Surely it'll all get cleared up soon, right?"

"A hundred percent. You've got nothing to hide, at least. I just hope Connor doesn't either, or you may get dragged into it."

I glance at Connor's house from my car window, convinced that if there's one person I'm right about, it's him. "No, I just feel like... I just trust him. I really do. He's different from most men."

"I know, I know. But he's blurring the lines of grief, friendship, and potential romance. You're the one who told me that no one is one-dimensional, Miss Writer."

I hate when she throws my words back in my face. It's like being hit with a boomerang between my eyes, a boomerang that, unfortunately, I threw myself. "Yeah, I know, but I don't know that he's trying to pursue anything but friendship with me. It's just, sometimes, I sense that he is, but I could be wrong about that. Plus, even if he were, he and Allegra were basically separated these past few years. So although he misses her and he's grieving, he's probably been ready to move on romantically for a while."

Connor opens the door and waves me inside, so I end the conversation with Violet and lock my car.

"I have to break up with you now. Well, 'fake' break up with you."

I've almost reached him, but I shuffle back a few steps as the words sink in. "You have to do what? What does that even mean?" Suddenly, I'm second-guessing myself.

He places his hand on the small of my back as he leads me inside the house and into the den. "Come, have a seat. We have a lot to talk about."

We sit side by side on the sofa, and he offers me a can of sparkling water that's sitting on the coffee table. "Guess who paid me a visit today? After the police came, of course. She actually just left."

I yank my hand away. "Don't tell me Ivy Richards met with me today then came straight here to bash me to you?" I instantly regret telling Ivy about Violet and me testing Connor's loyalty, and I wonder if she told him that story as well. But of course she did; it's the perfect way for her to end our friendship. "What did she tell you?" I cringe.

"Apparently, your friend 'Vivian'—I think that's what you told me her name was—is actually Violet? The lady I visited for a consultation the other day, whom I genuinely thought was bat-shit crazy by the way." He laughs.

Butterflies dance throughout my stomach as I wonder whether he's hurt, mad, upset, or indifferent. His sarcastic laugh tells me he's either mad or upset.

"Listen, I was unsure about you at that point and was looking into every avenue to properly work on the case, and I probably never should've—"

He cuts me off. "I'm really not upset. I was just giving you a hard time. I honestly think it's hilarious *and* ridiculous, totally something you would do."

"Totally something I would do? What is that supposed to mean?" My neck jerks backward. It's not like I've made it a habit to test men's loyalty by using my best friend as bait. And if I had, Connor definitely wouldn't know about it.

He chuckles. "It's not supposed to mean anything, really, only that you were checking facts. That's all. I'd expect nothing less from a journalist."

"You're not mad, then?" I'm surprised he's taking it so lightly.

"No, not at all." Connor grins. "But we've got to make Ivy think I am."

I sigh with frustration at the mention of her name. "And why is that?"

"Because me getting mad and cooling things off with you proves to her that we really weren't together before Allegra died. If we had been, you wouldn't have needed to put me through the test, because we would've already been in a relationship. You see?"

I scratch my head and wonder if that just made perfect sense or if I've been around too many crazy-ass situations lately. "Yeah, okay, I think. Yeah, that makes sense."

"Can I get you something to eat while I'm 'breaking up with you'?" Connor laughs as he stands and heads toward the kitchen, and I realize our fake-up will also get "a source" off my back about Connor. Two birds, one stone.

"Some tea would be nice. I'd hate to get dumped and dehydrated at the same time," I quip. "Actually, I'll go to the kitchen with you. I need a post-break-up snack as well now."

We gather cheese slices, crackers, and tea. Then we head to the den to sit by the fire. On the way, I really focus on the Restoration Hardware furniture filling the den. The pieces all ooze expensive simplicity and charm, but I wonder if I would ever be comfortable spending twenty thousand dollars on living room furniture.

A silver-covered book lies on the coffee table behind me, and I pick it up as Connor stokes the fire. "This is pretty. Is it a photo album?" I flip it open for a quick peek.

He looks down at the white rug and answers, "No, it's the guest book for Allegra's funeral."

I place the book down quickly, now noticing there's an urn that matches it on one of the bookshelves. "Oh, Connor. I'm so sorry. I didn't mean to—"

"No, no, no. I was looking through it earlier. That day was such a blur. I don't remember seeing half of those people who signed it or what I even said to them. I really would like to have spoken with Fran and Sarah. I didn't even know they made the long trip down here till I was looking it over just a few hours ago."

"And who are they?" I ask around a mouthful of cheese.

"Fran was Allegra's literary agent, and Sarah was her editor. They both came down from New York, which would've meant a lot to Allegra, especially after she had to let Fran go a few weeks before she died."

"Had to let her go?" I perk up at the sound of a new motive. This could be something everyone has overlooked. "That's kind of a big deal, right?"

"Well, yeah. It was such a shame. They worked together from the very beginning without a hiccup, but Allegra had these two new manuscripts, and Fran just wasn't willing to sell one of them. They couldn't agree on the big ending, and Allegra wouldn't budge. She said it was the only way the story made sense. Fran refused to represent it if Allegra didn't make her suggested changes. So Allegra let her go."

I swallow my bite with a loud gulp, wondering whether Fran could've been angry enough to hurt Allegra. "And how did Fran take it?"

"She was hurt. Devastated, really. She and Sarah were particularly close friends with Allegra, and they'd had a tight bond for years. I know what you're thinking, and the answer is no. Fran's not a killer. Never in a million years. Plus, she was all the way in New York when Allegra died."

"Well, it's definitely interesting if nothing else." I grab a cracker.

"And why is that?" Connor leans forward and takes a sip of tea.

"Because authors tend to get a surge in readers when they pass away, and as her agent for all of those years, Fran will get a hefty payout from her backlist. A lot heftier than if Allegra were still alive and had moved on to new works with another agent."

Connor seems to think on that then takes another sip of tea and changes the subject. "You know what? I wish we weren't fake breaking up. I really enjoy our brainstorming and time together." He frowns.

"We still have the investigation to do. So there'll be legitimate reasons for us to be around each other, even if we don't hang out in formalwear as friends anymore."

"True, and it can be a short 'friend break-up,'" Connor explains.

"When Ivy told you what I'd done, what did you say to her?"

"I acted like I was cut to the bone. She totally bought it, too, and said it was for the best. She thinks it's too soon for me to be seen with another woman around town, even if we are just friends."

My blood boils as Ivy's treachery slices me all over again. "I guess I'll have to send Ivy a biting text or something to let her know she ruined our friendship." I roll my eyes. "She was right about one thing. I'm the only person taking this case seriously. Wentworth is only interested in wrapping this case up with a nice, election-winning bow for his cousin. I'm not certain and don't have proof, but it seems like he paid the ex-girlfriend of Claude Van Morrison, who lives over off Marigold, to say he killed Allegra. In return, she got her drug charges dropped."

"God, I don't even want to know how you found that out, but do me a favor. Don't go running around in a dangerous part of town like that by yourself again. I'd be happy to go with you."

I wrinkle my face as I picture Ivy. "I guess what you consider 'dangerous' is all relative. For all I know, it may be just as dangerous to engage with Ivy Richards. I really don't want anything to do with her right now, even if it's only a text."

"I know you don't, but she does need to think I'm upset with you so she'll cool off for a bit. Otherwise, she'll keep coming after us."

"Yeah, I guess. This whole thing is just so strange, isn't it?"

"What part exactly?" He lifts his head and looks at me like he thinks I might be talking about more than just Ivy's behavior.

"I know you and Allegra have basically been separated for the past few years, but to Ivy, this *is* a quick jump into another relationship." I hope he won't take offense.

"Yeah, but she's wrong," he says.

I feel my face flush. "I know. I just meant, in her head, it... well, you know. We'd never, um... You'd probably go for someone older, anyway, and not someone like me, when you're ready to move on." I stumble all over myself and can't figure out what I'm trying to say.

"Are you saying I'd never be interested in someone like you... hypothetically?" Connor asks.

The crackling of the fire is suddenly as loud as thunder. "I mean, Allegra was so special, and you could have just about anyone you want, I imagine. You're like the perfect guy." *Oh God. Why did I say that? Now he's going to think I'm hitting on him or something.*

"Perfect? That, I certainly am not. But I could definitely see myself going for someone like you. We're so like-minded, and I feel so comfortable around you. Even if there is a big age difference. It's almost like I've..." Connor rests his hand on top of mine and looks me straight in the eyes. "Like I've known you forever, the way we talk and get along. Or that's how it feels, at least."

He reaches toward me and carefully tucks my hair behind my ear. We lock eyes as my heart threatens to beat out of my chest. Despite my better judgment, I lean in and part my lips. He meets me halfway, and we pause for a second before our lips gently touch, melting away all the sexual tension that's been lingering between us. We breathe each other in and explore one another as our relationship takes a step in a new direction.

Connor stops and takes a breath, his hands still under my top. "Doesn't it feel that way to you, too, Alleg—" He stops.

Neither of us seems to know what to say next. He's clearly slipped and almost called me Allegra. The sheer awkwardness of the situation is beyond words. I stand up from the rug, readjust my sweater, and begin picking up the mess we made. "It's getting late. I should probably go."

After I've gathered my things, I kneel down to him as he sits on the rug with his back to me, likely embarrassed. "I'm not so sure that this isn't too soon for you. Maybe we really do need to take a step back with our friendship or whatever this is, just until you figure out how you really feel about her and about me," I whisper, hoping it'll ease the sharp sting of truth.

His voice breaks. "I know how I feel. It was just a slip. It doesn't mean I'm not ready."

He looks up at me with droopy eyes, and I see fear. It's fear that he's lost something else before it even really began, something else he can't bear to lose. So I sit on the rug, pull him close to my chest, and hold him tight.

"I'm not going anywhere, Connor. I'm right here."

Chapter 13

Thanks for ratting me out to Connor. Now he wants to take a step back from our friendship because he isn't sure he trusts me. I wish you would've given me a chance, Ivy. I thought we could be friends. I text Ivy the next morning before I curl my hair at my vanity mirror. I'm ready for this drama to end so I can continue the investigation without any more hiccups.

I research Allegra online for what seems like the millionth time, looking for any shred of evidence that she might have had a darker side, but come up empty-handed again. She was every publicist's dream author: Attractive, witty, encouraging, smart, social media savvy, and engaged in nothing questionable or controversial—minus the QVC incident. Everything appeared ideal.

After coming up with nothing, I make the mistake of googling the most recent pictures of Allegra, whose movie-star good looks make me notice my flaws all the more. I've got a good twenty pounds on her skinny ass, even though I'm on the smallish side. Her slender nose makes mine look too wide, especially when I smile. Her icy-blond hair makes my dirty-blond locks look, well, dirty. So I try to step up my game by spending more time on my hair and makeup, especially since Graham spent the night at Mom's, and I have extra time for prep.

I really am sorry I hurt you. It's for the best. He's not ready for whatever you guys are, and it would only hinder you from finding out the truth about Allegra. I had to be sure you were telling me the truth about not being in a relationship before Al-

legra passed. Now that I feel like you were probably telling the truth all along, maybe we can start over? I don't guess Connor would be so upset with you if you really hadn't tested him. And you wouldn't have tested him if you'd already been in a relationship.

Ivy has texted me back quickly. She's taken the bait, hook, line, and sinker. I know why she's done what she's done, but I still can't get over my overwhelming sense of betrayal.

Maybe I'll give Mayven Bennett another visit to see what I can find out from the Queen Bee of Sequoyah Hills herself. Lord knows if there's anyone who has all the dirt on Ivy, it's Mayven.

I'll still be in touch with you and Connor regarding my investigation. As for being friends... That, I'll have to think about. I write her back before misting my hair with flexible-hold hairspray.

I get that. And I'm truly sorry you got hurt.

Despite her reply, I'm still not sure what I think about her, even when the haze of my anger clears.

I feel a smidge better about my appearance after I've contoured my nose, cheekbones, and jawline. It helps chisel my face, but I would have to get a nose job, lose twenty pounds, and brighten my shade of blond about four levels to come anywhere close to measuring up to Allegra. I shrug in the mirror, giving up. I wonder what Connor thinks when he looks at me. There must be something he likes. Maybe he simply likes how Allegra and I are different.

THIRTY MINUTES LATER, a woeful song plays on the radio as I steer my way toward Mayven's house. I instantly recognize the tune as one of the tracks on the melancholy album I tortured myself with for months after Clayton died. The playlist was full of love songs I cruelly used to inflict a deeper level of suffering upon myself. The self-torment made me feel better, like I'd gotten what I deserved—more pain. But now, the brutality of the song makes my throat tighten, my head throb, and my stomach knot up. An intense headache appears, and I pull over at the park in Sequoyah Hills, where I leave my car and spill over into the grassy knoll to catch my breath.

Like a truckload of bricks falling on sheets of glass, haunting images fill my mind. Every once in a while, random triggers hit me like this, and there's nothing I can do about them except relive the harrowing scenes that play out in my head.

I see myself at twenty-one, married and with Clayton at our apartment. We'd planned to go to his aunt's lake house that weekend and use the new kayaks we'd bought for our one-year anniversary. But I'd come down with a horrible stomach bug. Clayton wanted to stay and take care of me, but I urged him to go on to the lake house—so he wouldn't get the virus himself. My anxiety over sickness runs deep, and I hated the thought of him puking his guts up.

"I'll be fine. I have plenty of Sprite, crackers, and full access to the bathroom." I weakly laugh. "Really. Go on, babe." I shoo him away as I try not to gag. "You do *not* want to get this! It's a bad one. The last thing I want is us passing it back and forth over and over again."

"Are you sure? I feel terrible leaving you this way." Clayton walks toward me and feels my head. "You don't have a fever. I may not even catch it. Could be food poisoning."

"We ate the same thing for dinner and lunch, babe. It's a virus, for sure." I'm certain I'm right. "Really, go on. It's probably one of those twenty-four-hour things. I'll see you when I feel good as new tomorrow. Just don't go out on the lake kayaking alone. They say it can be dangerous," I beg him before he goes. He's always had daredevil tendencies.

"All right, babe. I'll go. Just take care of yourself and promise you'll call me if you need anything. I'll only be about forty minutes away, okay?" He gathers his bags.

I make him a deal. "I'll call if I need you to come back, as long as you don't go out there by yourself."

"All right, babe. I love you," he declares one last time before he opens the door and leaves my life forever.

"Love you too," I answer, not knowing he would get up early the next morning for a workout in his kayak all alone, just like I'd asked him not to do. A workout where he would flip upside down and get trapped inside his kayak until the lake water slowly filled his perfect lungs. Before he hit the water that day, those lungs had had plenty of years left in them to breathe in and out with me and the child we didn't yet know was in my belly.

That was the Graham Cracker he'd never have the chance to know, the one who would look like Clay's little twin and who would also be too adventurous for my liking—just like his daddy. Clay would never walk through the door to kiss me, bring our baby home from the hospital with me, or sigh at the end of a mundane workday and say, "Honey, I'm home. What's for dinner?" He would never walk through the door to love me—ever again.

I'm sitting on the near-frozen grass with my head in my hands, close to hyperventilating from my own breathless sobs and mumbled words. The keys are still in the ignition, and my car beeps incessantly, though I barely hear it. Someone's voice is muffled by my cries, then I see Connor's face in front of mine.

"Is it Clayton? Did you say Clayton, Madeleine?" I read his lips and nod as he throws his coat on top of me. He sits in the grass next to me, pulls me to him, and rubs my back as I weep.

I cry, knowing I was to blame for Clay's death and that Connor will surely think I'm an awful person. "I shouldn't have let him go. I knew he would go out on the water. I knew it. He never listened to me about stuff like that. I should've been there, or I shouldn't have let him go."

"It wasn't your fault. You couldn't look after him every second of every day. He was a grown man. He knew there was some risk involved in going out there on the water alone. Don't put that kind of pressure on yourself. He made a choice. A choice that unfortunately ended very badly. It's no one's fault. It just happened." Connor wipes my tears away with his thumbs.

I cease crying and stare at him with narrowed eyes. "I never told you exactly how he died, though. How did you know?"

Connor sighs. "I tried to tell you. I've heard the story before. I know it quite well, actually. We have a mutual friend, Clayton and me."

"Yeah, you did say that. Who is it?" I ask as I try to calm myself.

Connor looks at the grass in front of me. "Allegra."

"Allegra? How in the world did she know Clayton?" Confused, I cry again.

Connor pats my hair. "I think they went to the same school or something."

"The same school as Clay and me? She was forty, and Clayton would only be twenty-five, like me now. That doesn't make any sense." I rub the base of my neck.

Connor explains, "Well, you can go to the same school and be different ages, you know? They knew *of* each other."

"Yeah, I guess." I'm too exhausted to question it further. It doesn't really matter how Allegra heard about it. She heard, one way or another.

"Were you coming by to see me?" Connor asks as he holds my hand.

"No, I was going to Mayven's to dig around a bit more."

"Dig around about Ivy?" Connor winces.

"Yeah, a little. Plus, I just need to talk to her again. She's hard to get a good read on."

"All you have to do is talk about her charities or about how you despise Ivy Richards. Then you'll get her lips moving." Connor laughs.

I frown. "You're right. But deep down, I think Ivy's all right."

Connor nods. "She is. She's good people, Mad."

"Yeah, I hate that." I giggle, and Connor gives me a squeeze—almost a congratulatory hug. Apparently, since I've gone from crying in the grass to giggling at a funny, it's worth celebrating. "I'd better get on over there, I guess."

As I wipe my eyes, Connor smooths my hair down where I'm sure it was sticking straight up.

"You sure you're okay?" he asks.

"Yeah, I am. Sorry you had to see that. I've not done it in a long time. It creeps out every once in a while, unexpectedly." I shrug.

"What triggered it?" Connor pulls me to my feet, and we approach my ever-dinging car.

I answer curtly, not wanting to go into details. "A song." The last thing I want is to get upset all over again.

"Ah. A song. Those are the worst, no?" Connor asks with big eyes like he's been there.

"They really are." I smile as I get in the car, shut the door, and roll down the window. Just seeing Connor's face makes things better. Through the open window, he kisses me on the forehead and holds my face with both hands like I'm a fragile doll he can't bear to see unhappy.

"Go do your thing, but call me when you're done. I want to see you and make sure you're doing okay." He smiles as he walks toward his car, parked on the street and the door wide-open. It appears that he jumped out as soon as he spotted me. *God help me, I'm falling in love with this man.*

I head toward Mayven's house but stop when I notice a scribbled note lying on my passenger seat. It wasn't there when I pulled over.

So many people were jogging and walking by when I was talking to Connor that the note could've been left by anyone.

You don't know what you've got till it's gone—a source.

It could be a threat against someone I love, but my gut instinct says "a source" has someone on their mind and misses them. Perhaps it's Allegra Hudson. Or perhaps they're softening their view of me and Connor.

MAYVEN OPENS HER FRONT door and looks like she's been prepped for a *Vogue* cover shoot. I'm magically put back together thanks to Connor—and the emergency makeup kit I keep in my car.

"Oh, hi, Madeleine. C'mon in. I've got about ten minutes until I have to go to an appointment, so I can't chat long. Are you feeling better?"

The last time she saw me, I was running out her front door in agony from the stabbing pain in my head. "Oh, yeah, much better. Thanks for asking. Migraines." I wink in a sad attempt to downplay the situation, knowing that I'm truly not a lot better in the random-headache department.

"I'm so sorry to hear that. I hear they can be quite the nuisance," Mayven says in her notoriously poised tone as she takes my coat and hangs it up. She's the definition of sophistication and refinement, basically the opposite of me, a hot mess. I can barely get it together when I know I'm expecting someone, so I can't imagine being prepared at all times for a drop-in visitor.

"So, what can I help you with?" She pours me a cup of tea as I take a seat, almost as if she was prepared for me to stop by.

I cut to the chase. "I just wanted to feel you out a little more on Ivy Richards."

"Oh, because she told Detective Wentworth that you and Connor might have been having an affair before Allegra died?" Mayven is as cool as an icicle as she pours her tea.

My eyes bulge, and my jaw plummets. "Do you...? She... How did you?" I try to form a sentence but fail epically. Perhaps well-to-do families like the Bennetts have personal contacts on the police force, maybe even higher up than that.

"Oh, honey, Wentworth came over here yesterday and asked me all sorts of questions about you, Connor, and Ivy." Mayven takes a sip of tea with her pinky in the air.

"What did he ask? What did you say?" I lean forward, almost out of my chair, barely able to wait for the scandalous answers that will drip from her mouth as smooth as honey. *This is terrible. What if I get framed for Allegra's murder? What if everyone gangs up on me?*

"I told him the whole thing was utterly ridiculous. There was *no* secret affair. Connor would never cheat on Allegra, and Ivy Richards is just jealous that Connor is clearly into you now and not her. She's always had a thing for him, if you ask me. She was always a little obsessive with Allegra as well, and now, I think she wants to be her." Mayven leans in closer and whispers, "It's kind of sick."

"Wow. Well, uh, thanks, I guess." I gulp a huge swig of tea, more than relieved that Mayven told Wentworth the truth. I knew Ivy was jealous, but I thought that perhaps her jealousy was also the result of her protectiveness on behalf of Allegra and *her* relationship with Connor. I'd never considered the fact that *Ivy* might have wanted to pick up the pieces with Connor.

Mayven crosses one leg over the other and sits closer to the edge of her seat. "No need to thank me. I simply told him the truth, dear. I don't mean to pry, but are you and Connor a thing or not?"

I knew this was coming. It was bound to with the information given to her by the police. I don't know how she's going to feel if I tell her that we might be a "thing." Maybe she'll see things from my perspective in a way Ivy never could.

"I'm going to be transparent with you." I sit back farther into my seat. "We became fast friends because of the mutual loss of our spouses. We had a real connection until Ivy told him something I told her in confidence. Nothing earth-shattering but something I didn't necessarily want Connor to know. Now we're sort of cooling things off a bit."

"I can't say I'm surprised. That sounds exactly like an underhanded Ivy Richards move, if you ask me."

Wheels of potential motives and schemes turn inside my frantic mind. I wonder whether Ivy truly is sick in the head. She has been tough on me, and she did go to the police about me, so it's not like the idea of her being a little "off" is completely unbelievable. I'm not convinced she's got a real problem, but it's something worth keeping in mind. After all, Mayven is likely to believe the worst about Ivy and vice versa. It's probably best to let each of them think I'm on their side so I can gain all the information possible.

"Thanks for the heads-up, Mayven. This is good to be aware of as I continue to deal with Ivy." I rise from my chair. "I know you've got to go, so I'm going to run. But thanks again for chatting with me. It's nice to know someone has my back here."

Mayven follows me to the front door and opens it as I throw on my coat. "I know you think we don't have a lot in common," she says, "but neither did Allegra and I at first. Just remember one thing when it comes to you and me. The lamps are different, but the light is the same."

"I like that," I say as I step down to the sidewalk and look back. She's growing on me, and I can sense she's letting her guard down around me too. "And your honest opinion about Connor and me being friends?"

Mayven cocks her head and scrunches her lips to one side. "I loved Allegra, but she's gone, and although we all loved her immensely and miss her terribly, we have to move on at some point. Connor's been through absolute hell over everything, and whoever can make him happy again is a friend of mine as well."

"Good to know." I smile her way as we part, surprised and glad to have her support.

On the way to my car, I dig for my keys in my bag, and the light from my phone catches my eye. Apparently, I've been a hot commodity for the last ten minutes. First, I see a text from Lane Stone: **I need to talk to you when you get a chance. Detective Wentworth and another cop were just here questioning me about you and Connor Hudson. Is something going on with you two?**

Another missed text from "a source," stating the obvious: **Oh, what a tangled web we weave...—a source.**

Chapter 14

The second hand on my watch ticks like a time bomb as I do my best to hold it together. He's five minutes late. It's not a big deal, but the what-ifs are creeping in. *What if he decided not to come? What if he went to the police? What if the media finds out about my relationship with Connor? What if Lane is selling some made-up story to them right now?* Whether it's true or not, he would likely make several thousand dollars if he shopped it around properly.

When I see Lane Stone's face through my apartment curtains, I exhale again. *Thank you, God.* Now if I can just gain his friendship, maybe he won't sell me out to the tabloids. I can't lie. He already knows from his police questioning that there's something between Connor and me. I have no clue how this will go, but I've got to calm the turbulent waters around me.

I let Lane inside my front door with a smile, and he's giving me his usual cheerful grin, which I take as a good sign.

"Hi. Thanks so much for meeting me at my home, Lane. I've got a few minutes before I need to pick my son up from school, and I thought this way, we could at least have some privacy. Here, have a seat on the couch. What can I get you to drink or eat? I've got all kinds of sodas, tea, sparkling water, and I can make just about any kind of sandwich you like." I scurry around the apartment in a tizzy of hospitality.

Lane doesn't sit but instead walks in a circle around my living room, taking everything in. "A Coke and a PB and J sounds great, actually."

I can't help but love his simple choice. My stomach grumbles. I'm not sure if I'm just hungry or if I'm subconsciously wondering whether asking Lane over was a huge mistake. The reviews on him are mixed, but I suddenly can't remember anything besides the clingy, crazy stories.

"Perfect. I made two of them for Graham's lunches this week, so they're already prepared." I throw the sandwiches on plates with napkins and bring over two cans of Coke to the coffee table. "Is this okay?" I lay his food down and sit on the recliner across from the couch.

"It's perfect." He moseys over from the photo collage of Graham and me on the living room wall. "How old is he?" Lane asks as he takes a seat on the couch.

I don't want to seem rude, but the last thing I need is to get into a conversation about Clayton with him, something he's surely going to try to dig out of me if I don't redirect the conversation. It's only natural for him to wonder where my kid's father is. "He's almost four. I've only got a half hour to chat with you, so I guess we'd better dive on in. So tell me, Lane, what all did Wentworth and company have to say to you?" I take a huge bite of my sandwich, forcing him to carry the conversation.

Lane laughs sarcastically. "I think I got more information from them and their questions than they did from me. It seems they were under the impression I was privy to information about you and Connor for some odd reason, probably because you interviewed me."

I take a swig of Coke and shake my head. "I'm so sorry you got dragged into this whole ridiculous thing."

"It's not a big deal. They just asked how long I've known you and how long I've known Connor. Had I ever seen you two together or heard of you being together in any way, things like that. It was obvious what they were getting at, and honestly, I was pretty shocked to put those pieces together. That's why I wanted to get the whole story from you before I jumped to any conclusions."

"Thank you for that. You definitely didn't owe it to me." I clear my throat to begin the unwanted but necessary conversation, and my head begins to hurt. "The truth is pretty simple. Connor and I met when Ivy brought me into this whole investigation, and we bonded and became fast friends. Ivy ran to the police with all of these crazy claims that perhaps Connor and I had met earlier and were lying about not being in a relationship. So now we're taking a step back, and that's it, really." I shrug, hoping that one, he believes me, and two, he won't run to the media and spread Ivy's lies.

Lane rubs his chin as if contemplating all that. "You and Connor, huh? I mean, I can see why he fell for you, but I can't say I understand what you see in him."

I gulp, afraid to say the wrong thing. It's so important to have Lane in my corner right now. "We're just friends, really. Or we were..."

Lane raises his eyebrows and cocks his head, likely trying to decide whether he believes me.

"I really do see why you aren't a big fan, considering what you two went through with Allegra. It's no wonder you and Connor have issues. But I like you both, so I don't really want to get in the middle of all that." I tread lightly, trying to stay neutral and avoid the details of what Connor and I are or aren't.

Lane nods. "That's fair, I guess. I just want to let you know one thing before I go. I hope you know you can do better. There are plenty of other guys out there who'd love to let Connor's loss be their gain. Plus, I'd be very wary of why he's warming up to you so quickly."

I giggle and take a huge bite of my sandwich to buy more time. Clearly, he still has a vendetta against Connor, and I'm uncomfortable with his declaration of feelings for me. It's a little too close for comfort to the Allegra-Connor-Lane love triangle. I wasn't even around any of them then, but I've heard about it enough times that it gives me déjà vu. "Can you do me a huge favor, Lane?" I ask with my mouth full, trying to seem less appealing.

"I sure can." He seems intrigued as he grabs his phone and keys.

I narrow my eyes, almost afraid to ask such a favor. "Can you keep this story to yourself?"

Lane approaches the door as I grab my purse and coat so I can pick Graham up from school.

"I can, if you do one thing for me."

I catch up with him at the door, and he grabs my hand and faces me. "Will you have dinner with me? No pressure at all for anything romantic right away. I'd just like to get one shot with you. You said yourself that you and Connor are on a break right now anyway."

What in the world is up with all the love for me lately? I haven't had a date in years, and all of a sudden, I'm irresistible. I can't lie and tell him Connor and I aren't actually on a "fake break" and that I'm sort of taken. So I'm stuck accepting a date with Lane in exchange for his discretion. "Okay, once, but as friends," I add as he shakes my hand, sealing the deal.

"We'll see," he says before he walks out the door. "I'll be in touch, Mad."

I lock my apartment door and head toward my car as I clasp my coat around my neck. My headache suddenly worsens, and I fall to my knees on the sidewalk, writhing in blinding pain. My head is splitting like a piece of wood being struck by a flaming axe, and I'm officially in agony. I can't see anything but darkness.

***

Next thing I know, I'm in Lane Stone's car, racing to the emergency room. The blackness comes and goes along with the siren-like beeping in my ears, and all I can think about is Graham waiting in line for his mommy to pick him up at school. If something truly is wrong with me, I don't know what'll happen to Graham. He can't be left without a father and a mother. I desperately yell over the beeps for Lane to please call my mother and tell her to pick Graham up.

Although I know I'm screaming, I can't hear my voice. Lane nods like he hears me and, at a red light, digs for my phone. Through blurred vision, I see his lips moving, so I assume he's gotten ahold of Mom. I shut my eyes and, despite the pain, try to take deep, relaxing breaths. After a few minutes, the pain is manageable, and my vision and hearing are almost back to normal. I turn to Lane, who just hung up my phone, and whisper, "You were still on the phone with my mom? Is everything okay?"

He grimaces. "Yeah, that last phone call was your mom. Everything's fine. I played it down for her. Figured if she's anything like my mom, she'd freak out if I told her the whole truth."

I sigh with relief. "Yeah, thanks. She totally would've. So everything's okay, then? She's picking Graham up?"

Lane nods. "Yeah, all that's good. She finally calmed down when she realized a killer wouldn't call the victim's mother and ask her to pick up her grandkid from school."

I narrow my eyes, knowing he was on the phone much too long to have talked to only my mother. "Did anyone else call? You said the last phone call was my mom as if someone else phoned me too."

Lane grimaces again, and I already know I'm not going to like what he's about to say.

"When you were yelling at me to call your mom, I unlocked your phone right as you were getting a phone call."

My eyes open so widely I feel my head begin to ache again. "Oh no, it wasn't..."

"Connor. Your 'friend,'" Lane answers with a cringe. "Between me answering your phone and all the screaming you were doing in the background, I'd say he'll probably be at the hospital before we are. He wasn't too happy, like I somehow did this to you."

"Oh God," I mutter as I throw my head back onto the headrest and whine in pain.

THE ER ISN'T TOO BUSY, and they take me back after only ten minutes. "Do you want me to go with you?" Lane asks as I rise at the call of my name, full of trepidation.

"No, no, no. Honestly, I feel fine now. I don't even really need to be here." I wave my hand at him. I've had several ads placed on my website this month, enough to pay the next two months' rent. But my COBRA insurance isn't cheap, and the tests the ER will likely run could end up putting me in a financial bind again.

"If this has been happening to you for a while, for the sake of your little boy, you'd better get it checked out." Lane gives me a harsh stare.

"You're right. I'll go back and see what all they want to do to me." I roll my eyes, grab my bag, and head down the fluorescent corridor that reeks of bleach. The moment of truth has unfortunately arrived, and I'm forced to deal with it. I've convinced myself it's only migraines, along with some tinnitus, but now that I'm here and about to find out for sure, the words "brain tumor" and "aneurysm" are the only things I can think of. Adrenaline shoots through my body like a geyser.

A few minutes later, my assigned doctor nods as I explain my recent health woes, and I divulge as much as I can recall. He says it does, in fact, sound like migraines and tinnitus, likely due to stress, anxiety, or possibly lingering PTSD from Clayton's death, but he would like to run a CT scan to rule out some more serious conditions. Thanks to Google, I know the "serious conditions" he wants to rule out but won't discuss—an aneurysm, brain tumor, abscess, or sinus blockage—but I try to keep them buried in the back of my mind, in a place I like to refer to as "Denial-ville," for the time being.

As they prep me for my CT scan, the nurse walks in with a question. "Ms. Barton, there's a Mr. Hudson here to see you. Would you like us to send him back? He seems a little worked up."

Poor Connor. I've really put him through the wringer today. "Yes, send him back, please." I wonder if he'll be upset that I let Lane into my apartment, a risky move that I probably should've thought through.

Connor's face appears in the doorway, nearly white with concern. He reaches for my face and gives me a good look over. "Are you okay? Did Lane do something to you? What happened?"

I grab his hands in hopes of comforting him. "No, he was actually really helpful. I had him over today because..." I lower my voice and whisper the rest as the nurse walks back in. "Because the police paid him a visit, too, asking about us. They also questioned Mayven." I sit up straight and speak louder again. "Anyway, we think it's migraines with tinnitus, but they're taking me over for a CT scan right now to rule out the more serious things."

Connor takes a seat while rubbing his chin. Then he announces, "Y'all do whatever tests you need to do to make sure she's okay. I'm paying for everything, so send me the bills. I want to make sure you're taken care of." He grabs my hand and squeezes it, and I'm taken aback by his reaction. But I guess I can understand him not wanting to lose someone else he cares about.

The nurse smiles. "I assure you, sir, we're doing everything we can."

"Wow, I didn't know things were so serious between you two."

My mother enters the doorway with unkempt hair, and Connor's face turns pale once more at the sight of her. I'm sure meeting my mother for the first time was the last thing on his mind today. He almost looks as if he's seen a ghost.

"Mom! Where's Graham?" I perk up and shuffle in my bed.

"Don't worry. He's with Violet and Brighton. I had to come make sure you were okay myself after speaking with a complete stranger on your phone."

"See, I'm not the only one who's suspicious of him." Connor winks, and his normal coloring slowly reappears.

I playfully glare at Connor before bringing my mom up to date. "You can go, really. I'm sure it's nothing."

"Now that I'm here, I think I'll stay. Besides, I can get to know Mr. Hudson while we wait." She grins as she looks Connor up and down.

"It'd be an honor to get to know you, Linda." Connor beams at my mom, almost as if he's confident he can win her over.

"Great," I sneer as they wheel me out of the room and down the hall for my scan. I can't wait to hear what Mom, Connor, and Lane talk about in the waiting area while I'm gone.

Chapter 15

The scan goes by quickly, but it feels eternal. I'm more worried about the three of them and their potentially dangerous conversations than I am about the scan itself. If Connor and Lane get into it, Lane might go straight to the media to spite him. And I hope Mom and Connor get along. I also hope she's not upset that our friendship has become romantic so soon after Allegra's death. *What if she's more upset that I didn't tell her about it?*

"All done, Ms. Barton," the nurse says. Before I know it, I'm back in the room and awaiting the results.

"Can you have them bring Mr. Hudson, Mr. Stone, and my mom back?" I ask before the nurse takes off. Maybe no damage has been done yet. It's only been about ten minutes, and surely they can all hold their tongues that long.

Moments later, my mom walks in by herself. "All done, then?" she asks with a smile.

"Where are they?" I crane my neck as I look for Connor and Lane.

"Connor's on the phone, trying to make sure his eldest picks up his youngest from school." She leans in and whispers, "He said he's at the hospital with a sick friend."

"What about Lane?" I shut my eyes and rub my forehead, trying to ward off another brewing headache.

"He left. After I thanked him profusely on your behalf, I told him to go on home. I thought it'd be best if those two weren't forced to be together any longer. They certainly aren't fond of each other, are they?"

"That's an understatement." I elevate my brows. My growing headache doesn't compel me to share more about their rivalry. "Gosh, I hope Lane didn't get his feelings hurt. I don't know what would've happened to me today if it weren't for him."

"Oh no, dear. I think he had to go anyway, something about his mother. He said to tell you to please call or text him later when you learn something." Mom takes a seat next to me. "So, this Connor guy, he seems really smitten. What did you do to him?" She laughs, clearly excited to gossip.

I throw my palms upward because I, too, have asked myself that question a thousand times. "I don't know, Mom. We just have this bond, like we've always known each other. I can't really explain it. We just click. Maybe we were together in another life, even though I don't believe in any of that reincarnation crap."

Mom's lips purse, and I assume she's thinking we've jumped into a relationship too quickly—a relationship she's worried will leave her daughter broken-hearted again. "Just be careful. He may not realize what he really wants right now."

I rub my temples and take a deep breath. This feels just like my conversation with Violet. "I know, I know. It sounds crazy. But he seems pretty sure about taking the next step, and I trust his judgment."

The nurse pokes her head in the door, ending our debate. "They're reviewing your scan right now, so it shouldn't be long. Just wanted to let you know, hon."

My stomach tenses, knowing that potentially life-changing news is just around the corner. But I smile at the nurse and say, "Thanks so much for letting us know."

Connor arrives at my room and is out of breath. "Did you hear anything yet?"

I sit straight up in the bed and cock my head at his sweaty appearance. "No, not yet. Are you okay?"

He takes a seat and wipes sweat from his forehead. "Yeah. I think my nose has grown about eighteen feet and my pants are likely to burst into flames at any second, though."

Mom hands me my phone. "It's been blowing up, by the way."

I scan the screen. Two texts, three emails, and one missed FaceTime call. Graham likely tried to FaceTime me from Violet's phone. I'm sure he's dying to know if I'm all right. I have several email leads for new stories and a text from Violet that reads: **Love you. Graham is doing great, hope you are too. Call when you get answers. Prayers.**

I smile thinking of Violet, Graham, and Brighton together. Thank God for Vi. My smile fades when I notice the final text is from "a source."

Connor, Momma, and Lane Stone in the same room? The web thickens... P.S. your scan is clean. The only thing wrong with you is that you're snoozing on the job. Ticktock, M—a source.

"Everything okay?" Connor asks.

I turn my stare of concern into an unnatural, toothy smile.

"Yeah, just a little worried about Graham being scared. That's all." I set my phone to the side, and the doctor walks into the room.

"Great news, Madeleine. Your scan shows no abnormalities. So your headaches *are* likely due to migraines, and accompanying tinnitus is not out of the ordinary for migraine sufferers. Keep your family doctor informed of your symptoms and take your medicine. If things aren't getting better and you think your symptoms may be due to stress, you might want to look into an antianxiety medication."

Mom and Connor beam as if delighted, but I completely check out of the rest of the conversation. *How in the hell did "a source" know my results? Who is this person, and exactly how much power do they have?*

A WEEK AFTER MY CT scan, some medication, rest, and a surprising break from "a source," I'm at the Crowne Plaza hotel, which is hopping with chatter from the who's who of Knoxville. The soft lighting, marble floors, and acoustics are perfect. Mayven smooths her dress and fluffs her hair. Looking into the camera, I check my teeth once more before joining her.

"Thanks for tuning in to my live coverage today of the Bennett Book Foundation fundraising event, a charity run by stockbroker Troy Bennett and his wife, partner, and a former financial advisor herself, Mayven Bennett. Mayven, can you please tell our viewers who aren't in attendance about the charity and how they, too, can donate?"

"Thanks, Madeleine. The Bennett Book Foundation gathers, ships, and distributes books to children in Nigeria who might never see a book otherwise. Over the past year, we've sent fifteen thousand books and twenty computers and e-readers containing two thousand digital books to Nigeria, thanks to the giving hearts of all of you. This year, I'm honoring my dear departed friend Allegra Hudson. As an avid writer, reader, and philanthropist herself, she'd have loved nothing more than to see people donating to benefit the children of Nigeria and their right to read and learn." Mayven holds back tears as she finishes.

"Thanks, Mayven, and to anyone who wants to donate to this noble charity, please visit TheBennettBookFoundation.com. That's Bennett with two *n*'s and two *t*'s. I'll post a link on my website and my Facebook page. We're going to continue our party here tonight, so this is Madeleine Barton signing off."

Mayven wipes her misty eyes. "Thanks so much for the coverage. You're a good person, you know?" Mayven hugs me in her scratchy emerald-sequined Zuhair Murad gown.

"No problem. That's such a cool thing you're doing, so selfless. What got you guys into doing so many charitable organizations?" I ask as we walk arm in arm to the dining hall.

"Troy and I were fortunate enough to go to good schools, which led to great careers, but there are so many individuals out there who aren't as privileged and educated, and we grasped that. Giving back has always been a priority to both of us. That's partly why we're so well-suited for one another. Oh, excuse me, dear. I must go speak with Mr. Griffith over there. Thank you again." She smiles as she crosses the exquisitely but simply decorated black-and-white ballroom.

"I heard you had a little scare at the hospital the other day." An artificially concerned voice behind me calls out from nowhere. I know exactly whose it is before I even turn around.

"Detective Wentworth, how lovely to see you again." I plaster on the phoniest smile I can muster as I turn to face him.

"I don't like to miss a charity event. You know, you shouldn't be getting yourself so stressed out over a case that's been solved, my dear. It's a waste of time and energy." He continues to walk past.

"It's not closed yet." I smirk with a finger in the air, noting how ironic it is that he doesn't like to miss a charity event but missed his friend Marcus's funeral.

"We're just waiting on the final paperwork, dear, but it's as good as done. Unless you think there's someone else I should be looking into. Someone who's inserted themselves into Allegra's place since she's been gone, perhaps." Wentworth laughs and walks on toward some snooty-looking rich people at table five.

A hand traces my back, and a warm breath in my ear gives me chills. "You're the most beautiful woman in this room." Connor grabs me by the waist. "Come sit with me at my table."

"But people might—"

"They might what? Think we're friends? So what? Come, eat, enjoy with me. Please?" He pouts like Graham did when he was two.

I pluck his bottom lip with my finger. "Okay. Just stop with that pitiful face, why don't you." I chuckle as I link arms with him, and we stroll to his table as friends. On the way, I take my seating card from table eleven and drop it on table one's empty spot next to Connor, which Mayven left open—just in case we changed our minds.

All throughout dinner, we make eyes at each other when no one is looking, like two teenagers out past midnight. When the dancing begins and couples make their way to the dim dance floor, Connor's legs bounce up and down on his chair. He rests his elbow on the table and his face on his fist, and I almost laugh at his energy. He's about to burst. After two songs, he pushes back his seat, which makes a loud squeak, and stands. His hand grabs mine, and he leads me out of the ballroom and down the hall.

A romantic ballad blares from the ballroom, and Connor pulls me close to him in a doorway where no one can see us. His body heat warms me as we touch, and our lips are dangerously close, his breath on my breath. Connor turns the doorknob behind him, and suddenly, we're in the empty ballroom next door, where our lips can finally meet.

"You sure about all of this? About us?" I interrupt his soft kiss, worried that he's rushing himself.

"I'm more than sure. I want this. I want you." He grins, gently touches my face, and kisses me deeply as his hands travel to my hair and hold me close.

CAN YOU MEET ME IN the morning? There's something I left out. I've got to tell someone; the guilt is eating me alive.

The following morning, I wake in my bed, and when I check for the time, I find missed texts from Lane. Graham is still sound asleep, and I sit straight up after I've read the texts for the third time. *Guilt? Guilt about what? Something about Connor? Or Allegra?* My pulse fires up past a hundred and twenty beats per minute. He sent this at three in the morning. Whatever it was must've really been bothering him.

Come now, if you can. After I reply, I bite my bottom lip.

Seconds later, **on my way** appears, and I dash to the bathroom so I'll look halfway presentable. I wash up and throw on some light makeup and deodorant. I'm brushing my freshly ironed waves when a knock comes. Graham's still snoozing, so I tiptoe to the front door.

I swing the door open and see a red-eyed Lane Stone. "Thanks for not ringing the doorbell. Graham's still asleep. Gosh, are you okay?"

As he removes his hat and coat, he reveals wrinkled clothes and disheveled hair. He's clearly not been sleeping or taking care of himself.

"No, I'm not, actually. Not okay at all. I've got to get all of this off my chest." His voice is weak as he slumps onto the couch. "Here." He hands me my pad and paper that were on the coffee table. "You're going to need this."

I sit next to him on the couch and scratch my neck as my pad and paper lie in my lap. "Okay. Whenever you're ready."

Lane wipes sweat from his hairline and rubs his cheek. "You have to understand, I didn't go to the police with this because... I didn't think they'd believe me. It makes me look bad. Maybe even guilty for more than I actually did." He tugs on his greasy hair.

I shift in my seat and take a deep breath. Maybe this was a mistake.

Lane ruffles his shirt around to fan himself. "Is it hot in here?"

I turn on the ceiling fan. "That better?"

"Yeah, I just—everything I say here, it has to stay between you and me. Is that something you can do?" He stares me right in the eyes and awaits my answer. "I'm only telling you because I think it may help your investigation, not because I want the police knocking my door down tomorrow asking how I know this."

"I don't know if I can promise that. I have no idea what you're getting at. If you tell me you had something to do with her murder, I—"

He holds up his hands and shakes his head. "No, no, no. No! Nothing like that."

I inhale a deep breath and blow it out loudly. "Good. You were making me a little nervous there for a minute. If it's nothing like that, then yes, I swear. I won't say anything to anyone," I promise, still freaking out over what he might say.

Lane sits back farther into the couch. "Let's just start at the beginning. The week before Allegra died, I ran into her at the grocery store, the Kroger on Kingston." He pauses, and I remember thinking that he was lying when he'd said his last encounter with Allegra was after the school incident over Garrett being in his class.

"Okay." I nudge him to continue as I jot down some notes. My throat is tight, and my fingers are shaky.

"Anyway, we literally turned the same corner with our carts and bumped into each other. There was no way to avoid a confrontation. So she told me hello and asked how I was, and we had a nice conversation. It was so good to see her face, her hair, to smell her aroma. She had Garrett with her. I saw how much he loved his mom and how great she was with him, and I wished... I wished they were mine and not Connor's. Why did he deserve them and not me?"

Every time he says Connor's name in a derogatory way, I bounce my knee. I'm uneasy, like he's about to crack. I hope and pray to God that Graham won't wake up until this conversation is over.

"I still wondered if she was okay. If Connor was treating her right and all." His voice breaks, and he stops. Then he buries his head in his hands and begins to cry.

"What is it? You can tell me." I pat his back as he slowly lifts his head, revealing his now soggy face. *Dear God, please don't let this man say he killed her and then turn on me as well, especially with Graham in the house.*

"After our run-in, I started following her around, just to make sure everything was all right. I knew it was wrong, but I just had to be sure. I thought if I was there at the right time, I'd find out Connor was abusing her or something, and I could save her."

My mouth rests on my clenched fist as I listen.

"So when she died that morning, I was there. Right before she died, I was there." He cries out and convulses. "Madeleine, I was there, watching!"

Chapter 16

Breathing quickly, I stand and pace from the living area to the kitchen and back a few times then bite my nails. Lane tries to collect himself while I think. "Okay, Lane. You have to pull it together enough to tell me the whole story. What exactly did you see and when?" I try to calm myself down as well.

Lane hiccups as he takes a deep breath. "It was about three in the morning. I left my car over at the park and walked to the house across the street from Allegra's. I hid behind their hedges because I saw the lights were on at Allegra's. *Now* I know she was getting ready for her six a.m. flight, but at the time, I didn't realize why she was up. I saw her walk out the front door with all her stuff, then she turned around abruptly, like she heard something or someone who startled her.

"She started speaking to someone, but I couldn't see who. They were on the side of her porch where the bushes blocked them entirely. She was talking like she knew them, but it definitely didn't seem like it was Connor. If it was him, she wouldn't have come off so polite at three in the morning, I imagine. Then I heard a noise from the house I was hiding in front of, so I took off, and that's all I saw. If I'd just stayed, or if I'd gone back, maybe it wouldn't have happened. Or maybe I'd at least know who did it."

I continue to pace, making another circle in my living room, partially relieved Lane isn't a complete psychopath who went into a fit of rage and murdered Allegra and partially intrigued at the possibilities this new information brings. "Okay. So we know she had a conversation with someone on the front porch. Someone she knew and recognized, but it *probably* wasn't Connor because she was super friendly after their presence startled her, plus we know he was asleep, according to the cameras. That's huge, Lane! You know what this means, right?"

Lane nods but with little enthusiasm. "Yeah, I do. It means the police are wrong. It definitely wasn't a random incident."

"That's right." I jump up, elated, and then it hits me—why he never told anyone. "But if you tell them you were creeping around her house—" I wince and try again. "Ugh, I mean, if you tell them you were keeping an eye out on her safety, then you might not be viewed as a reliable source, and you might even become their top suspect."

"Exactly!" Lane roughly runs his fingers through his hair.

"This is beyond frustrating." I toss my notes across the living room. "This is huge, and we can't use it!"

Lane picks up the notebook and tranquilly hands it back to me along with my pen. "We can. We just have to think of what we're missing here."

"What made you change your mind?" I shake my head, already knowing in my gut that I believe him—even though he has every reason to lie. Even though I have every reason to believe he *is* lying.

Lane weeps and shakes again as he continues. "That day you and I were at the hospital opened my eyes to who Connor truly is. I saw how he cared for you and worried about you, and I have no doubt he loved her the exact same way. He's a good guy. Listening to him talk to his sons on the phone crushed me. I knew then I had to tell you—for them, for her—even though I wanted to go on hating him forever. If I'd truly loved Allegra, I would've wanted to see her happy even if it wasn't with me. And I don't know what to do with the information about what I saw without incriminating myself. Maybe you can use it to help find her killer now."

Lane continues to cry on my shoulder, and I open my arms and offer him a hug. He seems to hate what he let himself become after his breakup with Allegra and how he's let Allegra and Connor's opinions of him define who *he* thought he was, what he thought he was worth, and what he thought he deserved. That's what I'm gathering, at least.

I can't help empathizing now that I know Lane has another side that not many people know about. I feel like I lost a part of myself along with Clayton, a part I'll never get back, and if I can help Lane help himself, maybe I can somehow help me as well. "I'll think of something, Lane. I promise. I'll figure this out."

My phone vibrates in my jeans pocket, and I gulp with dread as I reach around Lane with one arm to hold up my phone behind his shoulder.

Keep your cards close to your chest—a source.

"MOMMY, WHO WAS HERE?" Graham finally emerges from his room and sees me twirling a pen as I reread my notes from every single interview I've conducted thus far about Allegra's murder. I'm desperately trying to induce some revelation, and I realize that with all that's happened in the last day, I haven't had a chance to call Allegra's literary agent.

"Hi, angel. Um, just a friend. Do you want some milk and cereal?" I drop my things to give him a hug and a kiss.

He giggles through my kisses. "Yeah."

"You know what today is, right?" I place his cereal on the kitchen table with a knowing smile.

"Brighton's birthday party!" Graham yells, spilling some of the cereal from the box as he throws his arms up in celebration.

"That's right. We need to eat and get ready so we can go celebrate. Okay, bud?" I muss his hair and start toward the TV. "*Paw Patrol*, *PJ Masks*, or *Hey Duggee*?"

Graham answers around a mouth full of Cheerios. "*Hey Duggee*."

"All right. You watch *Hey Duggee*, and I'm going to study my papers for a while over here." I grab my notebook and begin flipping through it like it's a fan. Maybe I should talk to Mayven and Ivy about Allegra's other friends and neighbors, because so far, no one I've talked to has given me a reason to suspect she was involved with anything sketchy. *Did she owe someone money? Did someone owe her?*

Graham hits the previous-channel button, and it goes to AMC. It's playing *Vertigo*, one of my favorites by Hitchcock. It's the very beginning, and Jimmy Stewart's character allows his vertigo to get the best of him. Along with a fellow officer, he's chasing a criminal when he falls on the rooftop and hangs onto the flexing gutter for his life. When he looks down, he can't see clearly, and his fears overtake him as he dangles from the ledge, helpless. The other officer comes back and tries to help him but falls to his own gruesome death. This trauma only feeds Jimmy's character's anxiety even more as he sways. It's exactly how I feel—stuck on a ledge. I can't piece this all together in my head, and I can't ask anyone for help either, or they might plummet to their own demise. It's up to me to save myself.

_____

That evening, Brighton is opening the last of his presents, and Violet hands me a trash bag to help her start picking up after the slew of tiny litterers who fill her house. "You care to start in the kitchen, and I'll start in here?"

"No problem." I collect endless Spider-Man paper plates half full of cake and pizza. *Don't these kids know now is the time to eat this stuff up?* I wish I could be on the toddler diet and exercise program: Coke, pizza, cake, a few bouncy house jumps, eleven hours of sleep per night, and a daily nap. Also known as the recipe for diabetes and obesity for adults, unfortunately.

My phone dings, and I laugh when a selfie of my mom and Connor shows up. **What on earth is up with this collaboration?** I text, tickled that they're bonding.

Connor said you mentioned my garbage disposal being clogged, so he came over to fix it for me. Now he's taking a look at the ripped flooring in the kitchen. Isn't that nice? Mom answers with a funny GIF that I'm surprised she knows how to use. Connor must have helped her with that as well.

He's pretty great like that. Perks of being friends with a contractor. Don't talk about me too much while I'm gone. I add a heart emoji to my reply.

Too late for that! Haha. Have fun, honey, we sure are. She adds a wineglass GIF. My heart soars as I think of them hanging out so well on their own. Perhaps we're well on our way to becoming a real family... again. It seems like a long shot given the circumstances under which Connor and I have come together. But for now, I can smile and pretend we have a hopeful future.

"Take this outside with me," Violet demands as she returns to the kitchen and pulls me toward the back door.

We walk outside, and she starts in immediately. "I haven't gotten a chance to really talk about everything with you. There's always someone around, and it's driving me crazy. What's going on with Connor? How was the charity event? Did you end up sitting at his table or what?"

"We're good, good, and yes, I did," I quip, knowing my vague answers will drive her nuts. Sometimes, it's just too much fun to mess with her. Lord knows she gives as good as she gets, or worse, actually.

She whispers loudly as my smile grows. "What else? I know you've got something else. I can see it on your face."

"I do." I taunt her as I shake my hips and throw the bags in the trash can.

Violet smacks my arm with a bag of trash. "Staaaahp. Tell me."

"Well, we sat together then left to go to another ballroom, and things got really, um, hot." I wink and head inside.

Violet throws down her bag, grabs my arm, and jerks me back outside. "How hot?"

"We just made out. A lot." I smirk as my cheeks warm.

"You guys are playing with fire, aren't you?" Her eyes bulge, and my shoulders fall. "Ugh, Mad. You sure you don't want to get out while you still can? When I said maybe something could happen between you and Connor eventually, I meant in the future, as in after this case is closed. This could go public. His kids could find out. This kind of drama can't be good for your anxiety either. I don't want you to end up in the hospital all over again."

I sigh and grab her by both hands. "Vi, I know you love me, but we know what we're doing. His boys aren't going to find out, and if they do for some reason, they knew their parents' marriage was hanging on by a thread for the last few years or so anyway. They're not babies."

"What about the media? They might spin it around to where you're this awful villain, and it could really ruin your career. I'm worried about you. Are you sure this is what you want?" Violet looks concerned.

I walk toward the door and grab the knob, knowing she's right. Yes, I'm letting my heart lead me while my head is floating elsewhere. But I know Connor and I belong together. And I also know I can solve this murder, despite getting emotionally attached with all the parties involved, maybe even *because* I have gotten attached.

"I know it doesn't make sense to you, but we're falling in love, just like y'all did." I tip my head and smile as we look at Nick, who waves at Violet and motions her inside to view something he's excited about.

Yet as we continue to clean up, I can't help wondering if maybe Vi is right.

AS I DRIVE DOWN THE interstate the next morning, I make a call, and the phone rings four times. Just before the fifth ring, Fran Marx answers with a raspy voice and a New York accent.

"Hi, this is Madeleine Barton. Connor Hudson gave me your cell phone number, and I was wondering if I could ask you a few questions about Allegra Hudson. I've been hired by her family to investigate her death." I wait for what seems like a lifetime for a response.

She clears her throat. "I'm sorry. I don't discuss my clients."

"But this is for a murder investigation. Is there any way I can have a few minutes of your time, just for Allegra's sake?" I try to work on her, but she's not having it.

"No, I'm sorry."

"What about her editor, Sarah? Do you think she would be able to speak with—"

"She's out of the country for the next few weeks, so you won't have any luck there either. Sorry." She hangs up.

The whole thing seems odd, and I know there's a confidentiality to be respected, but Fran seemed abnormally bothered about someone trying to find out the truth. She probably has, however, been bombarded for interviews and statements about her departed ex-client and friend, even though they parted ways. I'm arriving in the parking lot for my next meeting, but I make a mental note not to take Fran's word on Sarah being out of town. I'll follow up with her later.

I clutch my arms to my chest as I enter Starbucks, our usual meeting place. Ivy's already sitting at the table with two coffees, so I take a seat across from her.

"Madeleine, hi. I'm so glad you wanted to chat with me." She smiles before taking a big sip of coffee.

"Thanks for this." I lift my cup. "I've gotta say, I didn't enjoy you ratting me out to Connor or the police. I hope all the drama is finally behind us." I purse my lips, awaiting an answer.

"For me, it is. And I heard you and Connor were 'friends' again. Some people said you two even dined together at the Bennetts' fundraiser two nights ago. That was pretty interesting." Ivy is nothing if not completely transparent. I've got to give her that. I never have to wonder where I stand with her.

My teeth clench. "I missed seeing you there. Mayven said she invited you. Connor and I are friendly again, yes. Is that a problem for you?"

She sneers, clearly annoyed, but holds back. "Nope, I was just sayin'."

My phone buzzes, and I pick it up and glance at a new message. **Follow the paper trail—a source.**

What the hell does that mean? What paper trail?

"I wouldn't be caught dead at one of her events again, not after she told everyone last year that I never paid the money I pledged. Which was a lie. Besides, I only pledged a hundred dollars anyway, so I don't know why she made such a big deal over it. Maybe she wanted to make an example out of me so everyone else would hold true to theirs. Hello, are you listening?" Ivy's head is cocked as I look at my phone.

"Yeah. Sorry. I heard you." I place my phone facedown and pull out my pen and paper to change the subject. "Let's cut to the chase, Ivy. Who would Allegra tell her deepest, darkest secrets to, in your opinion?"

Ivy tucks her hair behind her ear. She wants answers too. I can feel it. "I wish I knew. If you asked me years ago, I would've said Connor then me. But now, I really don't know."

I make some notes to review later. "Let's start with what we do know. You read her books, right? As a beta reader?"

Ivy nods. "Yes. I would read through her early drafts and give her my notes before she let her agent and editor read."

I look up from my paper, thinking I might be onto something. "Okay, so what was the tone of the books she was working on, the ones she was taking to her editor in New York the day she died?"

Ivy slumps like she's guilty of something. "I don't know."

My brow furrows. "What do you mean you don't know? You read them, right?"

Ivy looks at the ground as if she's ashamed. "I never did. Not the last two."

"Why not?" I frown, my words sounding like a mother who feels sorry for her kid after they've done something wrong.

"To tell the truth, we weren't very close anymore. I felt like reading for her was the only thing she still talked to me about, and I didn't like being used." Ivy shrugs. "So I never got around to reading them."

"Hmm. Okay, then. Do you still have them?"

"I suppose I do. She gave me the original rough drafts she'd handwritten out with a pen and paper, so I could easily jot down notes. They're still around the house somewhere. I never had it in me to look for them after she..." Her voice wobbles, and it's as if she can't bring herself to complete the sentence. "I felt like I'd failed her in a way. You know?"

A tear falls from her right eye onto the table, where she blankly stares at it then wipes it up with a napkin.

I place my hand on top of hers. "You know what? Something I've learned the hard way is that people don't die according to our plan. Even if we know it's coming someday, it's still a surprise. Sometimes, it's right after you've had a fight. Sometimes, it's at the most joyful time of your life, and sometimes, it's just on a normal day where nothing special happened, when you never would've thought hey, this is going to be their last day. There are a million things we'd all change if we could, but we can't. We can only remember the good times we did have and try to forgive ourselves for the things we'd do differently."

Ivy blinks and sniffs. "Thank you. I really don't think I deserve your sympathy right now. I haven't been very kind to you lately."

"No, you haven't." I laugh, trying to bring a smile to her face. "But I know a wounded heart when I see one, and I know what that kind of pain can do to a person. It changes you, makes you act in ways you never imagined you could."

"So that really is what you and Connor have in common, then, isn't it?" I imagine a light bulb flipping on inside Ivy's brain. "You've both lost someone you deeply loved." She frowns.

I lift my eyebrows as if to say yes.

"You know, I think I get it now. I see how that could be a great foundation for a friendship, and I'm glad he has someone around him who gets it. I really am. I was afraid getting too close to him would deter your investigation, and I have to say I was impressed with how you and Mayven paid tribute to Allegra with the donations to the Bennett Book Foundation." Ivy checks her phone, stands up, and grabs her bag. "I'm sorry. I've got to go, but I think I understand."

I nod, believing she means it. "Good. I hope so."

"I'll let you know when I find those books, okay?" Ivy promises before she heads out the door with a smile.

I leave, too, and head to my car, where I touch up my lipstick and brush my hair before I go see Connor. A beep reveals that I have a new message from my favorite person.

Better get out your fine-tooth comb—a source.

Chapter 17

When I pull up at Connor's, news vans line the street. The hair on the back of my neck lifts, and my trembling fingers struggle to open the car door as the beeping in my head begins. I race past the crowd as a headache starts to form. Finally, I reach the front door, and Connor opens it and pulls me in.

"Are you okay?" I'm panting and out of breath. "I'm sorry I came in the front like that. I was just so worried."

"Yes, I'm okay. Everything is okay. Wentworth made a statement today. They've ruled Allegra's death a murder at the hands of the late Claude Van Morrison." Connor's eyes roll into his head so far that I think they'll be stuck forever.

My headache suddenly disappears, and I take a deep breath. "Oh, thank God! I thought something else had happened." I lean against the wall, exhausted from my pain and misplaced adrenaline.

Connor walks over and reaches out. "Come here." He kisses me deeply as our hips touch. My bag slips down my elbow, past my hand, and hits the floor with a *thud* as I melt into him.

"I guess all the reporters out there think I'm in here getting some exclusive interview, huh?" I say as we come up for air, then peer out the curtains in the dining room.

Connor snickers as he cranes his neck toward the living room, where he can view live reports from his front yard on his TV. "Probably. It just sickens me that the police let things go, just like that. What are they thinking? I swear, if you hadn't come back, I don't know what I would've done with my life."

I cock my head, confused. "Come back? You mean today?"

Connor shakes his head as if he's confused himself. "Yeah, I mean, came into my life when you did. Sorry, I'm thinking about the boys. I keep going back and forth on whether I should go get them from school or not. I want them to go about their lives as usual, but if the other kids at school are going to bring up what's going on in the media, maybe I should keep them here for a while, until the story dies down. What do you think?"

"Ooh, that's tough. Maybe text them or their teacher and ask how things are going? Can you do that?"

Connor runs and grabs his phone. "You always know what to do," he says as he dials.

"I do?" I laugh, not knowing what he means, since I assume raising preteens and teens is much harder than raising toddlers, who are quite difficult in their own right but don't have as many crucial, real-life problems yet.

He whispers with a smile as he covers the mouthpiece of his phone. "Mothers always know."

He leaves messages for Mason and Garrett's teachers on the school phone and texts both boys as well. "Hey, while I wait for them to get back to me, I have something for you." Connor reaches into a drawer in the pristine white kitchen and pulls out a black box with a red bow on it. "I think you'll like it."

I rip the bow off and open the box, which reveals a smaller box of black velvet. "Jewelry?"

Connor shrugs with a smirk.

I lift the lid, and the beautiful pendant and chain inside take my breath away—yellow-gold scrollwork laced with rubies and sprinkled with diamonds. "It's gorgeous!" I give him a big hug. "How did you know I'd love it?"

Connor kisses me on the lips and pulls me even closer. "I guess I know your taste that well, huh?" His phone rings from across the room. "I gotta get that." He dashes to answer it.

He's talking to one of the boys' teachers when the doorbell rings. I pull back the dining room curtain and see Mayven at the front door, so I scurry to let her in.

"Come on in," I say over the sea of voices outside as camera flashes blind me. She doesn't react quickly enough, so I reach outside the door and pull her in, careful not to be photographed again. "Sorry about that," I say as Mayven flattens her now-wrinkled skirt.

"It's quite all right. What a mess it is out there. I saw you run in a while back, and I wanted to give you all a minute, but I also wanted to make sure everything was okay. Anything I can do?" Mayven rubs my arm as if she's concerned.

"Well, they knew this was coming, but..."

Connor walks to the foyer from the kitchen. "Mad, I've got to—" His cell phone rings, and he holds a finger up in the air before he runs to answer it again. Why he doesn't just keep it in his pocket, I'll never know.

I turn to Mayven. "Connor's worried about the boys being at school with all of this hitting the fan today. He's calling to see how they are. He may end up going to get them."

Mayven frowns sympathetically. "I can call the principal at Garrett's school if you like. I'm close to his wife."

I grin, appreciating her sweet offer. "No, that's okay. I think he's talking to both of the boys' teachers right now, and he'll text the boys too. I just hope they tell him the truth if they're having a hard time."

Mayven nods and bites her bottom lip, obviously concerned. "I think *they* are the hardest part about all of this. Collateral damage, those poor innocent things."

"Breaks my heart too." Losing Clayton was awful, but having to see Graham lose Clayton would be even worse. Although I wish

Clayton had known Graham, I'm grateful Graham didn't have to work through that kind of pain, especially not in the public eye like Connor's kids.

Connor reappears in a complete tizzy. "I'm so sorry, Madeleine. I've got to go get the boys. They're having a rough go of it. Just let yourself out. But if you two want to stay and talk a few minutes, I'll be back with them in about half an hour."

I give him a quick hug and hand him his coat. "I wouldn't dream of being here when you guys get back. I'll talk to Mayven for a few and take off. Call me later?"

He gives me a thumbs-up as he heads toward the garage and adds, "Yeah, it's best they don't see you. They'd totally freak out."

Mayven's eyes grow large, and I wince as we all walk to the kitchen together. The boys are in such a delicate state already that meeting their dad's new girlfriend would surely go over like a lead balloon. But at the same time, I'm slightly offended by his statement.

"Mind if I use the restroom really quick?" Mayven asks before scurrying down the hallway toward the bathroom.

"Go right ahead. Make yourself at home." I reply as if it's my home, even though it makes more sense to go to the bathroom next to the kitchen.

While she's gone, I peer out the dining room window again, although nothing's changed. Vans filled with reporters line the streets in hopes of getting a killer story. I know the feeling. I've been on that end of the lawn many times. But I will say that I never harassed people like many of them do. Some cross the line of professionalism by ringing the doorbell and knocking on the front door incessantly, at all hours of the day.

Mayven reappears with fresh lipstick for the cameras. I was beginning to wonder what was taking her so long. She obviously did some serious primping in there.

"Sorry about that. My bladder just couldn't wait! I'd better be going, but I have to ask. What does all of this mean for your investigation? With the boys being so upset, and the police and media declaring it a random act, does this mean you guys are going to let the story die?" Mayven's hand is on the front doorknob.

"Gosh, I really don't know. Connor hasn't expressed any interest in letting things go. I don't know if he ever could." This may be a knot in the chain, though. He loves those boys so much. Their well-being would trump getting the truth.

Mayven takes her hand off the doorknob like she's conflicted. "I know it isn't my place, but I just can't help thinking... Allegra was so selfless and such a great mother, maybe all this is the exact opposite of what she'd want us to be focusing on right now, you know?"

My lips purse. Perhaps she's right, but it feels like she's giving up on her friend. "Yeah, I get that. To an extent."

"It's just a thought, though." Mayven grabs the knob once more. "I really need to go. Let me know how the boys are doing, okay?"

I wave goodbye with a smile but suddenly feel guilty for trying to get justice for Allegra but at the boys' expense. "I will, and hey, thanks for checking in. We appreciate it."

"Anytime." Mayven winks as she throws herself to the hungry wolves outside.

My mom, Ivy, and Violet also call to check on everyone, and I wonder what Connor will want to do regarding my investigation. It feels like defeat to give up, but I have to wonder what's the most important thing here—answers or a peaceful environment.

I lock the house up before I escape through the backyard to avoid being seen again. I climb over the fence with my phone and necklace stuffed down my bra and creep through a neighboring yard before I make my way onto the street and to my car. I successfully avoid the reporters, who haven't given up on getting an exclusive story from or about Connor.

I throw off Allegra's scarf, put on my new necklace, and hook my phone up to the charger in my car. I start to drive away from the reporters, who are still down the street, and pass the park as my phone lights up. I pull over to have a quick look. **You shouldn't keep souvenirs of a killing—a source.**

I jump when I read the text, because it's alarming and somehow familiar. I decide to reach out, despite my orders not to.

What does that even mean? Did someone take something from her?

For five minutes, I wait in my car for a response, and nothing comes. I hope I haven't pissed "a source" off to the point of not telling me anything anymore. I guess I'll let it go for the time being. Surely they'll clue me in when they think of something else important to say—via frustrating text message riddles, as usual.

I'm living a real-life game of Clue, except I'm the only one taking risks in the dark. I always do my best thinking when I drive, and I have a few extra minutes before I pick up Graham from school. I cruise around and ponder why "a source" might think this particular tip will be helpful.

I obviously don't know who tried to kill Allegra, so how else could this be helpful? The last tip said to hold my cards close, as if I had something they viewed as an asset. The only asset I have right now isn't usable—Lane Stone's admission about seeing Allegra the night she was murdered. He didn't give specific details about that night, such as what Allegra was wearing or what she had with her that might have been taken. No one would be able to recall those details unless they were trained to seek them, like a spy or something, which he clearly isn't. If only he could press Rewind and relive the moment.

Wait... Maybe he can.

I call Lane as I'm pulling up to Graham's school. "How about meeting me for dinner tonight for that raincheck? I've got something kind of crazy I want to discuss with you."

Lane laughs half-heartedly. "Crazier than our last conversation?"

I snicker. "Well, just as crazy, I'd say."

"I don't know how it could get any crazier than that, but I'm curious. What time and where?" Lane asks as a school bell rings in the background.

"Six o'clock. Café 4," I quickly respond so he can get back to work.

"See you there. Gotta go." Lane hangs up as I imagine students filling his classroom.

"Mommy!" Graham yells and waves when he spots my car as his class walks inside from the playground. I wave back and text my mom before I exit my car. **Can you come have dinner with Graham tonight? I have a last-minute meeting. Let me know—Love you.**

THIS WINTER IS UNENDING, and instead of a beautiful winter snow enveloping the landscape, all we get is frigid, crisp, completely dry air. I walk down Gay Street downtown, puffed up like I'm heading into outer space. Despite my down jacket, another jacket underneath that, gloves, hood, and scarf, I shiver like a nervous Chihuahua. I walk into Market Square and feel warmer—inside, at least—when I see a plethora of people enjoying the lights, ice rink, and winter boutiques. I open the door to Café 4, and the heat rushes at me like a beachy breeze. *Oh, how I wish I were somewhere in the Caribbean right now. Winter is so not my spirit season.*

I grab a table in the "seat yourself" loft area upstairs. I've barely been here a minute, and already, I'm chomping at the bit for Lane to arrive. If I can convince him to trust me and my idea, we may have a chance of solving this case. The waiter arrives, and I order a Sex on the Beach because why not. This is a risky conversation, and liquid courage never hurt anybody.

Lane arrives looking like someone who doesn't intend to lose at strip poker. "I'm so nervous about this, by the way." He takes a seat across from me and sheds a few layers. "So, what's this craziness you want to talk to me about? I don't think I can do the small talk thing right now. The suspense is killing me."

My second Sex on the Beach already resembles the skating rink outside—just ice—and I'm feeling looser than normal because I haven't had time to eat much today. "Oh, come on. Let's have a drink first." I signal the waiter.

"Yes, ma'am. Another drink for you?"

"Yes, another. And he wants a..." I twirl my hand, waiting for Lane to fill in the blank.

"An IPA." Lane grimaces at my state, and the waiter takes off to gather our drinks.

"I don't want to rush this conversation, Lane. You've got to let me build it up for you, okay?" I slur my words, and Lane laughs.

"God, you are such a lightweight," he jabs.

"Shut up! I've hard a had day. I mean, I hard a—whatever. You know what I mean."

Lane cracks up as the waiter hands him his IPA and places my drink to my right.

"I think I've come up with a way we can gain some valuable information, Mr. Stone." I lean across the table and speak in the deepest voice I can muster. "Are you willing to do whatever it takes?"

"No, I'm obviously not. Because I don't want this to get pinned on me," Lane quips after a sip of his beer.

"Well, okay. This is the thing. You have to trust me one hundred percent and one other person involved who is legally sworn to secrecy. It's a safe place, I promise. Can you trust me?"

Lane shakes his head and looks at his watch. "I guess so. Yeah."

I whisper across the table, "I happen to have a very good hunch that whoever killed Allegra also took something she had on her that night."

Lane leans into me and whispers back, "That's huge. Are you sure?"

I shake my head. "Well, no. I'm not certain, but I do think so."

"You're awful convincing tonight." Lane grabs his face and laughs as I chug some water in a sad attempt to become less loopy.

"I know, I know. My delivery is sloppy, but my head and heart are in the right place. I know this psychiatrist named Dominic. He used to be my neighbor growing up. Anyway, he hypnotizes people to help them recall certain lost memories. I think if I can observe you and take notes while you're hypnotized, we can unearth some of those small details about Allegra while she was on that porch."

"Hypnotized?" Lane furrows his brow. "I don't know about that."

"Why not?" I'm not whispering anymore.

Lane shuffles around in his seat. "You really think that'll work? Seriously?"

I stand up, walk behind Lane, and whisper again. "You want to know what I think? I think it's all we've got right now, I think I need some traction here, and I think this is a good way to clear that conscience of yours so you can look at yourself in the mirror and live your life again, Lane Stone. So what do you say?"

Chapter 18

Two days later, Lane and I are at an appointment with my psychiatrist friend, Dominic, at his office downtown. With my foot shaking back and forth, I sit in his green velvet wingback chair and tell him, "Don't forget, I don't want to be in the room when you start."

"I know. I'm not starting just yet. We have a few things to go over first, as a group." Dominic reads from his notebook and looks to Lane and me for assurance. "So we want to know about one night and one night only, the night Allegra Hudson was murdered. We want to know what she was wearing, what she had with her, and who she was talking to, even though the last part you likely won't recall because you didn't have that person in your line of sight. Is all of that correct?"

"Yes," Lane and I say in unison.

"Madeleine, you may go now. When it's time to come back in, I'll text you, and you can sit right here and take notes. If you think of anything else you want me to ask him, don't speak, just pass me a note."

I nod and say, "Good luck," before I scurry back to the lobby like I've escaped a grim fate. The last thing I want to do is listen to Lane be hypnotized—and accidentally be hypnotized myself. I can't exactly be Johnny-on-the-spot with the note taking if I'm trying to remember the night Allegra was murdered as well, especially since I wasn't there. The receptionist asks if she can get me water or coffee, so I gladly take a bottle of water and sip some as I glance at my phone.

Nothing from Dominic yet. But Violet's tried to call me once and Ivy as well. There's no way I have enough time to return their calls right now. Plus, I don't know what I would say to them when Dominic calls me into his office. "Sorry, I've got to go watch Allegra Hudson's ex-boyfriend-slash-stalker get hypnotized so he can recall what he saw the night she died while he was spying on her." I chuckle as I imagine myself saying it, especially to Ivy, whose brain would likely implode. I set my phone on my lap, take a deep breath, and try to be patient, but as soon as I do, it lights up. It's time to go in.

After I quietly enter the room, Dominic continues.

"It's the night Allegra Hudson is murdered, Lane, and you're across the street, watching her house. What do you see? Try to give as many details as possible."

Lane lies on the couch, seemingly in a trance, and answers softly, almost like a child. "Allegra is walking out her front door toward her car parked on the street, and it's very dark out, but the streetlight shines on her face, so I can see her. She's going somewhere, probably the airport, because she's carrying a large purse, luggage, and some stacks of bound papers that she's thumbing through. She's wearing black leggings, a pink sweatshirt that says Gucci, and black-and-white tennis shoes. Her hair is down and curled. She looks beautiful."

"Does she wear any jewelry?" Dominic inquires.

Lane replies, "Her wedding ring is all I can see as she goes through her papers."

"Is there anyone else around, Lane?"

"No, but a bright-green Jeep Wrangler has driven by a few times, and it just went by again."

My eyes open wide as I look at Dominic, waving my hand in a circle, indicating for him to press Lane for more about the Jeep. It has to be Marcus's. There aren't that many bright-green Jeeps in the world.

I wonder whether Marcus's big story could have had anything to do with him driving by Allegra's house so late at night. Since he knew I was covering her murder, surely he would have told me if our stories were connected.

"Have you ever seen who drives the green Jeep, Lane?" Dominic asks.

"A younger man. I saw him driving around here during the day once too."

I nod at Dominic to move on, knowing this must be Marcus, even though his involvement makes zero sense. Allegra was already dead when Marcus told me about his big exposé, but I guess that doesn't rule her out as an important figure who had an interesting job, as he put it. Perhaps he knew a secret of hers and was watching the house, trying to confirm something. It's just like I thought from the beginning. If I solve Allegra's murder, perhaps I'll prove that Marcus was murdered as well.

"She flips through her papers a bit. They're bound together, kind of like a book printed on computer paper. She looks startled and turns around like she heard a voice. Then she smiles and speaks to someone behind the hedges," Lane continues, and I scoot to the edge of my seat.

"Does she seem friendly with this person?" Dominic prompts.

Lane confidently answers, "Yes, she does. I feel that she likes whoever it is, but they're not supposed to be there."

"Can you see them? Maybe a hand, an arm, or a shoe?"

"No, I can't see anything. It looks like she's talking to no one at all from here."

"What happens next, Lane?"

"I hear something from the house behind me. They're going to walk out and see me. I need to go!" Lane raises his voice as if alarmed and starts to shake.

Dominic nods my way, my cue to go, and I tiptoe to the lobby once more. I study my notes and try to find some Easter eggs within them. Allegra's hair was down, so she could've had earrings on, which Lane wouldn't have seen. She wore a sweatshirt, so she could have worn a watch, which Lane wouldn't have seen either. She had bound papers, likely the manuscripts she was working on. Any of these items could've been taken, but it still doesn't make sense to me. I don't know why anyone would risk taking any of these things from her while she was awake. They could simply wait until she was asleep and rob her like a normal person. *It has to be about more than just stealing something, but what?*

I need to speak with Connor and see if maybe something is missing that he didn't notice at first, perhaps a piece of jewelry. I need to look over the police report one more time to see what they found at the scene of the crime and find out if it matches what Connor told them. I also need to talk to Ivy and Mayven about her books. Maybe they'll know what she was working on. Perhaps I can speak with her editor as well and learn what their meeting was supposed to be about and gain some insight into her beef with her agent.

Once I reenter the office a few minutes later, Lane is back to himself and seems refreshed.

"Was anything I said helpful?" he asks like a perky child who's excited about Christmas.

I smile and hold up my notes. "Actually, Lane, I think it was *very* helpful."

"Whoa, I'm long-winded, aren't I?" He laughs as he cranes his neck toward the paper and squints through his glasses.

"That, and you had a great prompter." I tilt my head toward Dominic. "Thanks, Dominic. Hopefully, we can use this to solve a murder and help a family."

"I'm glad I could help you out." Dominic pushes his glasses up his nose. "Anything else I can do for you two?" He rises from his seat as if to walk us out.

"No, I think that's it. Right, Lane?" I pat him on the back, proud that he's overcome his fear.

"Yeah, that's it for now." Lane laughs, glances at Dominic, and points at me. "If you're ever going to pick my brain again, I definitely don't want this one here taking notes."

"Hey, careful now. I won't let you read what you said if you aren't nice to me." I snap back playfully, thinking of how fond I am of Lane despite all he's guilty of. He seems oddly innocent, like a victim of his own immaturity.

"You two have a great day. Let me know how things turn out." Dominic smiles, waves, and shuts the door behind us.

After I share with Lane what he divulged while hypnotized, he immediately jumps on board with my theories about potentially stolen items and is equally confused about why someone decided to take them at that specific time. "Let's just go through each item and make up some reasons why they might've been desirable," Lane suggests as we walk through the parking lot, studying my notes.

"Okay, sounds logical. Let's start with the books." I feel drawn to them somehow.

Lane clears his throat. "Allegra's a pretty big deal, and now that's she's gone, if those typed, personal copies are the only ones that remain, they'll be worth a lot of money to someone. Right?"

I'm impressed, and my eyes widen as I halt. "You have quite the criminal mind. That's a good point, but would someone kill her just to do that? I don't know. I think there's more to it. I'll get in touch with her editor and see if she actually emailed her the books yet, saved them on her computer at home somewhere, or if the typed copies were all there was. This is a good start, though."

"Glad I could help." Lane shrugs as we continue to walk.

"Okay, moving on to possible earrings or a watch. We know it wasn't just a random attempted break-in, based on what you saw. Unless she saw this person, had a conversation, then was coincidentally robbed by someone else, but I find that highly unlikely."

Lane nods back at me. "I agree. So, why would anyone care enough to kill her over some jewelry or a watch?"

On my pad, I scribble some notes to ask Connor later. "I'll talk to Connor and double-check with him about what items the police recovered. That should eliminate or confirm what we should be paying attention to. I just don't see anyone killing Allegra over some jewelry unless it was either stolen from them originally or had some sentimental value."

"At least you have some direction now. Even if they all come up as dead ends, at least we tried everything," Lane says.

"Right." I grin to appease Lane, but I know we're onto something. We're on the verge of something big.

"Thanks, by the way." Lane continues past his car and toward mine with me.

"For what?" I ask.

Lane looks me in the eyes. "For trusting me. For taking this seriously. And most of all, for not taking me to the police."

I click the button to unlock my car, and Lane reaches around and opens the door for me. "Some of the things I've done, some of the things I've told you... have been sketchy at best. I'm not delusional. I realize that. I almost judge you a tiny bit for not running for the hills, from me and this whole case." He forces a smile.

I grin. So he *is* self-aware after all. "You do have a point there. I think I'm a pretty good judge of character, and you know what?"

Lane lifts his eyebrows. "What?"

"You're not perfect by any stretch of the imagination, but none of us are, and I know in my heart you mean well." I touch his shoulder.

Lane's eyes well up with tears. "When it comes to you and Connor, I'm going to let sleeping dogs lie. Looking back, I wish I'd done that for Allegra. I just let my crazy theories and pride get the best of me."

I throw my purse and notebook into the passenger seat on top of Allegra's scarf. "You're a decent guy, Lane Stone. Someday, you'll find someone so perfect for you and you alone, she'll make Allegra and me look like sliced bologna." I take a seat and start the engine.

Lane shuts the door, and I roll down the window and blast the heat in my car.

"I hope you're right, Madeleine. I hope you're right."

"WHERE EXACTLY ARE WE going?" I ask Connor as we walk arm in arm downtown on the Friday after Lane's hypnosis, bundled up like Eskimos.

"You'll see." He squeezes my hand three times. "You aren't a big fan of surprises, are you?"

"Not so much. Nine out of ten times, they're bad news." Knowing what's coming is important to me, and I don't cope well with being caught off-guard. It feeds my anxiety.

Connor walks faster. "This, I assure you, is not bad news, my dear."

We're taking a stroll by the performance lawn, the fountains, the Sunsphere, the Tennessee Amphitheater, and the carefully manicured festival lawn of the World's Fair Park, which are all almost deserted tonight. The one popular restaurant in the area closed ten years ago, and all of Knoxville anxiously awaits the resurgence of the area, which hosted the 1982 World's Fair. Everyone wants to see it become one of Knoxville's hot spots.

I don't generally miss a meal, and my growling stomach is all I can think about as we walk. Getting low blood sugar turns me into a bear. "There will be food where we're going, right?"

"Yes, I promise." Connor chuckles and squeezes my hand again as we reach an elevator at the base of the Sunsphere.

"Are we touring the top? I've always wanted to do that." I grin as I lean back to see the whole thing. It stretches into the sky just high enough to be a thrill without giving me vertigo.

"Something like that." Connor pushes the button for the top floor.

"For something that's essentially a giant gold-plated golf ball sitting on top of a tee, it sure is pretty. Right?"

The antique elevator slowly propels us upward about two hundred fifty feet.

"I always thought it was more of a big gold disco ball, kind of like a live version of that *Dancing with the Stars* mirror-ball trophy, but what you're saying makes more sense." Connor laughs.

A new sign on the elevator describes the top floor as a posh new restaurant called The Sphere.

"Stop the presses. This is a restaurant now?" My mouth gapes open, and I turn to Connor.

He smirks as if he has something up his sleeve. "It is."

We walk out of the elevator and past the hostess table to a restaurant decorated in black, blue, and white—black textured walls, white marble floors, and sophisticated blue table décor and chandeliers. It's regal and elegant but empty. "First ones here?" I ask as a man approaches us with two menus that have our names printed on them.

"Your menus." He nods and doesn't offer any more information, as if he's a butler from the early 1900s. My forehead wrinkles, but he and Connor appear to believe this is all perfectly normal. Connor takes the menus, and we head toward the only table set for two, right by the window overlooking World's Fair Park.

I gaze out as Connor takes a seat, and as my eyes drift to the sidewalk below, I notice a man looking up at me. And not just any man. It looks like... no, it *is* Lane Stone. I gasp and step back to see if Connor's looking at him as well, but he's already eyeing his menu. I glance below us again to see if Lane's still out there, and he's gone. I blink slowly and shake my head, wondering if I imagined the whole thing.

Connor drops his menu and looks at me. "If you'd rather see downtown or UT's campus, we can sit—"

"No, this is perfect." I take a seat at our exquisite table and smile. "Is this place going to give us food poisoning, or did you rent the entire restaurant?" I joke in an attempt to move on from what I just saw then look around for other diners, feeling like I've missed something.

Connor snorts. "No, it won't, and yes, I did. I wanted to take you out on a proper date, but I also want to be sensitive to the boys. This way, no one will take pictures that might end up online for them to see later. And I had a hunch you'd love to go inside the Sunsphere."

"How do you always have these 'hunches' about what I'd like?" I lean across the table to peck him on the lips, thankful he knows me so well but confused about how he does.

"Spot-on intuition, I suppose." Connor winks as he grabs his menu.

I scan my own, and at the bottom is an asterisk noting the availability of the listed items "or anything else you'd like to have." I guess when you rent the entire restaurant for the night, you're privy to any meal you want. "What are you going to have?" I place my menu down, prop my elbows on the table, and place my fists underneath my chin.

"Mm, probably the salmon." Connor squints as if he's unsure. "How about you?"

"I was thinking of the salmon, too, but I really want some spinach dip as well. Is that weird?" I wonder if Connor thinks me unsophisticated.

"It's not weird. Appetizers and entrees don't have to complement each other. They're separate beings entirely, but both are delicious." Connor scans the sides.

My wheels are turning, like these insightful words of wisdom aren't just about food, but I can't piece it all together.

"Fancy or not, they both end up in the same place together in the end, right?" I laugh to lighten the mood.

Connor agrees. "A hundred percent."

We both end up ordering the salmon, and while we wait on our meals, we walk around the Sunsphere, taking in the views. As we gaze out the windows, Connor holds my hand like we're a real couple, and I kiss him and rest my head on his shoulder.

"The boys doing any better?" I ask hesitantly. If I don't ask, I'm a jerk, and if I do, it may ruin the mood Connor's trying so hard to create.

"A bit. I think it'll just take some time. They're strong, just like her. They can get through this." Connor pulls me in for a hug. "Thanks for asking about them."

Still hugging, I pull my head back to look Connor in the eyes. Lately, he seems to avoid talking about Allegra with me. I get that he's trying to focus on me, but she was a huge part of his and his children's life. And I am still running her investigation, so it concerns me that he's holding back. "You know, you can talk about her to me... if you want to. It won't hurt my feelings. I'm strong too. I can take it."

Connor laughs under his breath and squeezes me even tighter. "I know you are."

———

The salmon is to die for, and I think we've managed to forget about everything but each other. Now that we're indoors and I've ripped off a few layers of outerwear, the ruby necklace Connor gave me is on display as we sit at the table. I paired it with a short black square-necked cocktail dress. It's very 1950s or 1960s, and Connor's suit is black as well. We look like quite the couple. Our romantic dinner goes off without a hitch, and I can't believe he went to so much trouble just for me.

Chapter 19

On our walk to the car, we take the long route through the heart of downtown so we can continue to talk.

"What prompted you to tell me that earlier? About talking about... her?" Connor asks after we've strolled by the shops in Market Square.

I held off discussing my concerns during dinner to avoid an awkward conversation, but now the topic is fair game. Getting this off my chest is vital for our relationship. I'm beginning to feel uncomfortable even mentioning Allegra, and that doesn't sit well.

"Since we've gotten together, you seem apprehensive of talking about her, like other than details about the case, I mean. I feel like my investigation is halted in a way. I know you're uncomfortable, and I can see it, but don't you still want to figure out what happened to her?"

Connor stumbles. He looks torn about what to say and what to withhold. "I guess, well... none of it feels real, in a way. I don't really know how to explain it to you."

"Try," I beg, feeling pushed away.

"Now's not the time, Mad. Do you have any new information? Is there something you need to talk about?" Connor's clearly reading between the lines about where I'm steering the conversation.

"Now that you mention it, yeah, there is. I have a few questions about information that wouldn't have been on the police report. I feel like it's going to upset you, though. So I need to know, are you still on board with the investigation or not?" I stop in front of a rustic new boutique that's now closed, then Connor follows suit. Suddenly, I wonder if he'll ever be comfortable discussing Allegra.

Connor angles his head to the side as his eyes grow wide. "Of course I am. You know that."

"I just don't know how to separate us and the investigation, I guess. That's what I'm having trouble with. What's off limits, and what isn't?" I shrug.

Connor pulls me forward, and we start walking again. "As far as I'm concerned, it's all blurred together. There is no end, and there's no beginning. So there are no rules. Anytime is fair game for discussing Allegra and the case as long as it doesn't make you feel weird."

So he thought talking about her was making me *uncomfortable?* I feel like there's more to the story, something he's not telling me.

"All right. What was found with Allegra that night? As far as clothes and belongings, is there anything you could have forgotten to mention?" I wince, hoping this question won't upset him. I know what it's like to recall the clothes that you last saw the love of your life wearing. It haunts you forever. Into my mind pop images of Clayton's khaki shorts and his kelly-green T-shirt that read Hard Knox Life.

Connor clears his throat and takes a long, hard breath. "She had her suitcase and her purse, which had her laptop in it. As far as clothes, she was wearing black leggings, her pink Gucci sweatshirt, and a plain white tee underneath that. Oh, she was also wearing her wedding rings, her diamond stud earrings, and her Nike tennis shoes." He looks away and clears his throat like he's about to be emotional. "Is that all you needed to know?"

My heart skips a beat. He didn't say anything about the books or papers. Perhaps the police didn't find them on her body. Maybe that's what was taken. "Are you sure that's everything? Did she have any paperwork with her or any copies of her books or anything like that?"

"No, everything she needed like that would've been on her laptop, I assumed. Why do you ask?"

"I'm just trying to get a better grasp on her trip that day. What was going through her head, who was she meeting, what were they going to discuss. Things like that." I don't want to get his hopes up in case my new information ends up hitting a dead end.

"Would it help if I gave you her editor's information?" Connor offers and holds my hand once again.

I smile. "Yes, that'd be great, actually, because Fran is refusing my calls, and I need to move on to Sarah even though Fran says she's out of the country for a few weeks."

Connor scrolls through his phone and texts me Sarah's contact info.

"Done. Feel free to ask her anything. She's really cool, and she adored Allegra."

"One more thing while we're on the subject. Do you remember a reporter named Marcus Roach ever coming around the house in a green Jeep? Did he ever come by and ask Allegra any questions?"

Connor scratches his head. "Not that I remember, but I'm not sure it would stick out. People often contacted her for interviews."

"Right. I kind of figured that."

"Why do you ask?" He slows down.

I sigh at his loaded question. "Friend of mine was working on a big story... and ended up dead because of it, even though I can't prove it."

"Wait. Do you think the same person who killed Allegra killed him too?" Connor stops walking.

I take another deep breath and wish I had the right answer. "I don't know what to think. All I know is they're connected somehow."

AFTER WE STROLL AROUND for thirty minutes, we find some extra room for dessert at Café 4 in Market Square. The carrot cake cupcakes are calling our names, so we devour one together as our forks battle it out over who gets more.

"We could just get two, you know." Connor laughs after our forks intertwine for the fourth time.

"True, but this is more fun." I accidentally drop some icing onto the table, and we laugh. Being with Connor makes me feel whole, like a missing puzzle piece is finally in place, and instead of a shiny, newly constructed piece, it's worn like the rest of the puzzle.

OUTSIDE THE DOOR OF my apartment, Connor kisses me good night. "Tonight was great, Mad. I'll see you tomorrow." He winks toward the window and leaves like a gentleman as my mom peeks at us from behind a curtain. I watch until he reaches his car in the parking lot below, and I blow him a kiss as he beams toward me again. I don't know how in the world I ended up with someone as wonderful as this man.

Once he's gone and I head inside, I realize Graham's already been in bed for over an hour, and I feel silly. Connor could've come in and visited with Mom and me for a while without Graham knowing. Oh well. It gives Mom and me some much-needed catch-up time.

One bowl of popcorn and a viewing of *How to Lose a Guy in 10 Days* later, Mom has gone home, and I'm finally tucked into bed. I check my phone to make sure Mom made it okay. **Home safe. Good night. Love you.** Before I can respond, another text flashes across my screen.

Enjoy that view from the top while you can—a source.

A pit forms in my stomach. This person always seems to know what's going on in my life before I do, and that doesn't make this tip seem promising. *Did I really see Lane earlier? Is he stalking me? Or is he "a source?"* It feels like the end of something is approaching, as if my window of time for finding Allegra's killer is about to close. Instead of panicking, maybe I should do just what the source suggested—enjoy what I have while I have it.

AS SOON AS I KISS GRAHAM goodbye at school the next day, I phone Sarah Patterson, Allegra's editor. I've wracked my brain about why someone might steal Allegra's books. Other than wanting to save the day by providing more reading material from a deceased beloved author, I can't come up with anything. Of all people, her editor is sure to have more information on what Allegra was working on. Maybe that will shine a light in the right direction.

"Hi, Ms. Patterson. I'm Madeleine Barton. Connor Hudson hired me to investigate the death of his wife, Allegra Hudson. I've heard you were her editor for a number of years. Is that right?"

"Yes. We worked together on all of her books, actually, and I considered her a close friend after all we've been through together."

"Out of the country" my ass.

I hadn't considered that the agent-author and editor-author relationships would be quite so tight-knit. I guess when two people spend that much time working on someone's innermost thoughts and feelings in the form of a book, they can't help growing attached.

"I'm so sorry for your loss, Sarah. What I'm trying to do is bring justice to the Hudson family by learning the truth about Allegra's death, because none of us down here believe the police have found the right killer. Would you be willing to answer a few questions for me about the meeting Allegra had scheduled with you on the day she was killed?"

"Oh, wow. I didn't realize anyone thought that. That really changes things, huh?" Sarah's voice trembles like she's taken aback at the notion of Allegra's killer still being on the loose. "Of course I'm willing to help. Anything for Allegra. She meant the world to me."

I ready my pen and clear my throat. "Great. Just tell me what your meeting was supposed to be about, and we'll go from there."

"Our meeting was primarily supposed to be about a romance-novel-turned-movie for Hallmark. She'd done romance in the past, although she excelled more at suspense and thrillers, but Hallmark wanted something very G-rated and for a great deal of money. We were going to heavily outline, create a synopsis, and make sure our overall tone matched up with what Hallmark was asking for."

"So she wouldn't have been bringing you books to edit, then?" I'm confused about why Allegra would ask Ivy and Mayven to beta read her new books if she wasn't going to take them to Sarah on her trip to New York.

"She did say she'd wrapped up two more suspense novels she was excited about, but she wasn't finished editing them quite yet. She did, however, have the rough drafts. She said she might bring them with her to show me, but she wasn't sure yet. She still wanted to hear back from both of her beta readers." *Okay. Jackpot.*

"Oh, wow. So those books are still with those beta readers?" My heart flutters as I obtain more information, hoping it leads to an epiphany.

"I'm really not sure if she'd sent them to her betas yet. Sometimes, authors just say that to buy themselves more time to write. There's no way to know for sure, I'm afraid, unless Connor can find those emails... assuming she sent them. Allegra was notorious for handwriting the first draft. She was very old-school like that." Sarah grows silent, and I can almost see the grief on her face. "I'm sorry. I'm not much help. If you think of anything else you need to ask, you've got my number, okay?"

Fortunately, I remember to ask about the agent. "Hey, one more thing. What's the story on Fran Marx, Allegra's agent? I heard you all came to the funeral together even though she'd just been fired."

I probe as if I haven't already spoken to Fran, hoping I'll uncover something useful.

Sarah sighs as if it's a long story. "I love Fran. I really do. She'd been Allegra's agent from the beginning, and they adored each other. But for some reason, Fran got weird when it came to Allegra's two new books. They had to part ways because they just couldn't agree on the plot for one of them. I've not read them yet, like I said, but it all seemed so strange."

"And why is that?" I ask.

"For an agent to refuse to bend for an established author they've worked with for so long is just unusual. Especially since I'd made it clear I'd be willing to work on all of her books with her. So there was really no reason for Fran to be so insistent upon it on the front end. The sale was a sure thing, you know?"

"Wow, that *is* strange. Was there anything going on with Fran that might make her act out of the ordinary?"

"I don't know. But I will say she was devastated afterward. I kept asking her to reconsider, but she kept saying she couldn't. Honestly, if I didn't know better, I'd say she was pushed into it somehow. I know it doesn't make sense, but it seemed like it wasn't something she wanted to do, like she was forced into it. And when Allegra died, it hit Fran hard. I don't think she showed up for work for a whole week."

"Hmm. So they were pretty close?"

"Just as close as she and I were. We loved each other like family." Sarah sniffs again and apologizes. "I'm sorry. I'm getting emotional."

"No, don't apologize. I completely understand. Let me ask you one more thing. Was there anyone Allegra ever mentioned that she feared or was afraid of in any way? Any enemies you knew of?"

Sarah pauses as if considering the question. "I don't think so. Most people really loved her. She was a sweetheart."

I sigh, wishing I'd uncovered a case-breaking clue. Instead, I have more questions.

"Thanks, Sarah. I appreciate your help. If I have any more questions, I'll give you a call back at this number, okay? And you have my number now, too, if you need anything or think of anything you forgot to mention."

"Yes, I do. Thanks so much. I really appreciate the work you're doing."

I end the call and bang my head on the steering wheel.

The Hallmark deal is the only thing I have that's new information. Maybe Allegra was hiding money from Connor or had a boyfriend. I wonder if Connor knew about this huge deal with Hallmark.

I know Ivy hasn't yet read the books Allegra gave her, but she does have them stashed somewhere. I need to check with her and see if she's found them. Perhaps the subject matter contains some clue that will help solve the murder. Maybe Allegra gave her main character a secret similar to her own. Or maybe the backstory holds a clue about something long-forgotten in Allegra's past.

I'll speak with Mayven. Allegra shared some writing with her as well, so maybe she has a copy via email or something. I'm amused that both Ivy and Mayven have the impression that they're Allegra's sole beta reader. And I could enlighten them, but I think I'll let that secret die with Allegra.

I phone Ivy and leave a voicemail asking her to let me know if she's found the books. Then I make my way downtown to record a public service announcement with the head honchos of TVA about being mindful of energy use during the bitter winter months. Afterward, I check my phone and find no messages from Ivy, much to my dismay. I head over to Mayven's house instead.

I really should call before just popping over to Mayven's, but I've learned that she tends to be home during the mornings, and since it's only eleven o'clock, I'll take my chances. Plus, it's not like I'm going to walk in on her with her hair in rollers, no makeup on, and her home a complete pigsty. If there's anyone who is always camera-ready with a pristine home, it's Mayven Bennett. Besides, if she isn't home, maybe Connor is.

Mayven has two gorgeous potted blue spruces wrapped in burlap on either side of her giant front door, and I wonder how they've managed to survive the harsh winter. Then I remember their owner and how she seems to turn everything into gold with minimal effort. I knock three times, and before I can count to thirty, Mayven opens the front door. Once again, she's dressed to the nines and has flawless hair and makeup. "Mad, come on inside. It's freezing out today. What a pleasant surprise. How are you?"

"I'm good, and you?"

She motions me toward the toasty living room as I thaw out.

"I'm good too. We really need to do another story together. That was such fun." Mayven heads toward the kitchen. "Hot tea?"

I nod, appreciating how she's always the perfect hostess. She makes me want to be better at it myself. "That'd be awesome, actually." Instead of having a seat, I follow her into the kitchen. "I'll help you."

She fills a copper kettle with water and points at a cabinet. "Top shelf on the far right." I open the door of the cabinet, which is full of fancy-schmancy teacups and coffee mugs, and grab two that say Vols.

"Those were a gift." Mayven eyes the mugs I chose, which clearly aren't up to par with the rest of her designer dishes. "It's fine, though. We'll rough it." She forces a high-pitched giggle. "So, what brings you here today? Have new information on the case, I hope?" Mayven leans against her marble countertop as I take a seat on a barstool on the other side of her island.

"I think you mentioned to me the first time we met that Allegra often asked you to read her writing before she sent it off to her agent and editor. Is that right?" I pull out my notepad and pen. If there's one thing I don't trust as of late, it's my memory.

"Yes, she valued my opinion since I'm an avid reader. Sometimes, she would have me do a read-through before she let her agent or editor lay eyes on it," Mayven says as she digs around in her pantry.

"The latest things she'd been working on were two suspense novels. Did she send you either of them?" I crane my neck to see her face, and while she's found the tea, she's still looking for something else, probably sugar.

She faces me with a sullen expression. "Yes, she did. Both of them, actually." Then she abruptly turns and starts digging again.

"Can't find it?" I ask with a sigh.

"No, worse. I accidentally deleted them."

She apparently doesn't realize I was referring to the sugar.

"And even worse, I asked her to resend them a few days before she was going to leave, and she said she wanted to see what her editor said first. So I never did get to read her final words." As the teakettle sings, she plops onto the stool next to me with a disappointed expression.

THAT EVENING, I GO to Connor's in an attempt to get to the bottom of this whole book thing. I ask to see Allegra's computer.

"It's on the desk in the library, but I'll warn you, it's toast." His shoulders slump.

I whip my head around. This can't be true. I was counting on this. It was all I had. "What do you mean, it's toast?" I hope I heard him wrong or that he's joking.

"I needed some tax information from it a few days ago, so I logged in, and everything's been wiped. I think she must've gotten a virus or something." Connor rubs his forehead. "I haven't told anyone yet because I didn't want to believe it was true. Everything she had was in there, everything she was working on... gone." Connor rubs his eyes like a wounded child, obviously upset.

I should comfort him, but all I can think about is the fact that I need this to figure out a motive for Allegra's murder. Now I've got nothing. "But it was fine when the police had it all that time, right?"

"Yeah, they said they dug into everything. They didn't see anything worth noting, really." Connor clears his throat, stands, and walks toward the kitchen. "You're more than welcome to have a look if you want. If you can fix it, then you're a miracle worker."

In the library, I stand behind the desk and open the computer to find all her files are indeed wiped. The internet is wonky, and it cuts off after a few minutes. When I attempt to reboot, it gives me all kinds of error notifications. Yep, it has a virus. A big, bad, ill-timed virus. A ding on my phone makes me jump as I stare in defeat at Allegra's ruined laptop.

CON-venient timing, huh?—a source.

A source is right. This is convenient timing for someone, and it's no coincidence. Someone went out of their way to ruin the last works of Allegra Hudson. But I can't seem to nail down the reason why. I slither down into the leather chair, prop my elbows on the desk, and hang my head in my hands, wondering why they alluded to a "con." How am I ever going to solve Allegra's murder when the killer is always three steps ahead of me?

Chapter 20

The next evening, Graham and I are chowing down on pizza as we watch *Spider-Man*—the *real Spider-Man* with Tobey Maguire—when there's a quick knock at the door. "Coming!" I yell as I creep off the couch with pizza in hand. When I reach the door and pull it open, there's no one in sight, but a yellow envelope sits at my feet.

"Hello?" I call as I take several steps down each direction of the hallway, seeing no one. I shrug and grab the envelope, which has my name printed on the opposite side. I snatch it and tear into it, although my better judgment says to grab a pair of gloves first, just in case. I wonder if the contents are going to be something huge, maybe something crucial to the case, and I can't open it fast enough.

What I see shocks me to my core, and my heart sinks to my feet. I was expecting something big, but not something so... personal. Inside the envelope are pictures of Ivy and Connor with their arms wrapped around each other in his den, looking as if they're about to kiss or like they just did. The pictures were clearly taken from outside a window, perhaps by the same person peering in at Connor and me that day I was over there. Accompanying the photos is a message consisting of letters cut out of magazines: "Are they playing you?" There's no signature.

The slice of pizza that was in my hand falls onto the door's threshold as I grow hot and cold at the same time.

"Who is it, Mommy?" Graham asks as commercials start to play instead of *Spider-Man*. I hear him talking to me, but I don't listen.

Can't listen. I shut the front door directly on the pizza and twist the dead bolt. *Are they playing me?*

My first thought goes to who sent this. *Is it from "a source" or someone else entirely? Do I believe this information is true?* It could easily be explained as an embrace between grieving friends or perhaps some good photoshopping. I wonder whether the photos indicate a truth I've been blind to, the truth about why Allegra was really killed. Suddenly, everything feels lost and upside-down, and I'm questioning everything, even my own judgment.

I put the pictures on top of the refrigerator so Graham won't see them. One of those blasted headaches is working its way back into my life despite my daily migraine medication. I pop two Advil as the ear ringing begins and drink a glass of water, hoping it will stop the headache from getting worse. But it only takes the edge off. I sit down and mindlessly eat another slice of pizza with Graham as we watch the remainder of *Spider-Man*. I don't recall a single scene.

After the movie, I bathe Graham and lay out all our clothes for the morning. I can't fathom Connor keeping something like this from me or pulling off something this despicable. *Could they be in on something together?* Ivy did recruit me for the "investigation job," and Connor did pull me into a relationship with him, a relationship he might have hoped would kill the investigation—or turn it away from him if I fell for him hard enough.

No. No one can fake feelings like that. It's not possible. I'm suddenly not sure who I can trust anymore, and I want to talk to Violet. At nine o'clock, once Graham has finally faded off into a peaceful sleep, I dial her number while sobbing. Once she answers and hears the state I'm in, she rushes over.

"In your heart of hearts, Mad, what do you believe?" Violet asks as we sit at the kitchen table where the photos now lie.

"I don't know. That our feelings were real, are still real. That it wasn't just an act for some sick, twisted game." I hiccup as I sip wine, hoping it'll numb my pain.

Violet passes me a chocolate chip cookie. "Is that what you think or what you want to think?"

"It's what I think and what I want to think," I say before biting off more than I can chew.

"Let's just talk through this, okay?" Violet closes the box of cookies. "They could've had an affair when Allegra was alive then killed her, and they're really these awful, horrible people. That's obviously the worst-case scenario, right?"

I mumble as a tear cascades down my cheek and into my cookie-filled mouth. "Yeah, I'd say so." The thought of such a betrayal makes me want to give up on love, on the case, on everything but Graham.

"Or maybe they started something after she died, when he was grieving and before you came around. Maybe they ended it when he started something with you," Violet suggests with lifted eyebrows as if this is clearly something more believable.

I mutter in agony before swallowing a bite. "Okay, but I don't like that one either."

"Or maybe whoever took this simply got the wrong idea by accident, and they were just hugging." Vi shifts her head back and forth as if considering that. "Or maybe someone saw it and knew they weren't having an affair, but they used it because they want you to think that they are."

I take a long sip of wine and grunt. "But why would that be? I can't think of a scenario where that makes sense."

"I don't know." Violet sighs. "But when you assume the worst, it doesn't always mean you're right. There's usually more information you don't know."

"So you're saying I should confront Connor about it, or Ivy?" I ask, not wanting to deal with it in any way.

"Maybe confront Connor, but for now, I think you need some insurance." Violet pulls her phone out of her pocket. "And I'm going to give it to you."

"Insurance?" I stand to look over her shoulder. "Why are you pulling up your camera app?"

"Because if your conversation with Connor doesn't go well, you'll have this as insurance. When I press Record, you're going to tell me everything you know so far, about everyone. Then if anyone decides to threaten you, I'll have this. Tell me the password to your Facebook page, and I'll post this if I don't hear from you by a certain point. That way, you have leverage. Understand?"

My hand goes straight to my hip. "You're saying I'm a sitting duck without this, right? Or a pushover? And you don't trust Connor?"

"No, I'm not saying that. I'm just saying you can't be too careful, Mad. There are people in your life you love who could be harmed just to hurt you. You've got to protect them and yourself."

Perhaps she's right. I have allowed myself to become too emotionally involved in this case, and it might just bite me in the butt. "Okay, okay. I'll do it. Just tell me when to start." I plop down at the kitchen table and rub my aching forehead.

Violet stands and makes sure I'm in the frame before she hits Record. "I just want to say, for the record, I don't think they're an item. Or ever were an item, for that matter."

A half smile crosses my face.

"All right, Mad. Go."

I CAN'T GO TO SLEEP, and it's already two in the morning, so I stare at my phone, expecting "a source" to drop me a riddle, quote, tip, clue, or Easter egg. And when I don't get one, I try to make it happen myself, even though trying to make "a source" talk hasn't proven to be very effective in the past. But what the hell, I'm desperate.

No tidbits on that envelope today? Was that you? Was the doll you?

Five minutes go by as I watch my screen for those three little dots that say someone's out there hearing me. Ten minutes later, I tuck myself into bed and turn out the light. Twenty minutes and I hook my phone up to the charger. Thirty minutes of waiting and I'm out like the light in my bedroom, minus my nightlight in the bathroom.

I have both of my hospital dreams again—the one where I wake up lost, confused, and hooked up to every machine known to man, and the one where I'm searching for room 101, only to find it and be wakened before I get to see whose legs are in the bed. This time, my phone is the culprit. It's four in the morning, and I've finally gotten my response.

I don't share an identity with "them." Don't believe everything you see; even salt looks like sugar—a source.

GRAHAM DIDN'T REST well last night either, or else he rested extra well. I'm not sure which. All I know is he is extra zombielike this morning. From the moment I wake him, he can't even. He immediately rolls over and buries his head with his pillow. "No school today. I'm tired," he claims like a dictator.

"Sorry, you've got to go. I have work, buddy. Besides, you love school." I jostle him and try to think of something to get him excited. "You're going to miss Avery's birthday party. Y'all are celebrating her at school today with cupcakes. I'd hate for you to miss it." Graham lowers the pillow just enough for his eyes to read my facial expressions; he can always tell when I'm fibbing.

"Cupcakes?" The pillow creeps down all the way, revealing his grin. "Okay. I'll get up." He flops out of bed and lies on the floor, expecting me to dress him like he's still a baby.

"No, no, you're a big boy. You can dress yourself now. Get up, Graham. We're going to be late, for Pete's sake." I hand him the clothes I laid out the night before, and he lets them fall through his hands onto his limp body.

"Who's Pete?" He smirks, knowing it's just something I say and not an actual person. He's trying to get me to laugh since he's won the battle if I do.

I turn on my mean-mom voice as he lies there with a huge grin growing on his adorable but ornery face. "Get up! One, two..." By the time I say two, he's working his way to a standing position.

"Okay. I'll get dressed." He finally gives in as I sigh with relief. Oh, the joys of toddlerhood.

I grab our bags for the day, and we head toward the front door, running only about four minutes late for preschool, thank God. I unlock the dead bolt, grab the knob, and am taken aback when someone's standing on the other side with her fist in the air like she was about to knock. I shriek then sigh with my hand over my heart. "Ivy. What on earth are you doing here? You scared me half to death!"

"Oh, I'm sorry. I was trying to catch you before you left for school." Ivy smiles as she crouches down and waves at Graham.

My suspicion levels are on high alert, especially after the photos in the yellow envelope. "How did you know where I live?" I ask carefully, studying her face as she answers.

She nods and says matter-of-factly, "Google."

"Were you here last night too?" My eyes narrow.

Ivy's brows furrow like she has no idea what I'm referring to. "Last night? No? What are you talking—"

"Never mind." If she's playing dumb, I don't want her to realize I'm onto her. "What's up?"

"Oh, I just found the two manuscripts the other day and thought I'd bring them over. I still haven't read them. I just... I couldn't do it. Not yet." Ivy looks at the two handwritten manuscripts as if they're made of gold. She hands them over with one palm on top and one on bottom. "You'll take care of them?" Her doe eyes make me question her innocence in all of this.

"Of course I will," I say as I drop the attitude. Maybe she *isn't* guilty. She sure seems emotional while handing these over. I glance at my watch. If I don't leave now, Graham will be seriously late to school. "I actually need to talk to you about something. Can you meet me back here in thirty minutes?" I ask as I lock my front door from the hallway.

"Um, sure. Okay." Ivy takes a few steps back as I throw on my coat and Graham's. I grab the manuscripts, and we all walk toward the parking lot.

AFTER DROPPING GRAHAM off, I get stuck in the infinite school-drop-off-lane traffic. While I'm in Park, I take the opportunity to eye the two books Allegra wrote. One is titled *Wordplay*, and the other is *Rest in Pieces*. Next to the titles are short pitches Allegra came up with. *Wordplay* is pitched as a suspense that centers around a woman who wants to give back to her community but gets wrapped up in an embezzlement scam. *Rest in Pieces* is pitched as domestic suspense about a woman who fakes her death so that she can escape her abusive husband and begin a new life as her dead friend.

The words "fake her own death" grab me, and I gasp. I don't know why this hasn't crossed my mind before. *Could this be a possibility? If she knew the right people in the right places, it absolutely could be.* Deep in thought, I stare at the gloomy winter sky. Multiple car horns honk, and I shift from Park into Drive with a new perspective. Maybe I should focus on whether Allegra is truly dead instead of on who killed her. And if she is alive, I wonder what the faking of her death has to do with Marcus.

My last tip from "a source" said, "Don't believe everything you see; even salt looks like sugar," and chills multiply over my skin. Ashes look like ashes. No one would ever be able to tell the difference if they didn't belong to the proper person as long as she had someone on the inside to declare her dead. Another clue from "a source" pops into my head: "You shouldn't keep souvenirs of a killing." It dawns on me that it isn't about what was missing from Allegra's body. It's a line from my favorite Hitchcock film, *Vertigo*.

In the movie, Madeleine Elster appeared to commit suicide, but it turns out it wasn't even her to begin with, and the Madeleine Scottie knew was alive and well, only her real name was Judy Barton. Several of the other tips and clues I've gathered from "a source" don't point toward this theory of Allegra somehow being alive, such as the one where they seemed to know Clayton loved me too—because I'm not sure how Allegra Hudson would know something like that—but some of them do lead me to believe Allegra might not be dead. If so, this changes everything.

I get so lost in my frenzied thoughts that I pass my apartment complex not once but twice. Once I park, I take a deep breath, open the car door, and walk toward my apartment. Ivy's sitting in my hallway, waiting for me as she checks her phone. Suddenly, I stop walking toward her, aware that Allegra had to have help if she faked her death, and *everyone* is a suspect, especially her old best friend. *What if Allegra no longer wants Connor but doesn't want anyone else to have him either? What if she sent me those pictures of him and Ivy to shoo me away? What if Ivy knows, and that's why she's so weird about me and Connor?* Suddenly, I'm Alice, stuck in a wonderland I don't trust or understand, and I don't know how to get out of my own head.

"Oh, good. You're back." Ivy rises to her feet.

I smile, not wanting to tip her off about my internal chaos. "Yeah, sorry. Traffic. You know how those school zones can get." I fumble with my keys. "Come on in and have a seat wherever." I throw my purse, coat, and keys onto the kitchen counter as Ivy has a seat in the living room. "Can I get you anything?"

"Um, water?" Ivy takes her coat off and lays it next to her.

I open the cabinet containing my glasses and take a shaky, deep breath before I grab two and fill them. I emerge from the kitchen with our waters and force a smile. "Here you go. After what I have to say, you may wish you'd asked for a bottle of wine."

Ivy's smile turns into a grimace. "Oh no, I thought we were finally on the same page. What's happened?"

I walk to the refrigerator, retrieve the yellow envelope, and hand it to Ivy without saying one little word. She opens it and studies the photos. She swallows, then she narrows her eyes as she reads the accompanying note. "Don't tell me you believe this crap?" She rolls her eyes, clearly offended and angry.

I shrug and have a seat next to her. "I don't know what to think," I confess.

She takes a sip of water and places the note and pictures back inside the envelope. "Well, don't let this keep you up at night. This is absolutely ridiculous! Who would even want you to think such a thing?" Ivy says. Then she perks up. "Wait. I know who. Someone who's trying to throw suspicion onto someone else."

Chapter 21

My mind races long after Ivy's left my apartment for brunch with her husband, Rick. Her theory isn't out of the question, but I don't know who to trust at this point. I'm deeply in love with Connor and our unconventional love story, and the thought of the book *Rest in Pieces* makes my breakfast threaten to reappear.

The questions come hard and fast. If Allegra is alive, does that also mean she faked her death to escape Connor, an abusive husband like the one in the book? Or are only tidbits of the story real? Is the whole thing just fiction, and I'm making mountains out of molehills? Could she have left him for someone else? Would she have abandoned her babies to run away with a lover? And did Marcus somehow figure this out and threaten to expose her or Connor? The Allegra I feel like I've come to know wouldn't leave her kids like this, but did anyone truly know her?

Maybe her stories were meant to be clues to her truth, her story within a story. I begin to read *Rest in Pieces* and wonder if this tortured character is based on Allegra's real life, or if these are even the exact words Allegra Hudson wrote. I'm assuming Ivy, or whoever is helping Allegra, hasn't tampered with her stories, but I honestly don't know what to believe anymore.

After an hour of reading, I slam the book on my coffee table, dying to know what Allegra's closest friends think of it. Once more, I have to ask Ivy and Mayven if they've ever suspected Connor of abuse. If I don't, I'll drive myself mad.

215

I ring Mayven first, thinking she might still be home since it's before noon and Ivy's likely still at brunch with Rick.

"Hey, Madeleine. How are you?" she asks as I hear some loud drilling in the background.

"Is this a bad time?" I'm barely able to hear her but desperate for her feedback.

"Oh no, let me just go inside. They're doing some light construction work in our backyard. We're having an outdoor planning meeting for our charity in a few days. It's bitterly cold outside, so we're putting up a nice tent with heaters and the whole nine. Can you hear me better now?"

I nod, even though she can't see me. "I have a serious question for you. Can you talk for a few minutes?"

Mayven's voice drops. "Yeah, I can. What's wrong?"

"I don't want to explain why I'm asking. I just want a straight answer from you. Okay?" I hope she tells me what I want to hear.

Mayven robotically responds, "Okay, I can do that for you. Go ahead."

"Did you ever suspect any kind of abuse from Connor when it came to Allegra?" The question comes out in one long breath.

Mayven pauses, and it seems like a lifetime passes before she answers. "No. I can't say I ever did."

Tension leaves my body like a fierce gust of wind. "I didn't think so, but thank God you didn't either. Okay."

"I'm not saying they didn't argue or that they didn't have their own unique issues. They weren't perfect, but abuse, no. Not that I was aware of, at least," Mayven adds.

When Ivy answers the same question a few hours later, she echoes Mayven's sentiments exactly. The irony is almost laughable considering how different those two are and how much they despise one another. I wonder how my opinion of Connor would've changed if they'd answered yes and whether I would have believed them.

Connor's never waved any red flags my way, and I'm hopelessly in love with him, whether I want to be or not. But this is a dangerous spot for me to be in, even if he isn't abusive.

A FEW DAYS LATER, MOM, Graham, and I are eating her home-made fried chicken, green beans, corn, and potato salad in front of the TV as we introduce Graham to the wonderful world of *The Lion King*. Mom's phone beeps, and she runs to my front door. I find it odd that she's expecting company at my house, but the movie is at its climax, and I can't look away.

"Ugh, I always hated that awful Scar. He's so evil," a familiar voice says from the doorway. I jerk my head around and drop a piece of fried chicken when I see both Connor and my mom smiling. I hadn't planned on introducing Graham to Connor, but it appears Mom and Connor have concocted some secret plan, and now I'm forced to make introductions.

"Connor! Hi." I wipe my mouth, pause the movie, and give him a platonic-like hug in front of Graham. "Connor, this is my Graham. Graham, this is Mommy's friend Connor."

"Hi," Connor says as he high-fives Graham. Connor high-fives him up high and down low, but when Graham gives him a hug out of left field, tears fill Connor's eyes. It strikes me as odd, but I assume he's having flashbacks of his boys at a younger age and feels nostalgic.

"The jig is up," Mom whispers in my ear. "We plotted against you since you've been too busy to hang out the past few days. I'm going to stay the night with Graham, and you two are off for a romantic getaway." Mom beams as she hands me a basket full of food and an overnight bag she's already packed for me.

I unpause the movie, and Graham is glued to the screen again. "Are you sure? We don't have to—"

"Yes, I'm sure." She pushes Connor and me toward the door. "We've worked it all out. Now you two go and have fun."

I walk over to Graham. "Mommy's going to be gone for a bit tonight and tomorrow, and Meems is going to stay here with you. Are you okay with that, bub?" I kiss his forehead and smooth his hair to one side.

"Yay, a sleepover!" he cheers.

I sigh with relief. "We're going now, okay? I love you, Graham Cracker."

"I love you, too, Mom," he says as he pecks me on the lips, revealing his dimples.

CONNOR WHISKS ME AWAY to a bed-and-breakfast resort in Kingston, the Whitestone Inn. The views, even in the dead of winter, make me forget all my troubles. The Inn calls their rolling hills a sanctuary for the soul, and they truly are. The inn also features a to-die-for view of Watts Bar Lake, a rustic red barn, two chapels, and farmhouse-like cottages on the property. There's a reason it's one of the area's top venues for weddings and receptions; it feels like nothing bad can happen here. On the way over, I fought a battle in my mind about the photos of Ivy and Connor and concluded that I'm right to trust him. The photos are probably a lie. But a small part of me wonders whether they *were* hooking up.

We arrive at the inn after dark, so we stay in the room and relax for the night. Connor gets flames roaring in the fireplace and brings me a glass of champagne as I gaze out the windows at the star-filled sky.

"This place brings you a certain peace, doesn't it?" he asks as he pulls me close.

"Like nothing else matters in the world except enjoying this view with you." I rest my head on his shoulder and forget the Allegra drama. My brain is dizzy from all the switchbacks of theories, and I just want Connor to take care of me. Even if it seems selfish and dumb.

The owner pops by to welcome Connor—apparently, they're acquaintances—and I step inside the bathroom to check out the oversized whirlpool tub and large custom waterfall shower with steam jets. Connor's probably used to staying in the lap of luxury, but this is new to me, and I'm not missing out on a single detail.

When I emerge from the bathroom, Connor is standing in the middle of the room, streaming Alan Jackson's *Remember When* through the Apple TV via his iPhone. He motions for me to come to him, and when I do, he takes me for a quick twirl before he pulls me into his chest for a slow sway. "I want us to always be this close," he says as he brushes my hair away from my face. "I just thank God every day that he put you in my life." He has tears in his eyes.

"I feel the same way." Loving how safe I feel in his arms, I'm beating myself up on the inside for ever thinking this wonderful man could be part of anything evil.

"Things change, and the busyness life brings can get in the way of love over time. That, I know." Connor's head falls to the side.

"I'm different. We're different. You won't have to worry about all of that with me. I know Allegra's success came between you two at times, but like you said, this is a second chance—for both of us. I know it's hard, but don't compare me to her. There hasn't been anyone between Allegra and me, has there?"

Connor doesn't hesitate to answer. "God, no. Why do you ask? I thought I made that pretty clear."

"Just making sure I understood correctly when you said you were separated. I didn't know what that meant exactly." I see truth in his face when he answers me, telling me all I need to know.

Connor gives me a half smile and looks me in the eyes. "I want you to know I love you, Madeleine."

I place my hands on either side of his face and kiss him deeply. "I love you, too, Connor."

"Also, don't feel any pressure tonight. I didn't bring you here so I could... I'll be sleeping on the sofa. Just so you know," he assures me.

"No, I can't wait to have you all to myself," I say, wondering how I could've ever doubted him. Ivy was right. Those photos are absolutely ridiculous, and someone wants to keep us apart.

I WAKE IN THE MORNING with Connor still wrapped around me, holding me like I'm a precious treasure. Being with him last night felt so right and so natural, and I never had a moment of hesitation or guilt about being intimate with someone other than Clayton. Connor has a way of making me feel safe at all times, like he truly understands me and my anxious ways. I love that about him the most.

We have a decadent breakfast and tour the inn's grounds as snow descends from the unyielding winter sky. We laugh, drink wine, and talk until our cheeks hurt. I haven't felt so connected to another person since Clayton, and it's wonderful and petrifying at the same time. I don't want to lose him too.

The drawback to having a secret relationship, though, is that there's never enough time: to hold their hand, to stare adoringly at their face when they speak, to soak them in entirely. The end is always in sight, ticking away in the background as it attempts to steal joy. And it's impossible to shout our love from the rooftops because, again, it's a secret.

When we return to Knoxville the following afternoon, Connor walks me to the door of my apartment. He's holding my hand and squeezes it three times. "This was one of the best weekends of my life, Mad. I want you to know that," he confesses before kissing and hugging me goodbye.

"I feel exactly the same way." I blush as I reach for my keys, feeling like a teenager again.

Connor starts down the hallway to the lot. "I love you so much." He beams.

"I love you so much too!" I shout back, not caring if the neighbors hear.

Once my keys are in the doorknob's keyhole and he's walked away, a text dings on my phone. **I'm not strange, weird, off, or crazy. My reality is just different from yours—a source.**

The line sounds familiar, like I've heard it before, but I can't place it. Maybe it's another clue and they want me to guess who they are now. After I jiggle my keys in the doorknob a few times, my door swings open. "I'm back!"

Graham sprints into the living room with open arms as Mom follows him with a grin but at a much slower pace.

"ARE YOU SURE YOU WANT to do that?" I ask Connor the next day. My fingernails are shorter from my incessant biting.

"Yeah, I'll just tell him you're a trusted reporter doing a piece on his mom. I'm not spilling the beans about us or anything. Don't worry. But believe me, if anyone would know the answers to your questions about the books, it'd be Mason. They always discussed her books as she brainstormed." Then Connor shouts, "Mason, can you answer a few questions about your mom's work to this nice reporter friend of mine?"

There's some mumbling in the background and some shuffling around, then I hear Mason's voice through the phone. For some reason, it's familiar, and a chill runs through my body.

"Hi, Ms. Barton. What was it you wanted to know about my mom's work, exactly?" Mason sounds almost like a grown man. I can't help picturing what Graham might look like at almost eighteen and how significant an age it is to be without a mother.

"I just wanted to know what the two books she'd just completed were about, briefly."

"The first one was about a woman who fakes her death so she can get away from her abusive husband and start a new life posing as her dead friend. That's the one she wrote based on what was hot in the market at the time. The other one was unique. Genius, actually. It's my favorite idea of hers so far, and it would make a great movie. It was about a socialite getting caught up in an elaborate embezzlement scam. It was suspense as well, very Hitchcock and noir-like. I didn't get to read them completely, but I know they would've been brilliant. Her work always was. Does that help you, I hope?"

His answer verifies that the books probably weren't changed, which is good. He's so enthusiastic when he talks about his mother and her incredible talent. He sounds proud. Allegra must've been proud of him as well.

"Yes, it helps more than you'll ever know," I counter as my voice cracks and my vision blurs with tears out of nowhere. I clear my throat and cough. "Hey, Mason, do you read a lot?" I'm still annoyed that I can't place the last line "a source" sent me. I'm not sure why I've asked Mason for his thoughts, but he feels like someone I can trust.

"Yes. Often, actually," he answers. "Why?"

"There's a line I can't quite place, and I feel like it's from a book I've read before. It's 'I'm not strange, weird, off, nor crazy, my reality is just different from yours.'"

Mason replies, "Sounds familiar. I think it's a quote by Lewis Carroll. I don't think it's from a book, just something he said once."

"Yes, that's it! Lewis Carroll. Thank you so much," I say, relieved to know its source without going to Google.

"My parents read his books to me when I was younger. They're very deep stories, actually."

I agree. My heart sinks when he says that Connor and Allegra read Lewis Carroll to him as a child because it gives each of them something else in common with "a source."

I thank him, but I feel sick to my stomach with new information I don't want to believe. "Thanks a million, Mason. You really saved me a ton of trouble."

"Glad to hear it. Anytime. Here's my dad again."

After more scuffling sounds, Connor is back. "Get what you need?"

"And then some," I reply as I jot some notes before I forget. *Allegra and Connor used to read Lewis Carroll to Mason. Which is who "a source" quoted to me. Coincidence?*

And my last note says, *Give Graham a five-minute bear hug and at least fifty kisses.*

AT TWO THIRTY IN THE morning, noise from my living room makes me stir. I'm not sure whether the noise was from one of my vivid dreams. But once I toss and turn a few more times, I realize I have to pee. Then there's no going back to sleep until I get up and go to the bathroom. After shuffling there half awake and with my eyes still shut, I can't help but think about the noise I thought I heard from the living room. I may as well go check it out.

A white envelope lies on the floor in front of my front door. *Great. Who is it this time?* Against my better judgment, I rip it open. I'm going to look eventually, anyway, and I'm not in the mood to waste time. An unsigned letter printed in Times New Roman twelve-point type reads: **Stop looking. I'm giving you twenty-four hours, then the whole world will know about you and Connor.**

Chapter 22

My website ads are sustaining me well financially thanks to the local spotlights I've been featuring. With Allegra's story, I feel like I'm on the edge of something new, so despite the warning to "stop looking" for clues, I spend the next day reading both of her books.

I read both quickly and am reminded of what a gifted storyteller Allegra was. She had a knack for giving readers just enough clues then a mind-blowing twist at the end. *Wordplay* ends when the main character exposes a nonprofit's scam at their annual gala. During a speech, the protagonist reveals where the funds supposedly used for food and water supplies in third-world countries were really going. *Rest in Pieces* ended when the main character's husband found her living a new life—as her friend—in another city, only to realize she'd lured him there to kill him and return to her kids after making it look like he'd held her captive there.

The novels have to mean something. I'm just not sure which one, or what part, but I have a hunch it's the fake-death part. I pace from the kitchen to the living room. I could try texting "a source," but that might be too dangerous. I don't know their ultimate goal, and I might know too much at this point. The questions eat at me as I chew my fingernails down to the quick, and they begin to sting. Safety is suddenly my biggest concern as I seem to draw closer and closer to the inevitable truth.

I grab my phone and stare at it, then the door, then the window. I dead bolt the door and slide down the other side until I'm sitting on the carpet. I text, **Is Allegra alive?** and send it to "a source."

The ellipses appear almost immediately. They disappear with no response, reappear, and disappear again. Someone is choosing their words carefully for a question that ought to receive a simple yes or no. My heartbeat is almost double that of the ticking wall clock, and my shaking hand grows weak from the increasing weight of my phone.

Finally, some words: **Is anyone really alive who lives?—a source.** Another riddle.

I hold my breath and ask what I truly long to know. **Are you her?** After I hit Send, I run and grab two throws from the couch and wrap up in them as I wait. My anxious shivering is debilitating.

The response is another riddle I recognize as a quote from *Alice in Wonderland* by Lewis Carroll. **It's no use going back to yesterday, because I was a different person then—a source.**

It's her! It's got to be. She isn't spelling it out on a billboard, but I can read between the lines. Allegra's been contacting me as "a source," messing with me—messing with all of us—and I don't trust her. Maybe she killed Marcus because he was onto her. *Will she kill me now?* If anyone can convincingly fake their own death, it's Allegra Hudson. Her characters have certainly done it time after time.

I grab my purse and keys, lock up the apartment, and sprint to my car. I feel faint. If she knows I know, she may come after Graham or my mom. I want to make sure they're in a safe place as soon as possible, so I race toward Graham's preschool and call my mom.

She answers on the second ring. "Hi, baby. How are you?"

"Mom, listen to me. I need you to drive to Violet's house right away and stay there until the morning, okay? Don't pack a bag, don't do anything, just get in your car and go!"

"What? Is everything okay?" Mom asks.

"For now, yes. I'm taking Graham there. Violet can catch you up when you reach her house. Just do what I ask, okay?" I beg.

I hear her car beep as she unlocks it, and I breathe a bit easier.

"All right, honey. I'm leaving now."

"Good. I love you, Mom." My vision grows cloudy from the mounting tears.

"I love you too," Mom echoes.

When I turn in at the school parking lot, my tires squeal. I run inside the school, not giving a damn about what people think of me or my driving skills. I reach Ms. Martha's door in less than five seconds and demand that Graham leave with me immediately.

"But Mommy, we're about to play outside for the rest of the day," Graham whines as his shoulders droop.

"Baby, let's get in the car now!" I raise my voice and grab the attention of every wide-eyed child in his classroom. Tears drip down Graham's cheeks onto his shirt. "I'm sorry. We've got to go," I explain to Ms. Martha, who stands there motionless. Graham finally quits crying when I tell him he has a sleepover with Brighton, one of his favorite people in the world, and we're off.

WHEN WE PULL INTO VIOLET'S driveway, I see Mom's car and realize I never informed Violet of my sudden plans. Mom and Violet meet us at the front door with concern on their faces.

"What happened?" Violet's complexion is paler than usual.

"She's alive. I think Allegra's alive!" I shake my head as I say it, wondering if any of this is real. It feels so bizarre.

Violet's hands cover her mouth. "What?"

"If I'm not back here in two hours, post the video," I demand as I wipe my eyes. "I've got to warn Connor in person. This isn't something I can just blurt out on the phone."

Mom gives me a quick hug, then Violet walks me to my car, squeezes me tight, and whispers in my ear. I know what she's about to say before she utters a word. It's her civic duty as my best friend to dish out the harsh truth and call me out when I'm not thinking things through, but I don't want to hear it. I believe Connor's innocent. He would never hurt me, never betray me.

The words fall from her mouth like a poison-filled dagger. "You can't go over there. What if he's in on it with her? This is too dangerous. It's time for you to step away from all of this and go to the police."

I wipe the beads of sweat trickling down my hairline as I try to keep the words from registering. "I have to. There isn't time to second-guess everything. He loves me, and he'd never in a million—" I try to think of a way to explain to her what I must do, but instead, doubts creep into my mind.

What if she's right? What if this ends in betrayal and I don't make it out of there unscathed? I can't do this to Graham, to Mom. A quote from an old college professor pops into my head. "You all are still young and full of optimism right now, but at some point in your life, you'll begin to question the world and its motives. One thing I want you to remember in that moment is *"What-ifs are a cancer to purpose. You'll never know the answers if you don't try."*

"Well, I won't know for sure if I don't try." With trembling hands, I open the door to my car. As much as I love Connor, I can't just sit back and allow harm to waltz in his door when I know about it.

"If I don't hear from you soon, I'm posting the video and calling the police." Vi gives me a pointed look as she backs up toward the front door beside my mom.

"Be careful," Mom and Violet say in unison. The same worried expression is on their faces as Brighton and Graham chat in the yard, oblivious to the potential danger.

I run to the yard and grab Graham by the face, kiss him hard, and squeeze him tight. "I'll see you in an hour or two, okay? I love you more than anything in the world. You know that, right?"

Graham shows me his dimples, channeling Clayton for a second before we part. "I know, Mom. I love you more than the whole world too."

I wave to everyone as I back out of the driveway and blow them all a very misleading kiss of confidence as I head toward Connor. If Allegra shows up on his doorstep before I can warn him, he may just shatter completely.

WHEN I REACH CONNOR'S house, the front door is ajar, and I wonder if that was Connor or Allegra's doing. She could have been sneaking into the house—or out of it. Perhaps she's hiding in the hedges. I hold my breath and listen as I spin around to study my surroundings. The air is frigid, the wind is calm, and the trees stand still, but the sounds of my heart pounding in my throat prevent me from hearing anything other than Connor's voice trailing off inside the house.

I push the door inward, and it squeaks. I leave just enough room for me to slip inside and leave the door ajar. I can't help speculating about whether Allegra recently did this exact thing. Once I'm inside, my eyes travel back and forth, making sure she isn't lurking in the shadows, although I don't have a clue what I'll do if I see her. I don't know why she isn't dead, whether someone tried to kill her, what her goals are, or what she wants with Connor or me. All I know is that I'll kill her before I let her harm him.

Preparing for something awful, I tiptoe farther inside to gauge the situation, but on my fourth step, the floors creak. I take another step and look down. The wood has been replaced and is relatively new, and the board that creaked must be part of the original flooring.

My knowledge of wood flooring is minimal at best, so the fact that I notice this means one of two things: I must be hyperaware of my surroundings because I'm in the most terrifying situation of my life, or perhaps I'm familiar with this particular patchwork. Maybe Connor mentioned it before. That must be it.

I pause and hear Connor's voice in the kitchen. I can't hear anyone else speaking, so perhaps he's on the phone. I creep past the living room and wait against the wall, craning my neck to listen.

"No, we had a wonderful time, Joe. Thanks for popping in to say hey to us," Connor says.

Joe—that was the name of the owner of the Whitestone Inn, I think.

A noise from the dining room window diverts my attention, so I stop to check it out. Before I can, my shifting weight causes the hardwood floors to creak again. I hang tight, stand still, and hold my breath as I continue to listen and pray the noise wasn't Allegra.

"The room was amazing, just like it was for our honeymoon. Yeah, it's my favorite room there too. Oh, you heard that? Yeah, that was our song. Our wedding song, actually. Yeah, *Remember When*. We wanted to relive our dance to it while we were there. Allegra and I both adore Alan Jackson." Connor pauses, and I assume Joe is speaking on the other end.

"Yeah, I'm sure I'm okay. No, no, I'm fine. Yeah, okay. No, nothing to worry about here. Nothing at all. It'll all make more sense soon. I promise. Great to speak with you again too. Bye."

He hangs up, and I can only gasp at the horror of his conversation. He took me to the place where he spent his honeymoon with Allegra, and we danced to their wedding song. That's beyond sick and twisted, and I can't decide whether I'm disgusted or if I pity Connor's apparent emotional instability.

A sick feeling in the pit of my stomach sends acid racing up my esophagus and into my mouth. Clearly, this Joe guy thinks Connor's nuts for referring to me as Allegra, because Connor kept assuring him everything was okay. I wonder what on earth he's thinking, or maybe this is just his way of grieving. I have to consider whether he ever truly loved me or just viewed me as a stand-in for Allegra. As I make my way toward the front door, I notice a turned-over picture frame on the foyer table. I've never seen it before, and I quickly turn it over.

There she is, in all her glory—*the* Allegra Hudson. Perfect hair, perfect smile, perfect everything. But there's something in the photo that was apparently hers all this time—something Connor gave to me. Intricate yellow-gold scrollwork laced with rubies and sprinkled with diamonds, all on a matching yellow-gold chain. It was always *her* necklace.

I creep out the front door, double over, and take five deep breaths. Then I knock on the front door, clueless about what I'll say or how this will go. All I know is that despite Connor's clear need for mental help, I love him, and I must tell him about Allegra most likely being alive. Maybe some way, somehow, this is all a huge misunderstanding.

"Hey." He beams as he opens the front door. "Didn't expect you today." He gives me a squeeze. "I'm so glad you came by. Come on in."

"Yeah, I was in the neighborhood and thought we should talk." I scratch my nose and scan the room for Allegra. "You're going to want to sit down for this. Okay?" I wonder if I need to sit down as well.

Connor studies me, his eyes wide, as he has a seat next to me on the sofa in the den. "What's wrong?"

"I don't want you to think I'm crazy for what I'm about to say. And I wouldn't say it if I didn't think it was true. There's... There's something I need to tell you." I grab his hands.

Connor leans toward me with glistening eyes.

"I think Allegra's still alive." I pause for a reaction, but Connor doesn't blink. He just stares straight through me as if I'm transparent.

"And..." he starts, clearly expecting me to finish.

"And..." I say, expecting him to finish.

"And... She's alive inside you?" he asks, his eyes even wider.

"Alive... inside... me..." I say in slow motion. It's not a question and not a statement either. My heart falls to the floor, and I feel like I might pass out. Maybe he's having a meltdown or a nervous breakdown. Whatever the case, he's not well.

Connor grasps my face and looks deep into my eyes. "You think I didn't know that? Allegra, I recognized you as soon as you told me about Clayton. You'd told me that exact story shortly after we met. I knew it right then and there. You'd somehow come back to me as you were fifteen years ago. I was consumed by grief and didn't even recognize you at first. I'm sorry for that. You looked so different at twenty-five, and it's been so long. I just, I just didn't... *see* you."

He pulls me to him and pats my hair as he weeps. My eyes no longer blink, and I'm numb.

"I'm so glad you remember now. I'm so glad I have you back! I don't know how we're going to explain this to everyone else, but we'll think of something, baby. We'll think of something."

My body feels like lead, and blood rushes away from my face as I stare at the wall behind Connor's head, taking it all in. I love him so much, but he's clearly suffering from some mental collapse. Our relationship wasn't real—none of it. He only ever loved me because he thought she was *in me* somehow, like I was actually *her*. This whole time. I echo his sentiments as I blink away a puddle of tears. "Yes, Connor. I remember everything."

Remember When starts playing through the TV in the living room, and Connor reaches for my hand. He beams as he tugs me upward.

As we sway back and forth to the tune, I rest my head on his shoulder and realize the word *sad* isn't powerful enough to describe my agony. The stabbing pain in my heart makes me wheeze, and I struggle over what's right and what's wrong anymore. I just want him to be *mine*. Since Clayton's death, no one's ever loved me with such passion, and I cry silently as we dance, knowing Connor's love for me wasn't for who I really am.

I kiss him deeply, knowing this is the end of us. It has to be. "I love you so much, Connor. But I've got to go grab something from my car really quick, okay?" I walk toward the foyer with a tear-stained face, knowing I've got to get him some help. But I also know this may be the last time I see him for a long time, and I can barely put one foot in front of the other.

"I love you, too, Allegra. Hurry back." He twirls to the music and, as I leave, smiles at me like he's just won the lottery.

"Okay," I call back as I turn toward the knob, twist it, step outside, and push the door shut with my back. When the door latches, I sob into my palms, and through the spaces between my fingers, I see two red high heels step right in front of me. I gasp with disbelief as I remove my hands and gaze upward at two perfectly toned legs and a red swing dress.

"Time to wake up and smell the roses, Mad!" she says with a simper as she forces a dampened cloth over my mouth and face. At first, I think it's Mayven, which surprises me. But when my body fades out and falls, I turn over to my attacker and see a face that shocks me to my core.

"Allegra?" I mumble before blacking out.

Chapter 23

The back of my head pounds, and I hear deafening beeps as I'm bumping up and down. My stomach turns and my head spins, almost as if I'm in motion. I open my eyes, but all I see is black. I lift myself up and bump my head on something cool and metallic. My whole body is thrown backward, and I slide until my head collides with a wall. Then I figure out that I'm in the trunk of a car—probably Allegra Hudson's. My adrenaline kicks in as I realize this is probably not going to end well.

We appear to be heading up a mountainside. The switchbacks are endless, and my ears are popping. *Does she plan to kill me? Does anyone else know she's alive? Why is she taking me away and not just killing me if she thinks I know too much?* Questions about my fate fill my panicked mind as quiet tears of shock stream down my face. Maybe Violet was right about me going to the police after all.

I don't know how I allowed myself to get into this situation or how I'll get myself out. I almost smirk, knowing one thing's for certain. It's been at least two hours since I left Violet's, and by now, she's uploaded my video. And I'm sure she's noted the last thing I said before I disappeared—I suspected Allegra Hudson wasn't dead. So even if I don't make it out alive, the world is about to learn that Allegra Hudson's possibly been alive this entire time.

After ten more switchbacks, we find a straight stretch and accelerate. Wherever we're headed, it sure seems secluded; I don't hear any other cars on the road. I wonder if I should try to kick out a taillight and stick my fingers through the hole to alert another driver that I'm in here. Something tells me no one would notice anyway.

Pretending I'm still unconscious when we arrive at our destination seems like a better option, and she would know I was awake by the noise from busting out the light. Even if she didn't, by some miracle, hear the kicking, she would still know I'd been awake when she opened the trunk and saw part of the taillight missing.

It's too late now anyway. We slow down on a gravel road or driveway, like we're at the destination. I don't hear anything except my heavy breathing and the crunching of tires on pebbles. It's hard to pretend to be unconscious when my breath is quick and my blood is pumping faster than Niagara Falls, but I shut my eyes and give it a shot. My life probably depends on it.

A few seconds later, the trunk pops, and someone lifts the lid. The sunlight makes me want to squint even though my eyes are closed, and suddenly, someone's breath is on my face. They smell great, like coconuts and lavender. Probably Allegra. Shadows come and go rapidly across my face. She's likely waving her hand to see if she can get some reaction.

"C'mon, you big faker!" Allegra laughs, taunting me. "I know you're awake, so go ahead and get up and walk inside yourself. I don't want to have to lift your one-hundred-and-thirty-pound body again, okay?" She huffs. "No one is around for miles, so you can scream and shout all you want. Or you can come inside with me and allow me to explain everything. I'm trying to help you. C'mon, Mad, I'm really getting thirsty." She heads off without me, clearly confident I'll follow suit.

My eyes open, and I look around at enormous trees and rolling hills. We're in the Smokies for sure, but where exactly, I'm not certain.

"This way," Allegra calls from afar as she walks into a cozy cabin about thirty feet away. I sit up slowly and follow soon after, still skeptical but also hopeful for some answers.

"Where are we, Allegra?" I've entered the threshold of the cabin and see her flipping all the lights on.

She grabs a remote and lights the fireplace.

"Is this where you've been hiding out?" I ask.

"Listen, I'm about to tell you everything you need to know, okay? Just have a seat on the couch, and I'll bring us both some tea and sandwiches."

"If you're a source, why did you want me to solve your murder if you're not dead?" I ask anyway, unable to help myself.

"I'll give you this one as an appetizer. Just because I'm not dead doesn't mean someone didn't try to kill me," she points out as she nukes two mugs of hot water in the microwave.

I look to the floor then the fireplace. "Oh."

"Four teaspoons of sugar, right?" she asks as she opens a big bag of it.

My eyebrows meet as I study her face. "Yeah. How'd you know?"

"I know you better than anyone else, Madeleine." She smiles and winks, and I wonder whether it's the wink of a psychopath or an ally.

I can't focus on anything except the fact that none of this makes sense—that, and the feeling I may be in an absurd amount of danger. I scan the room for knives, bats, fire pokers, shovels—anything to use as a weapon.

"The handgun I keep in the end table would probably be your best bet, but only I know which end table I'm actually referring to," Allegra scoffs as she sets our mugs of tea on the coffee table. "I'm not going to hurt you. If I wanted you dead, I'd have killed you by now. During my time as a source, did I ever once harm you?" She sips her tea. "Let me ask you some questions first, Madeleine. Then you can ask me anything you like. Deal?"

With trembling fingers, I take a sip of tea then scan the room again. "All right."

"Has it been fall and winter for an extraordinary amount of time for you?" She leans in close as she awaits my response.

I purse my lips at the absurd, irrelevant question. "Yes, it does kind of seem that way. Why? Aren't all winters eternal?"

"Have you been forgetting things, or is your timeline a bit screwy lately?" Her eyes narrow as she studies me.

I start to answer, but she continues to her next question before I can finish. "All these times you've met with Ivy Richards, have you ever once seen her husband or her house?" Allegra's head tilts to one side, almost as if she's playing a game with me.

"No, I haven't, but I do know where she lives," I answer, irritated. "What are you getting at?"

She sets down her mug and grabs my hands. "Think about where Ivy Richards lives. Really think about the details of her street."

"Okay, I'm thinking about it." I lean away, not sure if I trust her and wondering where in the world this is going. I've driven by Ivy's place before, but I've never actually been inside. It's an updated 1960s white brick rancher, so I'm not sure what the big deal is.

I imagine I'm driving by her house, just as I have many times, but this time, I slow down the snapshot in my head and zoom in to study the house. It's a 1960s white brick rancher with an updated Crafts-man front porch, black shutters, and brick-paver driveway. The yard is full of auburn leaves that fall from the big, beautiful maple trees. The front door is a bright, shiny, freshly painted shade of red, and it has an abnormally high peephole just like Violet's. No, it's... *identical* to Violet's.

Sweat drips down my chest, and I scoot backward in my seat. I imagine Violet and Ivy's houses side by side. The white brick houses merge, and I realize they *are* the same home. Pieces of broken bricks fall into the yard, where I stand fixated on the view, and they tumble up to my feet as I continue to stare at the red front door.

I visualize both Ivy and Violet opening the door. They have not only the same home but the same *everything*, only Ivy's an older version of Violet. Their faces, their hair, the inflections in their voices, their personalities, their mannerisms, and all their stories collide as my entire existence dissipates into nothing. The back of my head throbs as my hands try to jerk away from Allegra's, but she squeezes them tighter and continues to tell me more.

"You haven't been there because it looks exactly like someone else's house, and your brain hasn't let you go there because it knows, Madeleine, it *knows*... that they're the exact... same... place."

I pull my hands away, not wanting to hear anymore, and my vision glitches. The room vibrates back and forth like something has malfunctioned, and nothing seems right any longer. My body mimics the movement and grows icy. I'm not sure how much more I can take. *How does she know exactly what's happening inside my head?* This feels like an episode of *The Twilight Zone* that won't end. It's like I'm stuck in a loop of bizarre events that make no sense whatsoever, yet at the same time, they make all the sense in the world when viewed from the proper angle.

"What is this? What are you trying to do, gaslight me?" I scoot backward, farther away from her. I'm horrified, exposed, and unable to process my reality.

"Just listen to me for a minute. Ivy couldn't see you properly as your old self—or the old me, rather—because of her loyalty to me as I am now. You created your own version of her, the old version of her, from fifteen years ago before everything changed for our friendship. And you called her Violet to separate the relationship we used to have from what it turned into. As for Connor, as soon as you told him the Clayton story, he saw you despite how much I've changed. He saw you and loved you all over again, like he did with me in the beginning, when I was twenty-five and widowed. And Lane, he felt a familiarity with you from the get-go, like you'd met before somehow."

Allegra reaches for my hand as if she cares for me, and tears roll down my motionless face. Connor *was* telling his truth before.

"Those dreams you've had about waking up in the hospital, about wanting to see that person lying in the bed, the severe headaches which stem from the injury at the back of your head, the beeps of the machines you're hooked up to right now... I thought the old me, the twenty-five-year-old me, would have clearer eyes. I thought you'd be able to figure it all out—for me, for us."

Allegra continues, "I kicked off this dream with you as the main character and me guiding you along as 'a source.' A type of self-hypnosis, if you will, so I could remember who did this to me. Things aren't exactly clear with this bump on the back of my head, and for some reason, I know I'm not going to be able to wake up until I figure everything out. That's where you came in... Me, but fifteen years ago, you're unbiased toward my current life and the people in it."

I jerk my hands away and stand up, eager to escape. This woman is clearly insane, and if she thinks I'm going to sit here and let her convince me that *I'm* the one who's crazy, then she's got another think coming. "Figure it out? Figure *what* out?" My voice cracks as I step toward the door, and I hate the way it exposes my fear.

"Figure out who tried to kill me. Who killed us, rather."

"Us? You mean you and Marcus?" I ask, confused.

She rubs the back of her head as if she's in pain. "No. Who killed you and me. Although I do feel that the same person killed him somehow, or like I know that person, but I can't quite remember."

My headache strengthens, and the searing ache forces me to close my eyes. I don't know what's worse, the physical agony or the emotional anguish of this confrontation. I see myself waking up in the hospital with cords and machines all around me, then I envision walking down the hospital corridor toward room 101. *Room 101.* The number remains the same backward and forward, and even it's turned completely upside down, like something from Wonderland. I run toward the door as usual, and it creeps open in slow motion. I see the feet at the edge of the bed, and I step in farther to see the face this time—only it's my own but also Allegra's. I shake my head from side to side until the pain subsides, and I open my eyes again.

"I lost about fifteen or twenty pounds after Garrett was born. Then, I took it even further by going blonder and getting my nose done. It's just like you said when you googled my photo. You'd have to lose fifteen pounds, get a nose job, and lighten your hair about four shades to look anything like me. And I'm here to tell you that you did, eventually."

I grab my nose and feel the pain of a thousand knives irrigating and chipping away at the bone from my rhinoplasty all over again, like it was yesterday.

"I'm a writer, and you're a writer. Although you did take a new path on the reporter-journalist front in this world we created, which I obviously didn't do in the real world. We changed things just enough to where it wouldn't be obvious to you or anyone else, I guess," Allegra explains. "We both have the same birthday and adore Hitchcock. *That*, you didn't change. *Vertigo*'s still our favorite film fifteen years later, by the way. And Mom, dear sweet Mom, she's still alive here. God, I miss her. She came as quite the shock to Connor, though, as you could probably tell when he saw her in the hospital that day. That was a glitch on my part. Somehow, control of the dream got away from me at some point.

"Poor guy. I don't think he saw any of this coming, but he loves us so much. I truly wish I'd done things differently with him now. There are so many things here I didn't see coming either. Now, I'd definitely put him first. Our love was so special, so surreal. The kind of love that transcends time and death, you know? At first, I wanted you to focus on finding my killer, but the dream took a turn, resulting in me learning more than who tried to kill me. As you were reliving my life, I realized how stupid I'd been with Connor.

"I tried to keep you on track with the investigation with the texts and the messages, but there were other lessons I needed to learn along the way. I couldn't control the dream anymore, and I realized the mistakes I've made in the last few years. Mistakes that pushed away the love of my life and ultimately put us all in jeopardy. Connor loved us all over again. Even here, where things are topsy-turvy and utterly insane. Then I realized it's not just about my death. It's about our life, together, and how that needed to change."

I shake my head in disbelief as I attempt to take it all in. I wonder if there's any possible way that this could be the truth. Flashes of my mom's funeral appear as if they truly happened, because they did, and I realize I've buried them somewhere deep within my subconscious where I couldn't see them. Images of Connor and me arguing and growing further and further apart flicker in and out as well, interspersed with recollections of my other life with Graham, Mom, and Violet. *Is Allegra crazy? Am I crazy? How can I be two people at the same time? Which life is real?*

My heart rate soars at what she and my own mind are implying, and I can't concentrate on anything she's saying until I can see it for myself. I need to keep her talking so I can sneak away and look in the mirror down the hallway to prove myself right and Allegra wrong.

As she spills more details, I slowly inch toward the mirror in the hallway. "Rick and Nick for Ivy and Violet's husbands. That one was easy, Mad. And Graham, I always loved that name for a boy. It was my absolute favorite."

At the mention of Graham's name, she's gotten my attention again.

"But remember, Mad, we *actually* named him Mason..."

And we finish the sentence together in perfect unison. "Because it was Clayton's favorite name for a boy."

My heart feels like it could stop beating any second, and my skin prickles as our entire lives fuse together. She knows everything about me because she *is* me, or I'm her, rather. No, it can't be true. It isn't possible. If we were the same person, there's no way I could split us up into two people and have a conversation with myself. This is just absurd. She's lying.

"Clayton mentioned it one night after we got back from our honeymoon. We decided to tell each other our favorite baby names, just for fun." I finish the story as I inch closer to the mirror.

"Mason for a boy, and Rose for a girl, he said." Allegra tears up.

I whip my head around to stare into her eyes. She appears genuinely emotional. I'm astounded at how she learned this information. She must have tricked me into telling her, or maybe my apartment is bugged and she heard me telling someone else. Only I've never told anyone else that story before. It was something I held close to my heart and never shared.

I'm finally close enough to the hallway to make a dash for it, but as soon as I peek in the mirror, I gasp. Like a mad woman, I back into the wall behind me. Beachy-blond waves, a perfect nose, and a slender frame in a red swing dress. It's not me I see in the mirror; it's Allegra Hudson.

Chapter 24

My hair is so much blonder, and my nose is considerably thinner. Hell, *I'm* a lot thinner. I run my hands down my slim body, and I feel my bones more prominently. "What did you put in that tea?"

"Four teaspoons of sugar, just how we like it." Allegra smiles, and I feel as if I'm smiling as well. "Now that you see we're one and the same, we need to relive the murder together. You've done your job and helped me remember who did it. I'm just not strong enough yet to go back on my own. But I'll see you again when the pages fall."

Allegra pushes me backward into a hole. I'm falling for miles. The wind is in my hair, my limbs flail helplessly, and my stomach feels like it missed the fall completely and stayed in the cabin with Allegra.

When I hit the ground, it's no longer the hardwood of the cabin but the floor of Connor and Allegra's bedroom—my bedroom—in Sequoyah Hills. I recognize it. I remember everything about my real life, her real life. The real world hits me like a jolt of electricity, and I suddenly recall being Allegra. Everything in my dream was a projection of how things really are now and, at the same time, also how they were fifteen years ago.

The relationships were the same with everyone involved, despite the slightly different circumstances I experienced as Madeleine. She wasn't a character I created. She was me, the exact person I was at twenty-five but thrust into my current life.

I remember when I landed my book editor, Sarah. I remember when my first book came out and how Connor, Mason, Garrett, and I celebrated at home with pizza, ice cream, and champagne. My brain pieces it together again. The things Graham did and said in my dream world were things Mason actually did at that age in the real world, only my name wasn't Madeleine but Allegra. In my dream, if I'd been at Connor's house and seen pictures of Mason when he was little, I probably would've gone into shock as Madeleine, because Mason would've looked exactly like Graham. I finally realize that's why Connor got so emotional upon meeting Graham. It was like traveling back in time to when they first met and Mason was almost four.

Madeleine Barton. *Why did I pick that alias?* The answer is on the tip of my tongue—*Vertigo*! In *Vertigo*, Kim Novak played two characters who were actually the same person, Madeleine Elster and Judy Barton. I simply combined the two to make Madeleine Barton. *Pretty clever.*

I glance at the clock. It's two minutes shy of three in the morning, and Connor's out like a light in our bed. My suitcase is packed, as is my purse, and I'm dressed in a pink Gucci sweatshirt and black leggings. It's then that I realize I'm about to die. This is my memory coming back of the night I was attacked. At last. But I'm not ready.

My printed manuscripts are on my end table with my phone, so I grab them and gather all my belongings and head down the stairs. I want to go back to the bedroom, wake Connor, and kiss him. I want to do everything differently than the first time, but I can't. I'm being pulled by an unknown force toward the events exactly as they happened. History clearly cannot be altered. Not even here.

I step toward the hallway but cry internally. *Why didn't I kiss him goodbye the first time? Why did we grow so far apart these past five years? Why did it take nearly being killed from a head injury to make me wake up?* Taking another step down the hall, I remember opening my eyes for a few seconds in the hospital, not knowing why I was there. It wasn't a dream. It was reality.

I step toward the stairs and closer to my fate. The headaches and ringing in my ears are from the head injury and machines beeping in real life, just like Allegra told me. They've been playing in the background of my medically induced coma, and every once in a while, the sounds made their way into my dream and interrupted it. I remember it all now—Connor holding my hand, saying they needed me to go to sleep for a while, to heal. Then I remember slipping away and waking up as Madeleine, eating dinner with Graham as the news of Allegra Hudson's "death" came to me via my mom.

What I don't understand is how I lived if someone tried to kill me, and clearly, they attempted to because I have this agonizing head injury as a reminder. I wonder whether it was an accident or if they feel remorseful. Maybe I took too many pills again and relapsed. But no, I haven't done that for years. Someone did this to me, and it's time I learned who. *Did Connor wake up and confront them? And who was charged with my attempted murder in the real world? Is there really a Detective Wentworth and a Claude Van Morrison, or did I make them up in my dream to push Madeleine forward?*

My memory continues to return as I grab the knob to the front door and twist it with sorrow, because I'm unable to do anything differently than the first time, though I try my best. I step onto the porch and check all my belongings. Luggage, wallet, purse, laptop, manuscripts. Check, check, check, check, check. Then a voice calls my name from the right side of the porch—in the dark. It's a voice I recognize, but I still jump as it catches me off-guard.

"Did you change the book, Allegra?" she asks.

"God, Mayven, you scared me half to death." I exhale and grab my heart.

Mayven remains hidden in the shadows. "Did you change the book? Yes or no?" I've never heard her use that low tone before.

"No, I think it works best as a nonprofit scam. It's juicier that way. Plus, I just love the name Raven for an antagonist. It's so dark and sinister yet beautiful at the same time. I tried changing her name for the version I handwrote, but it just didn't feel right." I smile innocently. "What are you doing up so early?"

Mayven steps closer to me with one of her hands behind her back. I try to force different words from my mouth, then I try to hit her, but all I can do is wait and let things play out.

"I tried so hard, Allegra. I tried so hard after I read it to politely suggest you change her name, to change the scam plot. Don't you understand? People will figure it all out if you leave it this way. Troy and I will be done! People will grow suspicious of the Bennett Book Foundation because everyone knows you and I are good friends. They'll start to look into where *our* charitable proceeds are truly going, and I can't allow that. Not to mention, the name Raven for the antagonist? Really? It literally rhymes with my name! All of this trouble over one little word."

I take a step away from her and try to clear the fog in my mind. She's telling me that I hit the nail on the head with her charity—and that I'm putting one in my own coffin as well. "But you guys aren't doing anything illegal like that?" I ask.

Mayven drops her head to the side and raises her eyebrows.

When we hear some scuffling across the street, we turn our heads toward the road, but ultimately, we see nothing and no one.

"What are you saying, Mayven? That my plot hit too close to home?" I look to see if anyone else is around, and Mayven snatches my manuscripts with her free hand.

It makes sense. In my dream world, she tried to cover her tracks. She thought the picture of Connor and Ivy might make them look guilty, but I still believed them. So she planted the headless doll, scared Graham at the playground, and sent the threatening note about the twenty-four-hour deadline after that to try to stop me. She's also the one who wiped Allegra's laptop.

"Listen, Allegra, I can't let you take these to New York. I just can't. Oh, and by the way, I accidentally deleted the emailed copies of your manuscripts after I read them. Sorry. So these are all that's left now, and I'm the only other person who's read them." She smirks, and I see a side of her I never thought I would—pure evil.

I lunge for my pages, and some fall to the ground, almost in slow motion. They cascade down like leaves falling from a tree, and when the wind hits them just right, I chase them down to the porch floor with open arms. "Why are you acting so crazy, Mayven?"

"I know you won't understand. You're far too virtuous. You'd have to run and tell on me and be the hero."

I gasp as I put the pieces together from my dream and see that it matches reality. I try my best to ask her if Marcus started digging around in Troy's records and if she put almond milk in his coffee cup somehow, but the words won't come out of my mouth. That's because I didn't say them the first time around. Which means that didn't happen in the real world at all. I created Marcus to help myself realize something, but what? I wonder.

Mayven continues, "I can't let my whole family go down for you, Allegra. If only you'd changed the story when Fran told you to. I really thought blackmailing her would do the trick and she'd convince you to scrap it."

I try my best to pick up the fallen pages and the fallen pieces of my life. I gather the papers and glimpse the title page of the book that saw through Mayven and Troy Bennett's lies and deceit. I open one helpless eye and see the word typed out in big, bold letters—*Wordplay*.

"Getting rid of you won't be easy. I might have to get my hands a little dirty. I'm sorry it had to be this way, Allegra. You really *were* a good friend." Mayven's voice cracks from above me as a tear drops from her face onto my arm. A sharp blow to the back of my head stings, and all I see is darkness as a car pulls up in front of my house and I tumble down the concrete stairs. I imagine it's Troy coming to finish me off with a quick jerk of my neck.

Since this is how it really happened, maybe this time, he'll wrap me in a garbage bag, throw me in his trunk, and dump me in a river somewhere. All I know for sure is that there isn't one thing I can do about it as I lie here. But if that were truly the case, how did I wind up in the hospital in a coma? It has to be someone else in the real world who finds me before the Bennetts finish me off and Connor finds my dead body. But who? And how? Footsteps approach me from the street as Mayven scoots behind the bushes, where she can't be seen.

Gentle hands are suddenly on my back and head. "Allegra, Allegra! Are you okay? Why are you lying here? What's wrong? Oh my God, you're bleeding!" He dials 911 and rings the doorbell five times as he yells for Connor.

It's Lane Stone. He came back to check on me, just like he said he wished he had come back in my dream. *Thank you, God!* I close my eyes and rest at last, for this has been a long journey.

All the things I found creepy about Connor while I was dreaming were actually him trying to help me remember who I really am; I wish I'd seen that then. The Whitestone Inn, *Remember When*, even regifting me the ruby necklace he gave me for our fifth anniversary in the real world. The one that, oddly enough, was a replica of the one Madeleine Elster wore in *Vertigo*, when she, too, was living a double life. He knew that movie was my absolute favorite, and a replica of the necklace from the movie would've been a perfect gift.

In the real world, I married Connor a year after we met at my mom's house. He adopted Mason the day after our wedding, before we even went on a honeymoon. He was a gem—no, a diamond in the rough. Just as he was in my dream. He even suggested we delay the honeymoon for a week since the wedding "hoopla," as he called it, had kept us so busy. He didn't want Mason to feel like we'd run off and left him right after the wedding, so we stayed.

Two years later, in 2005, Garrett was born, and our family was complete. Mason adored having a father figure and a baby brother; Lord knows he'd put up with so much estrogen from my mom and me for far too long. Those were the early years, though, before my writing took off and the busyness got out of control and my priorities shifted. I don't completely regret my career keeping me busy—it's who I am, who I was—but there *is* this thing called balance, and my life became incredibly uneven after Mom died.

When I lost Clayton so young and so suddenly, it hardened me. I'd depended on him far too much, and he was my everything. Everything I needed in a best friend and husband was wrapped up in him and him alone. When he was taken from me, I found it hard to stand on my own again. Then I had Mason depending on me, and me alone, and I wasn't ready. So with Connor, I wanted to love him with all of my heart yet still be able to take care of myself and my children financially if something ever happened to him. I guess I overcompensated, though, to the point of almost ruining a great thing.

When Mom died and my books really took off, my fans demanded more of me, and my friends began to ask for favors and appearances almost every day. I kept saying yes. That's when everything truly started to fall apart, not when Mayven hit me.

If I ever wake up, I hope Connor can forgive me. I hope I can see Mason and Garrett one last time, even if I don't make it for very long. I pray for God to heal me if it's his will, and I understand if it isn't. I beg him to please take care of my babies and to help Connor move on with his life and find happiness. I pray that Connor won't blame himself for the dissolution of our marriage. It was all my fault, and I want to apologize for my mistakes before I go, if that's at all possible.

Light and shadows dance before my eyes, and I squint to make sense of them. Voices mumble softly around me, and I can't under-

stand them at first. "She's awake!" I finally hear and recognize it as
the sweet voice of my youngest son, Garrett.

"Shh. You're going to give her a headache!" Mason says as if annoyed. "Mom, it's us. Can you see me? Can you hear me?"

My eyes dart back and forth to the three pieces of my heart in
human form.

"Allegra, we're right here. It's okay. We're all right here." Connor's
hands are clasping mine.

Chapter 25

The first few minutes, I can't say much to Connor and the boys except "I love you" and "I'm sorry." Nurses and doctors rush to my side to check my vitals, and we all cry every few minutes, hugging one another as often as possible without tugging on my cords. When the staff decides to let me have a moment of peace, the boys run down the hall to order us some food, per my request, and I ask Connor to shut the door.

"How long have I—?"

"Four days, seven hours, and four minutes." Connor beams and squeezes my hand three times. "I missed you so much." He breaks down and weeps on my shoulder.

My tears flow onto his head. "I dreamt of you. I wasn't me, but I was. You found me, and it was like old times. Like in the beginning, before I screwed it all up. I'm so sorry for everything." My voice is raspy.

"It wasn't just you. I should've done more, tried harder. It takes two, you know?" He smiles as he wipes his wet cheeks. "I dreamt of you, too, every night. It was back to the good times for me too. And I want it all back like it used to be, and I know we can get there together..."

"We can, and we will." I scan the room and notice the bouquets of flowers and plants. "So who do they think did this to me?"

"You don't remember?" Connor asks as if the answer is quite obvious. "The doctors told me not to discuss it. They thought it might be too much for you to speak about at first."

250

"I've been doing nothing but trying to remember it for the past four days. I don't think it'll be too much now. So I'm curious. Who did they pin it on?"

"Lane, of course. I caught him with you red-handed. He was screaming for me, even though he denied doing it, and Detective Wentworth arrested him on the spot. It was obvious to the police and me that he was guilty. He'd been watching you for days. Mayven saw him on her security cameras several times, scanning the neighborhood and such."

"It wasn't him, Connor," I whisper knowingly.

"What?" Connor leans in as if baffled.

"You heard me. It wasn't Lane Stone. I remember."

"Then who?"

"I don't want to say until I'm ready to leave the hospital because I'm still vulnerable here. Plus, I still have some details to sort out before I'm a hundred percent sure of the whole truth and what I want to do. Just tell anyone who asks that I don't remember. If you know, you won't be able to resist doing something you'll regret, and I don't want that on your conscience or mine."

I explain further, "Let's just allow this to play out how they wanted it to for now. It's the only way we're all going to be completely safe. Not one little word. To anyone. Got it?" I raise my croaky voice and purse my cracked lips.

"Not even your own kids?" Connor rubs his forehead, making it wrinkle.

"Not even the kids. I don't want them to know *anything*. Don't trust anyone, even people we're very close to. Okay? Didn't the doctor ask you not to upset me?" I narrow my eyes.

"Okay, fine. But you have to set this right as soon as you get out, then." Connor reaches over to me.

"Fine. Deal."

We shake on it. "Wait, so Detective Wentworth is real? Is his cousin the police chief? And does he look like Santa minus the beard?"

"How do you...?" Connor pauses. "I guess he did come into your room a few times, and maybe you created your own version of him in your dream. But no. To answer your question, his cousin isn't the police chief." Connor chokes up as his eyes grow glassy. "One day, I told you he'd make a good Santa minus the beard, hoping you'd wake up and have a laugh about it. I can't believe you remember that. You heard me all this time?"

"And Marcus, is he really dead?" I hope it was only in my dreams. I know good and well his death was no accident.

Connor pauses and obviously can't come up with an answer. "Who?"

My head is fuzzy about him, and I can't remember anything except what I dreamed as Madeleine. "You know, Marcus. He drives that green Jeep, and he's my friend from..." It doesn't even make sense to me as the words drip from my mouth. I never actually worked at WKNX.

Connor scrunches up his face and looks confused. "Doesn't ring a bell. But you honestly don't sound so sure about him yourself. Maybe he represents a theme of some sort. You're usually all about an underlying theme, so maybe you just got bored and dreamed him up for fun." He pats my knee as if reassuring me that I'm not completely nuts.

I smile and look around at the floral arrangements lining my room to distract myself. "So, who are all these flowers from? You'd think I'd kicked the bucket already and this was my funeral," I joke.

Connor walks around to several of the plants and flowers and explains who they're from. Ivy, Sarah, several women in my Sunday school class, some of Garrett's teachers, Garrett's principal, Mason's teachers, Mason's principal, and fans and other friends are on the list of givers.

A pang of nausea comes when I think of no longer seeing my mom every day. Even if it was just a dream, I felt her presence, and I miss her all over again. My head jerks toward Connor as he points at a large vase filled with beautiful white alstroemeria accented with soft green hydrangeas and says, "This one is from Troy and Mayven. It's gorgeous, isn't it? Probably set them back a few hundred, I'd say." Connor smiles.

"Yes, it's lovely." I clench my jaw, enraged. If it set them back a few hundred, they can certainly afford it with the extra cash they're bringing in from their fake charities. Troy has a great job, so I wonder why they needed to do all of this. Maybe his job isn't as great as they would have everyone believe. Maybe they got into financial trouble and couldn't find a way out without having to give up their life of luxury.

Life of luxury. Ugh. It sickens me to think of going back to our house—a house that changed me, a house I was nearly murdered in, a house that derailed us from the path we knew we should've taken. I think of our quaint farmhouse in Powell, the one we never finished renovating but should have.

"Connor, I want to move," I blurt to my own surprise.

"The nurse said you couldn't get up quite yet. Maybe you could shuffle your legs around a bit, though?" Connor wiggles his own legs as he stands in the corner, as if I've forgotten how to do so and require instructions.

I laugh, or I try to, but my raw throat doesn't allow it. "No, honey. I meant move, as in houses."

Connor whips his head toward me and backs up. I've awakened as a new woman, and he's thrown. "Move? Really? Maybe you shouldn't make any big decisions just yet."

"No, I've thought about things a lot lately. I've made so many mistakes, and I want to go back to Powell, to the farmhouse and the barn. Let's do what we were supposed to do years ago." I smile confidently. "Besides, I can't stay in our house anymore. Too many bad memories there after all this." I point at my body and scrunch my face.

"Even if we do move there, it won't be immediately. It'll take several months to get things renovated, you know." Connor walks over and takes my hand.

"I know." I gaze into eyes that still sparkle just for me.

Connor kisses me on the lips. "Then that's what we'll do, as long as the boys are okay with it."

I beam, feeling like the luckiest person in the world. "Agreed. I love you, Connor. So much."

"I love you too." Connor pushes my hair back and kisses me on the forehead.

"Yes, she's right here in room 101. You up for another visitor, Mrs. Hudson?" the nurse asks.

"Maybe. Who is it?"

"It's me." Mayven Bennett stands on the threshold of my room.

I swallow with panic but grin on the outside. "Of course, Mayven. I'd love to see you."

The nurse warns, "Only a few minutes, though, and don't speak of anything upsetting, hon."

"Of course not," Mayven agrees as she approaches the side of my bed opposite Connor. "I heard you were supposed to wake up today, so I *had* to come by and see you for myself." Mayven musters some fake tears as she places her hand on mine, and Connor glances at her with misty eyes. Hook, line, and sinker. And I must play along as well until I sort out what to do.

I place my hand on top of hers and give it a gentle squeeze, as if we're still truly friends and she didn't try to murder me. "It's so great to see you. I've been so out of sorts with my memory, and I'm just trying to figure out how I got here. The last thing I remember is packing for my trip to New York and going to bed. Then I'm somehow here, hooked up to all kinds of machines. It's been overwhelming, but it's so nice to see a familiar face. It helps me feel like I'm at home."

I imagine that my hand is made of iron and I'm crushing her metacarpals into a million pieces. When I get out of here, I'm going to make that charity of hers legit if it's the last thing I do. The kids in Nigeria deserve books and food and water. I won't let this charade go on any longer. The kids won't suffer for her greed and lies.

"Oh no, you're having memory issues?" Mayven gasps, and I imagine she's doing a happy dance inside, assuming she's buying what I'm selling.

Thank God Connor chimes in, because I'm growing weary of being fake-nice. "Yes, the doctor said she may never get those memories back. It's pretty common for this type of head injury. We're just lucky she didn't lose more time." Connor nods with a frown, keeping up his end of the deal.

"Oh my, how unfortunate." Mayven pouts. "But at least you're here, and you're okay." She grins again.

I wonder if Mayven thinks I'm going ahead with rewriting and publishing the book. She can't know that Ivy has that original hand-written copy somewhere, even though Mayven probably destroyed my laptop like she did in the dream. If she suspects I'm going forward with the book, she'll have a reason to harm me and my family all over again. But I can't tell the police about Mayven yet, not until I figure out this whole Marcus thing. There's something I'm missing, and I can feel it.

"I'm quitting writing, too, for a while. I'm going to take the next few years off and focus on my family," I say to seal the deal.

"Oh, really?" Mayven says. "Maybe that *is* best, considering."

I want to laugh and smack her at the same time, seeing how quickly she jumps on board with the idea of me quitting, like a true, supportive friend.

Connor furrows his brow and looks at me like I've gone insane. "You don't need to go that far, honey. I'm sure you can still write but maybe scale back some other things. Like all the appearances and stuff like that."

I agree wholeheartedly, but I have to convince Mayven I'm no longer a threat. I smile at them both. "Maybe in a few years, Connor."

"Well, I'm going to go and let you get some rest, dear." Mayven kisses me on the forehead, the same skull she struck and left for dead. It's the kiss of death averted.

When she leaves, Connor looks at me like I have three heads. "What was that?"

"That was me sticking to my story, and doing it pretty damn well, if I say so myself."

"We've got to sell it this way to everyone?" Connor sighs. "I'm sorry she came by, by the way. I hope it wasn't too taxing for you to speak with her. I asked everyone to wait a day or two," Connor explains as the boys run inside my room with enough food to feed the entire ward.

I mutter with a knowing grin, "I guess she just couldn't help herself."

Chapter 26

Later the next night, Connor rushes home to take a much-needed shower. As I attempt to drift off to sleep, exhausted from trying to rehab mind and body, I wonder if the rest of my dreams will feel boring and underwhelming after the life-changing revelations my coma brought. One thing still doesn't make sense, and I can't quite fall asleep or tell the police about Mayven because of it. The hole in my story, the part that doesn't add up, is that Marcus wasn't real.

He wasn't a friend of mine in real life or someone who even existed. He was no one, just a figment of my overactive imagination. But somehow, I miss him just like before, and the thought of him existing for no apparent reason in my dream bothers me to no end.

So what was the point of dreaming up a male work figure, then? Maybe Connor was right and Marcus just represented some underlying theme I haven't pieced together yet. Or maybe my mind was too busy building an elaborate and intricate world to trick me into learning more about myself and decided to add a random character just for good measure.

Could Marcus possibly represent a person rather than a theme? Someone who's also in danger from the Bennetts as well, perhaps? I finally nod off as I speculate about Marcus to the sound of my own vitals beeping on the machines around me.

MARCUS IS SITTING AT his desk, drinking his Beanery coffee, as I approach him inside the WKNX offices, only this time, it's as myself and not Madeleine. He turns to me and smiles as if he knows me and opens a book as I sit next to him.

"One of mine?" I crane my neck to see the title, although there isn't one.

Marcus nods. "*Wordplay*, my favorite. You know, this one will make such a great movie one day." He sounds excited, yet it doesn't quite sound like words Marcus would say or like the tone of voice he used in my dream.

"Who are you?" I ask as the scenery changes to that of my living room in Sequoyah Hills. Here we are, suddenly on my couch together as he rests his head in my lap like a child. Then he lifts his head and looks at me before he speaks.

"The other one was unique. Genius, actually. It's my favorite idea of hers so far, and it would make a great movie."

And just like that, I wake up. I haven't been up from bed except for bathroom trips and a few laps around the hallway with Connor, the boys, and my nurse. My doctor says that by some unexplainable miracle, I've got a clean bill of health. My vitals are solid, and I feel pretty good. I'm just severely bruised, tired, dizzy, and weak from the trauma.

But none of that matters right now, because I missed something important. Marcus represented someone, and that slipped right by me at first, but now that I know who it is, I must get to him as soon as possible. I grab my phone to call Connor and see that he's left me a voicemail, so I quickly listen as I yank off every cord attached to my body.

"Hey, honey. I'm just getting out of the shower. I'm going to run to the store for a few things, and then I'll be back at the hospital. Garrett's over at Ivy's spending the night, and Mayven asked Mason to help with her annual charity event or gala thing down at Crowne

Plaza. She's offered him five hundred dollars to help make sure the event runs smoothly since her assistant bailed at the last second. Isn't that nice? So everyone's accounted for, and I'll see you soon. Call if there's something in particular you want me to pick up. Love you. Bye."

My heart rate soars when I hear that Mason's with Mayven. The whole point of Marcus's existence was to remind me of Mason. In my dream, Mayven killed Marcus because he was onto her and Troy. Although Mason hasn't read *Wordplay* in its entirety, he knows the synopsis of the story and how it ends with the main character outing a nonprofit's embezzlement scam while she's at their annual gala.

Why didn't I think of this earlier or realize he may be in danger as well if he speaks about my book? Mayven may realize he knows about it somehow, although I don't remember ever mentioning it to her or anyone else. I wonder if he would tell her if she quizzed him on what he knows about my latest books. Is him working the event a trap, her way of trying to get rid of him, too, for knowing too much?

I grab my phone as I throw on the coat Connor left behind and proceed to sneak out of my room. I dash down the hallway to exit through the badge-only doors with a group of visitors who were just buzzed through by a nurse. Suddenly, I'm out.

In my bare feet, I head down the hall on the other side of the double doors and toward the elevators with a slew of other hospital visitors. My hair is disheveled, and I look like a hot mess, but that's the least of my worries. Not even the weird looks I receive in the elevator bother me as I dial Mason, whose phone is apparently off and goes straight to voicemail. Then I call Connor.

The elevator door slides open as we reach the first floor, and I rush out with adrenaline soaring throughout my weakened body. My phone finally gets a proper signal and dials Connor. Four, five, six rings, and it finally goes to voicemail. "Call me back immediately. We have to get to Mason before Mayven tries to kill him! I should've told you before that it was her. I think she may try to hurt him or something. Call me back." Panic fills my voice.

A few steps later and I have to pause and bend over to catch my breath. While I recover, I call for an Uber. Nothing will stop me from getting to my son, even if my body falls apart limb by limb.

I call Connor a few more times. He doesn't pick up. I imagine him happily shopping for groceries, his phone silenced as he reads labels and loads his buggy. I don't bother wasting my breath on repeat voicemails.

Soon, the Uber car arrives. I'm trying to salvage my remaining energy for when I step out of the car and onto the sidewalk of the Crowne Plaza to face one of my biggest nightmares.

The hotel isn't far away, but the ride is a blur of dark skies and passing city lights I fear will never look the same at the end of this night. My hands tremble, and tears cascade down my cheeks as I consider the worst possible scenarios. But I decide they won't happen, can't happen, because I'll sacrifice myself before I let her touch a hair on his head.

As we're pulling up to the building, I tell the Uber driver to call 911 and have them meet me at the Plaza—and that Mayven Bennett is about to commit another murder.

"Lady, what on earth?" As I exit his car, he eyes me from head to toe like I'm some crazy homeless woman or drug addict.

He pulls out his phone with apprehension. "Who do I say that you are again?"

"Allegra Hudson, the almost-murdered author," I answer and shut my door as he rolls down his window with his mouth gaping open.

With a face full of recognition, his voice rises. "Heeeey, ain't you supposed to be in a coma?"

I turn to him and shrug. "Woke up." I continue into the hotel lobby without turning back for his reaction.

Cold marble tickles my feet as I trample toward the front desk and past the black grand piano to find the party. "Which ballroom is the Bennett party in?" I ask the attractive brunette girl at the counter, who looks like she's about to call the police to come pick up the homeless lady standing in front of her.

"I'm sorry, who are you? Are you... a guest?" Doubt fills her eyes.

I look around, hoping to recognize someone who can vouch for me. "I should be. I'm Mayven's bestie, Allegra Hudson."

The girl's eyes widen as her neck stretches my way for a closer look. She's likely trying to decipher whether *the* Allegra Hudson could be found underneath my unkempt appearance. "Ms. Hudson, I'm so sorry. I didn't recognize you at first. Of course, the party is actually up on the rooftop tonight. Head on over to the elevators on your left and push *R*."

My face falls as I picture Mason's limp body falling over the edge of the hotel rooftop as Mayven looks on with a crafty smile. With knots filling my nauseated stomach, I run as fast as I can toward the elevator but trip on the carpet just before I can hit the call button. A few people look at me as they pass by, and I slowly pick up my frail body right before the elevator opens.

A man in a suit scrunches his eyebrows at me as he exits, and no one joins me for my ride up. As the doors close, I picture Mayven shedding fake tears of agony and explaining Mason's fall as an accident. Otherwise, I don't know why she would change the event's customary location to the roof. She must have an ulterior motive for doing so, because everyone knows they always deck out a ballroom for their galas. It's tradition. I wonder who's going to hurt Mason, her or Troy. Mayven's obviously not afraid to get her hands dirty, but I'm not sure she could actually kill an innocent teenager to prevent her own financial ruin.

Music from a live band fills my ears as the doors open again, and I step into a land that looks like it could be inhabited by fairies. Greenery and twinkling lights fill the roof as upbeat classical music blares from all sides. I walk through the crowd until I find a server doling out champagne near an intricate concrete fountain. "Where can I find Mayven Bennett?"

The server looks me up and down. "Oh, I like your, uh, costume?" she says as she tries to figure out what I must be.

"Thanks. Where is she?" I ask again.

She points and smiles. "Oh, she's in the staging area behind the black curtain over there with some of the staff."

I'm gone before she even finishes whatever she was going to say next. I stop at the fountain and steady myself as I lean against it for a second. A rush of weakness attacks my deteriorated body, but Mason needs me, and I have to press on even if it kills me.

I approach the black curtain and peel it back to see a fully staffed outdoor kitchen, where busy workers happily buzz around as if someone's life weren't in danger up here. Mayven and Mason are nowhere to be seen, but a slim hallway in the back looks like it wraps around the stairwell to the other side of the open rooftop. I instantly know that's where they are.

The brick corridor feels like it's closing in around me as I race to the other side of the building. My feet speed along the stone path toward a questionable fate as the voices from the kitchen behind me trail off into faint whispers. I rush toward my son, and when I reach the other side, Mayven and Mason are talking near the rooftop's edge, all alone.

My heart drops. I have to warn him and get him away from her *now*, even if Mayven attempts to play dumb or make me sound crazy.

As I reach the opening past the galley, Mason's face falls, and his brow furrows as he turns and stares at me with confusion on his face. He looks absolutely dashing in a black-and-white tuxedo, and Mayven looks beautiful as usual in a one-shoulder sequined white gown.

"Mom?" Mason says as Mayven's eyes meet mine.

For a split second, I wonder if she knows that I know, but her next move proves that she does.

"What are you doing out of the hospital, Mom?" Mason starts to walk toward me just as Mayven grabs his arm and pulls him back.

My heart catches in my throat. She's waiting on me to make a move, and I don't know how not to panic in this situation. Mason turns to Mayven then me. "What's going on? Mom, are you okay?"

Mayven continues to hang onto Mason's arm as she stands slightly behind him. "Are you all right, Allegra? You don't look well at all." Mayven's normally assertive voice shakes. She reaches into the cleavage of her dress and pulls something out. The object catches the light overhead and shines as it's whipped out. The pointed end lands next to Mason's throat. The metal is pressed there hard enough to threaten but not penetrate. Not yet.

"I will be as soon as you let my son go, Mayven. It's me you want. Despite what you think, he doesn't know a thing. You can let him go, and we can finish this up, just me and you." I inch toward them, but we both know Mason isn't going to leave me alone with her now.

Mayven rolls her eyes and kicks her heels off as she steps up on the ledge. Her knee pokes through the slit of her dress. "Get up here beside me now, or I'll plunge this right through your little neck!" she yells at Mason as she pulls him up on the edge beside her with the dagger barely poking the surface of his throat.

I hold my hands out and plead for her to stop but don't dare walk toward them. My fear is that she'll push him over. I'm a good ten feet away, and there's nothing I can do to make this situation end well. Maybe I can offer her my silence, but I doubt there's any way that she would ever believe me.

"We're friends, Mayven. You and me. Why didn't you ever consider confiding in me about the book? If you'd come to me and told me what was really going on, maybe I would've dropped the whole thing and changed the book for you. That's what friends do."

Her anger seems to elevate, and her face grows redder. Mayven rolls her eyes again as she laughs. "Yeah, right. What do you take me for, an idiot? There's no way in hell you'd align your squeaky-clean public image with someone operating an illegal business, and you know it."

"But you don't know because you didn't try!" I yell as Mason's eyes meet mine. His slight nod indicates that he's about to do something. My eyes widen as if to say no, but he makes his move anyway.

In one swift maneuver, he pushes Mayven backward with his right arm. As she falls down, her knife slices his right ear, and blood spills from it. Mason jumps down to the rooftop floor in front of me while clutching his ear. After hugging him and seeing that he's safe, I lunge toward the ledge to see Mayven's tiny body dangling by one hand. I don't even think about all she's done to me, my family, or my son. I just grab her wrist and hold on.

"Could you really have killed my son?" I grip her hand harder and begin to slip over the edge with tears of betrayal at the loss of someone I thought was my good friend.

"You know I couldn't, Allegra. I was only bluffing. I panicked!"

My body loses its strength and shakes uncontrollably, begging me to let her go. My feet start to rise as I inch toward the edge, about to go over right along with Mayven, when Mason grabs me by the waist and holds me down.

"Let her go, Mom!" he yells.

But I can't because her grip is too strong. Not even if I wanted to. "I loved you, Mayven," I tell her as tears fill my eyes.

She smiles back with tears of her own as if she's made a decision. "Loved. I see. Well, then, we're just going to have to let the chips fall where they may." She loosens her grip on my wrist and lets herself go just as police cars pull up to the hotel.

With every fiber of my being, I regrasp her hand at the last second. My shoulder tendons and ligaments stretch then rip, and the socket of my right arm pops out of place with a *crunch* as I swing her to the left then back to the right as I wail in agony. When she's as far as I can get her to the right, I let go, letting her fall to her fate.

She falls into the open air below with a look of panic that only grows with the distance between us. She heads toward the end of her story as she's always known it, our story together— and my nightmare.

Only she lands just where I intended her to—in the hydrangea bush on the balcony of the Presidential Suite.

Epilogue

Connor and I walk hand in hand down a dark cinder block hallway. The odor of shame, guilt, and pain fills my nostrils, and misery is written all over the walls.

"You sure you feel up to this?" Connor pats the sling on my right arm, but I already feel relief in my bones just by being here.

"I'm sure." I narrow my eyes with a smile.

"Do you want to speak to him alone first?" He squeezes my hand even tighter.

"I do, actually. I'll turn around and peek at you when I'm ready for you to join us. Is that okay?"

Connor waits on the other side of the two-way mirror while an officer escorts me inside the visitation room. "Glass of water, ma'am?"

"Two, please." I smile then take a deep breath as I wait.

A few seconds later, the other door opens, and an officer escorts a handcuffed Lane Stone, clad in an orange jumpsuit, inside the room. At first, he beams when he sees my face, then his appearance turns pallid as he looks back and forth between the officer and me. "Allegra, I swear, I didn't do this!"

I keep a straight face, not letting him know why I'm here. Our relationship in my dream wasn't entirely real, but I still see him in a different light now because of it. "Sit down, Lane."

The officer gently pushes Lane into his chair then stands in the corner of the room.

"I want you to know while I was in my coma, I relived the past in my head in some weird way, and you were there. I know you were following me around so much because you wanted to make sure I was okay, but you have to know that Connor and I are happy. Not perfect but truly happy. Can you acknowledge that and live your own life?" I lean in and study his reaction.

"I know that. Especially after he found you that night, he wanted to kill me! If the police hadn't arrived so quickly, he might have done it. I get it. He loves you," Lane cries.

"With that said, I need you to let us be after today. Okay?" I tear up, relieved that he'll stop obsessing over me, grateful that he saved me and guilty that he's been wrongfully accused. I'm also a little depressed after realizing that the Lane in my dream isn't the same Lane before me. Not completely. The Lane in my dream had to let go of me entirely, and through the circumstances in my dream, he learned he was wrong about Connor, something I hope this Lane realizes, too, after being falsely accused and having so much time to think.

"I will, but it's not like I have much choice anyway." He raises his handcuffed hands in the air.

"If you did, would you? You could get some professional help." I angle my head with curiosity.

"Yes, absolutely. I read you, loud and clear. But do you even believe me? I swear, I didn't—"

I interrupt. "That's why I'm here, actually." I shuffle in my seat. "Now that I'm awake and healed, I've told the police everything that happened that night." I smile.

Lane gives me a half grin, full of optimism. "You remember?"

"I do." I nod to the officer, who walks over and removes Lane's handcuffs. "I've already jumped through all the necessary hoops to release you from this place with a clean slate. Effective, well, right now." Another officer comes in with Lane's belongings and hands them over while Lane and I cry. "Thank you, Lane, for coming back.

I wouldn't be here right now if it weren't for you." I hug him with my one good arm and look in the mirror to Connor.

Connor opens the door seconds later, and I see Mayven being pushed in a wheelchair in the hall. She has two broken legs in casts, and Troy Bennett is being escorted in handcuffs by two officers next to her. Mayven catches a glimpse of Lane and me embracing, and our eyes lock. Her stare isn't one full of anger but of shame, and mine isn't full of hate but of disappointment and hurt.

Connor walks in and reaches a hand out to Lane with tears in his eyes. "Thank you, Lane, for bringing her back to me. I'm so sorry I didn't believe you. We're prepared to make full statements to the media with you later today, to clear your name and to let everyone know what really happened to Allegra."

Lane looks at us both and says, "It was like a little voice inside my head told me to go back and check on you one more time, a voice that sounded a lot like... Well, it's weird, but it sounded a lot like you, Allegra."

***

It's been about four months since we saw Lane in jail, and today, the boys are both at school. Garrett's in the seventh grade, and Mason's starting his freshman year at UT. It's a sunny day, and I'm sitting outside on a brick bench that Connor built for me, joined by my new Great Dane puppy named Marcus. We're underneath an overgrown maple tree in Powell, Tennessee. I'm sitting and relaxing, waiting for Connor to bring out our iced teas from the kitchen.

The house is a freshly painted shade of linen white with dark-teal shutters. We even have the event barn painted to match, and a few goats are feeding on the grass in our backyard. I take a break from reading a book to eye the beautiful man walking my way. The man who's all mine for the rest of our days.

About four and a half months ago, the pieces of my life began to crumble, but the story of our life fell back into place because of our love. The final pages of the book I'm reading make me giddy. I guess Mayven got what she wanted after all. I did change the title, the antagonist's name, and the plot of *Wordplay*, although I doubt she appreciates her exact name being used now rather than the name Raven. I close the book's cover and read the new title with a smile—*One Little Word: A Memoir* by Allegra Hudson. Marcus's ears perk up.

The beeping of what I assume must be ambulance sirens or firetrucks in the distance grows closer and closer, momentarily making me nervous that maybe I'm hearing the beeps from my dream again and this isn't real life. Finally, they pass us by and fade away. All I can focus on now is the man walking toward me, the man I love who also loves me. The man who can find me *anywhere*.

Acknowledgments

Writing this book was such a wild ride, and first off, I have to thank God for bringing me along to this crazy idea of being an author. It truly is something I now realize I'm passionate about for many reasons, and I've been blessed to meet so many amazing people and grow in the Spirit on this journey toward publication.

Daniel, my favorite person in the world, my best friend, my partner in crime, my husband, my baby-daddy, and the man who can find me anywhere... I can't thank you enough for getting on board with this huge career change that didn't make a lot of sense for a long time. You've been such a great source of support through the roller-coaster ride that led to this story getting out into the world, and even when I tell you the details about the sketchy books I'm writing, you always know my true heart and aren't scared to sleep next to me (that I know of). I heart you. Forever.

Hudson and Graydon, I love you all more than anything, and even though you won't get to read this book for a while, you have a huge part in it. You two mixed together are Graham, and I love that you'll get to see that one day. Mommy loves you to the moon and back, and you inspire me every single day. You all are my heart and soul.

To my parents and my sister, your approval and encouragement mean the world to me, and I hope you won't fear what you now know lies inside my already twisted brain. I love you all so much and hope you love this story.

To the girls who don't write but are the best cheerleaders a girl could have (Brittany, Erin, Rachel, Courtney, Kaycie, and Amie), thanks so much for listening to me go on about things that probably don't make any sense, for asking how this writing journey is going, and for being supportive. I hope you ladies love this book and the female friendships in it.

To my beta readers and critique partners for this book and other ones (Kellie, Nicole, Jennifer, CL, Kimberly Brock, Tasha, Peggy, Kaitlyn, Kathy, Ella, Elizabeth, Heather, Kimberly Belle, Rea Frey, Sheila, Bradeigh) I cannot thank you guys enough for your input and wise advice. This is a group effort, and I appreciate each and every one of you.

To Jennifer Klepper, how will I ever repay you? The way you've mentored me and provided me with the most useful and intelligent feedback doesn't go unappreciated or unnoticed. I am honored to call you a friend.

To Kris and Autumn, sharing our ups and downs on the way to publication has been incredible. This road hasn't been easy, but we did it. I love you girls and our friendship.

To the Fictionistas in the Ink Tank, I mean, what would I do without you? We share way more than writing tidbits in our tank, and I'm so grateful for our comradery and companionship. Without it, I probably would've quit writing a long time ago (and I might have also had a nervous breakdown or two). So, a huge thank-you to you ladies for doing life together.

A special thank-you to Kimberly Belle, Rea Frey, Samantha Downing, and Jeneva Rose, who provided the kindest feedback and blurbs. I admire you all so much and still can't believe you've read my words. Much love.

To Lynn McNamee and all the staff at Red Adept Publishing, thanks for believing in me and my stories. I'll forever be grateful for the incredible opportunity Lynn gave me, and I can't wait to work with you on the next one. And to my fellow WFWA Rappers, you all are so wonderful.

To Erica (my mentor who came up with my amazing cover), Sara, and Angela at RAP, I can't thank you all enough for your input and love for this story—you truly helped it come to life with your priceless feedback, edits, encouragement, and support.

To my amazing agent and manager, Liza Fleissig, when you know, you know. Thanks for jumping off the cliff with me and for your unending kindness. I am so glad we were brought together the way we were, and I'm so thrilled to keep working with you and your team at Liza Royce Agency.

To the rest of my family and friends, I hope this story entertains you and lives up to the hype since you've heard me talk about it for quite a while now.

To anyone who has read this book, I thank you from the bottom of my heart. And please share with your friends on social media—I'd be forever grateful. These kinds of things help authors much more than you know.

To Knoxville and Powell, you are characters in this book because I love you with all of my heart. And to Sequoyah Hills, thanks for being a place so charming and beautiful I could practically write a whole book about it.

And a special thanks to Taylor Swift, who is always a huge source of inspiration for my writing.

About the Author

Audra McElyea loves to write suspenseful stories that read like modern-day Alfred Hitchcock films. She's a former corporate buyer, magazine writer, college head majorette, and personal trainer who has always loved to tell a story?whether it be through the movies she wrote and made her friends act out growing up, the secret songs she penned and never showed a soul, or the choreography she created for numerous dance and baton-twirling teams.

Audra has a bachelor's degree from the University of Tennessee in consumer services management. She currently lives in Tennessee with her husband, two boys, and their dog and cat. In her spare time, she enjoys reading, exercising, and listening to Taylor Swift songs over and over.

Read more at audramcelyea.com.

About the Publisher

Dear Reader,

We hope you enjoyed this book. Please consider leaving a review on your favorite book site.

Visit https://RedAdeptPublishing.com to see our entire catalogue.

Don't forget to subscribe to our monthly newsletter to be notified of future releases and special sales.

CPSIA information can be obtained
at www.ICGtesting.com
Printed in the USA
LVHW032033280422
717483LV00011B/1803